THE THREE ANGELS AND THE SEVEN DEADLY SINS

by.

Stevie Chandler & Gregory Burson

Same Old Story Publishing

VICTOR FERUS, PRESIDENT and CEO

The Three Angels and the Seven Deadly Sins

Copyright © 2018 – Stevie Chandler & Gregory Burson

Cover Artwork Copyright © 2018 Amanda Scharf

ISBN - 978-1-945450-08-2

First paperback edition,2018

SAME OLD STORY PUBLISHING 2018

THE THREE ANGELS

AND THE

SEVEN DEADLY SINS

S.G. BURSON

To Dad and Granny,

Thank you for the stories. We wish we could show you this one. In loving memory of Mark Chandler and Margaret Donthnier.

1
SENIORITIS

An angel on my right and a devil on my left.

One high and mighty, his judgment looks down upon those who seek his guidance. His wary eyes ever vigilant as his cryptic tongue speaks riddles that no man could hope to understand fully. His humor gone from years of petty losses and wisdom forgotten, it is he who presents fits with grave intonations. For it was he who gave the idea to his disciples to set ablaze habit and forgo the trivial matters such as happiness and riot pleasure. He stands high above the heads of others and leads with a voice of thunder. Order controls the land, and it is his order alone that dictates the century-ridden seconds of his teachings.

Sounds pretty fancy huh? Well don't get used to it; that's my entire vocabulary.

Mr. Scott with his belly-line far outstretching his belt leaned over the desk to my left. His pale face was red with stress and the "thunderous commands" sounded somewhat like a mixture between a dog's squeaky toy and that chipmunk that used to live in my Dad's old truck, *you know, before I started it.*

His dark brown hair combed back in an attempt to hide the unhideable as his bushy eyebrows tried to make up for what wasn't there. His sweat-stained, yellow-buttoned-up shirt seems misplaced in a room of jeans and t-shirts. But no one was that worried about his shirt, *in fact, the only thing I was concerned about was that his butt was only a few inches from my face.*

Mr. Scott was ironically barking at Scott. *Scott Milter was...um...a few short of a...not the bulb... He wasn't very smart, and I'm not very good at metaphors.*

Anyway.

Mr. Scott attempted to fan away the smoke as he explained to Milter that when he said "Burn your old tests for all I care," he did not mean right now in the classroom. *But I'm still impressed that Milter managed to do it without a lighter.*

Then comes the angel. The clock that counts down to my very last seconds of this place.

School is fine and all, it's not even that I mind going to it that much. I'm not a bad student; I'm not that good of one either. I'm perfectly average. No really, I get the average grade on every single assignment. Even my teachers can't explain it. It doesn't matter how much I study either. I always get the middle grade, always.

But my grades don't really matter anymore. School is almost over. Just two minutes left, and I'll officially be done with high school. Only two more minutes of this one-sided-yell-fest then we'll all be free. I can hardly wait.

A tap on my left shoulder gained my attention. I turned back to see Thomas Colleen. He had a bronze tan with clear outlines from his shirt that revealed pale skin below it. He was a bit shorter than me at six-foot on the dot. His hair was kept short and buzzed leaving a dark brown line that framed his face. He wore a dark green baseball cap along with a T-shirt from the last fair and reliable jeans. Thomas was a bit bigger, but it wasn't fat, I've worked morning shifts on his family's farm before, there's no way he could be fat with days like that. But Thomas was still one of my closest friends ever since we could remember.

"Terrance," he whispered then stroked my face with the back of his hand.

"What is wrong with you?" I snapped back in the same hushed tone.

He laughed a bit, and a snort sounded from his nose. "I'm just messing with you. I've tapped your shoulder like six times. You've just been staring off into space for the past ten minutes," he said.

"So petting my face was the best way to get my attention?" I asked.

"Hey...it worked didn't it?" Thomas replied with a shrug.

"Remind me why we're friends?" I chuckled then sighed. "Okay, you got my attention. What do you want?"

"I don't know," he replied, bluntly.

I blinked a few times and rolled my eyes. I smacked my hand against the table and threw my head to the right side.

"You're such a good talker aren't yah?" I huffed with a smirk.

"I try my best. Hey, that does remind me. Do you want to come over to my place later? A couple of us were planning on going down to the riverside for a couple beers and BBQ. Kind of a party for the end of the year, you know? So are you in?" Thomas asked.

I thought about it for a moment before replying. "I'd honestly love to, but I got to help out my Dad tonight. We have to get everything all cleaned up before tomorrow. Dad says those suits are coming down to see if we are a sanitary milkery. They've been trying to get Dad to hand over the land for months now, and this inspection is just more garbage their throwing our way. But that doesn't mean we can't ignore it," I explained.

"They're seriously still gunning for you?"

"Yeah, but there won't be much they can do if we have everything clean. So Dad and I are making everything look real pretty for those inspectors. After that we can tell them where to shove it," I added.

Dad and I have always been alone on our farm. It's small, but we make enough to get by, and we treat our cows like family; at least till they get old and die then we treat them like dinner, but still. We do more for them than some big company.

"Okay well if you have time after come check it out. We'll probably be there awhile, but we're heading back when it gets dark. Mabel says she is going to set up the bonfire at my place maybe you can swing by?" Thomas reasoned.

"I'll try. If not let's hang out sometime this weekend," I suggested right as the bell rang.

I stood from the desk as a rush of excitement ran through my body. Those around me seemed just as excited to get out of the classroom. I followed Thomas out to his car. His younger brother, Andrew, was waiting against the passenger door.

I ran over to the truck and jumped into the bed with excitement painted on my face.

"Woo!" I called happily.

I wasn't that excited before, but with so many people around me who are excited, it's hard not to copy.

Andrew frowned and swung open the passenger side door. "It's not fair. You two get to graduate, and I still got two more years," he muttered.

"Nah it's plenty fair you just don't like it," Thomas ensured.

"Hey at least you get to goof off for a while longer," I added.

"Terrance I know damn well how you're going to spend the next month; you'll be doing nothing but goofing off, don't give me that crap!" Andrew teased.

I laughed and sat down on the bed of the truck. "You got me there. Just thought you'd appreciate the bright side."

"I never understand you," Andrew sighed.

He sat down and closed the car door, and Thomas got behind the wheel.

The warm May breeze flew against my short tangled brunette hair. As the sun shined against my tan skin, I felt the hope that summer might just be coming early this year.

We drove down the back country roads for some time till we reached the dirt path that was home. Thomas dropped me off first since my house was the first one on the street. Still, it was a good two miles from the top of the road till my driveway appeared.

I hopped out of the beaten gray truck. I waved my goodbyes to Andrew, who crossed his arms and shrugged, and Thomas who replied with a half salute before driving down the path; sending dust up as they went.

I walked towards my house on the gravel driveway. It was a nice home, nothing too fancy. Just two bedrooms, one bath ranch. The windows were new and freshly installed; last year proved to be a bit too much with the storms for the old house. The siding was a slight yellow tint where white used to stand; although that white was back when I was about knee level to my old man and now, at six-foot-two, I stand an inch and a half taller.

A large wooden porch attached when I was about ten rested against the front of the house. All three of my big mutts laid sprawled on the white porch. They barely lifted an eye as I arrived, just a flick of the tail and a puff of air.

Some guard dogs y'all are.

My Dad rested on the far right side of the porch on the squeaky porch swing. He rocked back and forth and raised his bottle towards me as I arrived.

He was forty-three, and it showed. *Not to be rude, my Dad is a hard worker and eat, sleep, and breathes this place. In all honesty, I would give anything to be like him and if that means my age shows and my hands are cracked from my work then so be it; you'll never find a more honest man.*

His hair, like mine, was a dark brown color that laid in a constant state of hat-hair, as Mrs. Robin cared to point out. With a suntanned mug and a hearty five-o'clock shadow, the old farmer nodded towards me as I reached the porch. I stepped over the mutts and sat in the rocking chair next to my Dad.

The man leaned forward, his beaten, barely washed, gray t-shirt moved against his worked defined muscles as his arms bent over his jeans. He pressed the dark brown bottle to his lips once more; the label was clear now, I could see that it was root beer.

"Any reason for that?" I asked and pointed towards the bottle.

"Doc says I need to lay off the Bourbon and I wanted a beer," he replied.

"Fair enough," I shrugged with a smile.

"Oh." He leaned back, "Terrance I need you to go clean out the pens a little earlier than I asked you to. Daisy had a bit of an...let's call it an accident. I would have gotten to it sooner, but I've been spending all afternoon working on that old truck we got from Mr. Millar. I think I got the darn thing finally running."

"You got that damn thing to turn on?" I asked. My Dad shot me a scornful glare. "Ah, darn thing working...pardon my language."

My Dad stood up and cracked his back. He finished his drink and turned back to me. A small smile was painted on his lips.

"That darn thing is your graduation present. You can take it down to the riverbed tonight if you can clean out the pens in time," he assured. "Now get moving, you don't want to be late."

My smile grew with the realization that my Dad already knew about the party. I didn't want to be late, so I dropped my backpack on the porch and ran out to the barn.

I went through the side door to the barn and the instant I walked in I knew what my Dad meant by accident. *It seemed that Daisy decided that the color of the wall lacked something, specifically a greenish brown.*

I covered my nose and gagged slightly. *I know I'm pretty used to cleaning up after our nineteen ladies, but this is a new level of fowl. Still, I want to go to that party, and I know better than to ask to help since he's been busy all day.*

I took a deep breath and walked over to the tools. I slipped on my cowboy boots and gloves. I looked over the two scooping shovels. Much like the devil and the angel these two shovels were opposites. One was old and splintery. Still, she's a hard worker, but I fear that at any moment she will break in half. The other on the other hand was more temptation than I ever thought I'd feel over a shovel. Clean, and brand new. The plastic and steel shovel, still wearing the price tag, laid tantalizingly against the barn wall. *My Dad just bought it, and I know I shouldn't, but it would make everything go so much faster.*

I'm sure it won't be a problem if I just clean it later...

There's a hose out back...

One little job...

Screw it; I'm using it.

I picked up the new shovel and turned to my work. With the cows out grazing in the field, the stalls were peacefully quiet. *I know when I am frequently cleaning, a few always tend to wander in and give a few kisses and moos in attempt to get a snack. I don't normally clean at this time so they won't be expecting me.* Still, one seemed to make her way in.

The sound of a loan bell rang as I continued to shovel the mess. The bell was shortly accompanied by the distant howls of the dogs. I turned my head slightly towards the noise, and I felt a wet tongue drag itself from the back of my neck to the top of my head. *Like I said before, our cows will sometimes give us little kisses with their tongues, but this felt different almost like this unknown licker was...tasting me.*

I slowly turned my head to get a view of my slobbering assailant and immediately wished I had kept my attention on my work.

"What in the world?" I stammered out.

It was one of the cows, at least that's all I could assume, but its figure was distorted. Its face looked as if it had started melting off revealing muscle and bone below. The eyes seemed to have expanded and had an orange glaze across them. The bottom jaw was hanging as if it was out of socket but the way it smacked it lips repeatedly proved it worked quite well. The teeth were no longer flat grazing teeth but instead were pointed and stuck out at odd angles even stabbed through some parts of the mouth. The body was not in any better shape with the same melting appearance as the head, but a black tar-like substance oozed out of it and bubbled as if it were boiling.

I backed up to the wall that I had been cleaning.

"Y-you okay there Daisy?" I shuttered. The bell belonged to Daisy, but this thing was far from her.

She was obviously not okay but to be honest; I had no idea what else to say in a situation like this. She seemed to respond by raising her head up and letting out this shriek that was a mix of moo and nails sliding across a chalkboard. Her boiling body charged at me; hooves kicked up the mud from the floor. I attempted to dive to the side, but she caught me just in time to slam me into the ground. The shock of it knocked the air out of me, but I still kept a hold of Dad's shovel.

A wheeze escaped me as I shut my eyes. The pain coursed through me and for a moment, everything seemed unreal. For that moment everything in my life felt like it was about to stop and I didn't have a word in edgewise.

Was I going to die?

2
MAD COW DISEASE

I might actually die here. Like, of all ways I end up being eaten by a cow? A cow that, might I remind you, has been raised alongside me for the last eighteen years. Now she was standing over me with drool that looked as if she had chewed a bucket of those black gumball eyes from the ice cream truck.

I felt the cold chill of the drool falling against my face. My arms were pressing the shovel against the creature in a desperate attempt to keep distance between us. I gritted my teeth as I tried to push the pole of the shovel further into the animal's mouth with no give.

When I opened my eyes, they were wide to match my shaking figure as my years of farm work fought desperately to keep the razor teeth from biting off my face.

"Get off of me!" I barked through struggled pants.

The creature's blood only seemed to boil from my demand. She stiffened her upper spine as it appeared to protrude from her skin. A crackle of bones and ripping flesh echoed with a sickening tempo the longer we stayed in our power struggle. With a few twitches of the neck and repeated crack, Daisy's head seemed to split down the center of her skull. With the overflowing waterfall from the self-inflicted wound, the harder it became to hold my own against the thing.

The shovel moved towards me at a frighteningly slow pace. I could smell the black substance that I began to think was tar. The scent was similar to a freshly paved street mixed with black licorice in the worst way possible.

I wanted to gag, but my attention was obviously in keeping my arms straight, which proved to be harder than it sounds.

With Daisy's blunt force against the shovel, my arms were obliged to bend. I gasped as the pressure pushed the air from my lungs. I continued to try and press the shovel back up. If I could just get Daisy off me for a second, I was sure I could make it back to the house. I just needed a little more of a push.

A growl, unlike the one that came from Daisy, sounded in the barn. I turned my head to the right to see Ralph. Ralph was one of our dogs; he was a large German shepherd mixed with what we think was a pit bull based on his face. His ears were back, and his teeth were shown. Ralph growled with his shoulders pressed forward. The mutt rushed forward and took Daisy by the neck. The force and power of Ralph's attack was enough for Daisy to bite down hard on the shovel. The handle snapped in half, but it gave me the opportunity to crawl out from under the beast.

I ran over to the middle of the barn where I felt there was enough distance between the monster and me. I watched Ralph tear into the neck of the creature with a fury. My eyes looked down at the now cut shovel with my body still shaking.

"Dad's going to kill me," I stated, quietly.

With a yelp from my six-year-old mutt, I looked up to see where the dog lay limp against the stable wall. The near entirely black figure rose from the ground and turned its attention towards me. A cold sensation burst through my body in the course of a single glare.

"It's going to kill me," I added.

Without any more hesitation, I turned towards the doorway I had come in. I bolted from the barn and towards the house without another thought. The grit of my teeth and the strain on my eyes from keeping them so wide began to burn as I bolted at full speed towards the home.

"Dad! Dad! Dad! Da-"

I tripped across the cheaply wired fence we had placed around the garden to keep the girls from grazing where they weren't supposed to be. I landed face first into the newly fertilized dirt, but I didn't have time to worry about that now.

I stood back up and continued to my call out to my Dad who walked out onto the front porch of the home. He stood with a stern posture as he seemed to look past me with a double barrel shotgun in his hand.

I managed to get to the porch where I could see at least six of those demonic cows. They ran towards the house, but it seemed as if more were to come. I swallowed dryly, and for the first time since I was a kid, I hid for a moment behind my Dad before I gained back a bit of pride.

"What the Hell are those things?" I barked.

"I'm not sure if you'd even believe me if I told you. But I'll try later. Right now get your ass to the storm cellar and don't touch a thing till I get down there," he ordered.

I have only heard my Dad curse about three times in my memory. It's not something that I would like to repeat. So without a second thought, I nodded and ran towards the cellar doors on the side of the house. I turned for a moment to watch my Dad and the two remaining hounds stand at the ready as Daisy, Millie, Coco, Heather, and Tina came running in from the field, all covered in the black tar.

I did not want to go into the cellar. I wanted to stand and fight with my Dad, but that look on his face was not one that I could match. He was serious and for what it was worth he looked like he knew what he was doing. I didn't want to get in his way even if the thought of hiding was infuriating.

I opened the cellar doors and went into the basement and closed the door, but I did not lock them. He said he'd come and for now, I'm choosing to believe that despite better judgment that urged me to fight.

I looked around the cellar for something that I could use to fight just in case things started to turn south.

The cellar was rather bare. We had shelves with food and water for when storm season hit. The shelves were covered with sheets to keep the dust off the items. I turned on the single light for the room which didn't provide that much visibility for the area. I squinted and rubbed my eyes as I looked for something useful.

I picked up a can. I threw it up and caught the can in my hand a few times before I decided that it wouldn't be nearly effective enough. I put down the can and continued to search around the room.

"Is it him..." a gentle voice whispered. It sounded like that of a young girl with an ashy tone.

"Who's there?" I asked.

I looked behind me where no one stood. There was the sound of shots being fired from outside. I jumped slightly and returned to find something to help with.

"It would appear so. I couldn't forget that birds nest atop his scalp. It's unmistakable," a man's voice replied. It was rough sounding, like that belonging to a veteran smoker who had seen their fair share of tough times.

"Where are you?" I snapped. "Show yourself!"

I know I hear these. There's no way that I imagined this.

"Did he forget?" the girl asked.

"Must have," the man replied.

"Forget? What the are you talking about? Stop hiding!" I commanded.

"The mirror. Have him look into the mirror," the girl suggested.

"Mirror? What does a mirror have to do with any of this?" I questioned.

Two more shots sounded.

"I don't have time for this I gotta get out there and help," I ensured.

I started to dig through the boxes with a desperate attempt to find something to help as the shots became much more frequent and the scream of the cows burned in the air.

"You seek power? You should know what you must do vessel. Look within the mirror and the power will be yours," he claimed. "It is straightforward and information you should know well, Homwell."

"You know my name? If this is your idea of a prank I'm going to be pissed off," I swore.

The scream from the monstrous cows called from outside the cellar. I felt the cold chill of my depleting timeline remind me of the situation.

"Fine. If you can help me then tell me what I have to do," I agreed.

I don't have time to wonder about what's going on or who these voices belong to. Right then I just needed to do whatever I could to help my Dad. I can figure out what these things are after.

"Now you are talking sensical," the man called in a hearty voice.

"Touch the mirror, it's on the third shelf, right side," the girl explained.

I walked to where she directed and pulled a small box off of the shelf. It was a simple cardboard box covered with a thick level of dust. I narrowed my eyebrows but I didn't waste time. I opened the box and dug through layers of newspapers. I pulled out a heavy shell bag. It was a dark and worn brown color with the symbol of a feather sealed onto the front of the leather.

I set the object to the side and continued to dig. I found a hunting knife covered in a matching leather sheath with the same feather imprint. I picked up the knife and unsheathed the blade. It was definitely a hunting knife, it looked similar to that of a skinning knife. The handle was a short oak color and the blade seemed a bit too long for the curve of the blade. It appeared to be bigger than one that would be used for a deer, it was for big game for sure, as to what game I am not sure. The blade itself was a light silver and heavy, much heavier than it should have been but manageable.

With this, I should be able to help. I can't just keep sitting here.

"The glass, touch the glass!" the female voice reminded.

"But I can help with this. Why do I-"

"If you try to fight only with that you will be killed the moment you walk from those doors. We do not have time to wait Homwell," the man scolded.

"But if I do nothing he's going to die!" I snapped back.

"And if you do not listen, then so will you. Stop being such a sniveling brat and do what you've been told," the man roared.

"I'm not a brat. I'm just trying to think but it's a little hard when I have some old geezer and a child yelling at me in my head while some kind of black-oozing cows are attacking my family," I snapped.

My face was heated and my eye felt as if any moment it would twitch. I don't know what's going on anymore, I'm not even sure I understood to begin with. This situation made about as much sense as a fever dream.

Silence enveloped the room. Not even the sounds of the gunshots made it to my ears. I panted a bit and tightened my fist at my side. My other hand held just as tight a grip on the hilt of the knife to the point that my knuckles were white.

"Just stop beating around the bush. Kids obviously not who we thought. If he wants his family to die then let them. We tried birdbrain, not our fault if he becomes mincemeat," the girl said.

I was expecting the man to reply but he didn't. I waited a moment and soon the sounds from outside filled the room. A scream echoed through the room and I turned white. Without hesitation, I turned towards the entrance to the cellar. I readied the shaking knife and ran towards the doorway.

Wait.

I didn't.

I wanted to. I wanted to run out of the cellar and over to my Dad, I wanted to burst through the doors and help him take out whatever those things are. I wanted to save him like he had me. But here I was; still.

I narrowed my brow and my body returned to the box. Without my control, I pulled out what seemed to be a pocket watch from the box. This left it empty. I looked over the watch with a bit of wonder but in the same, fear. I still possessed no real control over my body. It seemed as if my limbs were not mine and my hands, although they were touching this thing...I couldn't feel it.

The watch was a golden color with detailed carvings across the metal in what appeared to be some type of symbol based language, *or scribbles to make it look cool, I'm not too sure*. On the front of the closed pocket watch there was the same symbol of the feather that was on the other two objects. I did notice that along with there were four lines meeting in the center of the embellishment.

I clicked the top of the watch to open it. In replace of the gears and clock face of the pocket watch were two clean mirrors. It looked like a makeup compact but seemed almost too clean for being left out in the cellar this long. I felt my right hand raise and my pointer finger moved forward.

I attempted to pull away but it seemed that all I could do was move my neck and head. I gritted my teeth and did what I could to move away from the object.

"Stop," I begged.

"It's for your own good Homwell," the man said.

The green color of my eyes reflected off the mirror but they didn't look like mine; more like those of a scared animal. I watched as the tan skin seemed to stretch from my square chin over my screaming lips to muffle them. The burning sensation of my face coursed through my body was the skin against my arms. The skin morphed and tore as the snap of what I can only assume were bones sounded. I tried to scream louder but the sound was covered by the skin from my neck and chin. The tears from my eyes fell down the morphing figure of my face. With each passing second my body became more and more distorted and the pain only increased.

I fell to my knees as the pain made it to my legs. My body twitched and convulsed as my nose flared in attempt to keep me breathing.

The gray color of metal bled from my wounds and over took my flesh. As the color rushed through my body became heavy. It felt weighted as if I had just put on twelve winter coats.

I tried to scream again, but again there was nothing but the muffles of my own skin gag. I shut my eyes as the pain was unbearable.

This is unreal.

None of this can be happening.

I can't. I can't. I can't...

3
SCHIZOPHRENIA AND A SHOTGUN

The thin line of my vision blurred as my body became aware of itself. I blinked a few times as I figured out where I was. The upturned grass and mud filled my sight. I tried to look around more but my vision was limited but one thing was clear, it was the dead of night, or I'm going blind.

I forced my eyes to look up. A black substance wet my dry hair. It was almost as if I had taken a shower an hour ago and now the hair was nearly dry but not entirely. The color seemed odd to me, but I was sure it was the blackness of the night that was doing that.

With a tired and slow motion, I rolled to my back. I looked up at the sky filled with stars. It was late, and there was no sign of the sun setting or rising anytime soon. My body felt numb as well. I felt like I had worked the entire day, and just now woke up.

I yawned and forced myself to sit up, as a shot of pain came from the back of my shoulder. I gripped my left side in agony. It felt like I had a knife under my shoulder blades. I leaned back in hopes to stop the pain, but it only lightened it. My hand slipped behind me and felt the space between the bones, but I felt nothing that would cause this pain.

With a few deep breaths, I managed to get to the point that I could move once more. I forced myself to stand and looked around the scene with slow and careful movements.

I was in my backyard. The air was a dead silent with only the night song of cicadas and crickets to lighten up the air. The dirt in the ground was upturned and thrown across the yard. *It looked nearly as if we had a football game with my uncle Jimmy and cousin Taylor after they had a few too many or after the Packers game; maybe both with the amount of damage there was.*

I looked back to the house and could see the faint glow of the porch light in the front. I swallowed shallowly and walked towards the light. My legs felt heavy as if I were wearing steel boots but I managed to get around the little white house.

The porch was in shambles. Wood split and stuck out towards every direction. The light flickered some but continued to function as if everything were normal. I looked over the rubble with a tight feeling.

Dad and I built that porch the summer I turned twelve. I remember just how cool it was when he taught me how to use all the power tools and how to sand the boards. I didn't even want to go and play with Thomas.

It's a real shame to see it like th-...Dad.

My eyes once again widened and the beat in my chest seemed to triple in a moment.

How could I forget? I mean I didn't, but I did let it slip my mind for a second. Dang it, where is he?

I looked around the rubble with a huffing breath. The white wood was painted with the same black goo on my hair.

Without a thought from my head, my hand touched the liquid. It was slimy and cold. It had the same feeling as curdled milk. I gagged and pulled my hand away.

It was at that moment I noticed something in the flickering light. There was a line of red from the rubble and to the front door or where the front door should have been. The only thing that was remaining now was a gaping hole where something at least a foot taller than the door and twice as wide pushed through.

"So it was real?" I asked myself.

"Wasn't it obvious?" The girl's voice called.

"Ah!" I yelled.

From the surprise, I lost my footing and fell into a puddle of the black tar and what seemed to be pieces of the remaining animal.

"Oh, fu-"

"That's enough time wasted," the man interrupted. "We must get a move on. You have wasted enough of our time with your lies. In return, you will follow my orders until we can part. Now get a move on. We must be on our way before those Leeches return."

"Wait? Lie? I didn't lie to you, and I'm not going anywhere...detached voice. I got to find my Dad," I replied.

"You claimed you were Homwell, did you not? Then you are not free from the sin. And because you insisted on wasting my time with your stories I nearly killed you. Do you know nothing of the training required to hold my soul? Of course not because you are not the vessel. You are not Homwell," he barked.

"Yeah, I am," I snarled. "I think I know my *own* last name."

"Waste no time with your fib. We know well that you are not the vessel. Unfortunately for the vessel, your body wasn't capable of holding me but a few minutes before you passed out," he claimed.

"You barely even lasted that. A cool transformation and you couldn't even manage to stay on your feet for ten minutes haha," the girl laughed.

"I'm not lying! But I'm not some vessel. I never said I was. All I said was that my last name was Homwell; which it is," I snapped. I took a deep breath and shook my head. "I don't have time for this."

With those words, I marched forward past the rubble of the porch and into the home.

The door creaked with an unsettling stillness followed. I looked around the house that looked as if a herd had run through it. The trail of red blood was washed out by the black stains. There was a puddle that took up the majority of the main hallway floor. Splattered black covered the striped wallpaper of the hall across from the kitchen.

I swallowed shallowly and began to walk through the silent home. The squish of my boots against the floor was somewhat nauseating. I followed the red, at least what I could see from it, down the hallway and to the point when the kitchen opened to the kitchen. I paused a moment without looking into the room as I noticed the red lined curved.

My breath was hard to manage as it seemed I couldn't keep it steady enough to hide what I was thinking.

"What will you do human?" the girl asked. "You know just as well as I do what this path will lead to. Are you ready to face the truth you've known from the moment you awoke?"

"Shut it," I snapped.

My chest rose and sunk as if I had just run a marathon. It was the only sound besides the creeks that came from such an old home. The salty reality began to stream down my face already. I quickly wiped away the few tears and took a ragged breath in an attempt to calm myself.

I'm making a big deal out of nothing. I know my Dad is okay. He's probably just knocked out cause he's so tired. I know my Dad, and I know he's the type of guy to work till he passes out. He's done it before. Yeah, just sleeping since he killed those things. Just a nap.

"You refuse to listen to reason do you? Although I do not agree with Luci's methods, she doesn't mean you harm. If you turn that corner, you will struggle with moving forward with our mission," the man warned.

"Why should I trust either of you? You don't even believe me about my last name. Besides you're just voices. You're not even real. Probably none of this is. I mean who would believe me if I told them all this?" I asked.

There was silence, as silent as it could get with the creeks and my breathing that is.

I turned the corner without a thought. My body stiffened as the smell became a lingering stench that I am surprised I managed to tune out until this moment. My stomach turned as I was sure that at any moment my lunch would become a part of the mess that coated the floor.

I covered my mouth and looked upon the sight where my Dad, I'm barely sure that it was my Dad at all, where my Dad laid.

He was slumped up against the kitchen wall. The table had been thrown to his right side, and much like the porch, it was in rubble. The whole kitchen was. It looked like a stampede had come through and based on the destruction I'd believe it.

My eyes shut. I couldn't bear to look at the mess of remains that was left of the man who laid slumped on the tiled floors, shotgun in hands.

My chest rose and sunk with an unreal slowness. I felt like I wasn't breathing at all. The tightness in my throat grew to the point that I felt as if I was choking.

"Ah..."

The tears that I had once tried to stop fell without restraint. I clenched the front of my tar stained shirt, and my teeth gritted. Grunts and whimpers escaped through the clenched mouth. The shaking sensation that began in my hands spread quickly through my body with no control.

My mouth opened and with it came a yell. It started deep in my chest and got louder as it moved to my throat. I opened my eyes and turned to my right. I pulled off the photos from the wall. I moved on to the calendar then to the bowls and decorations around the kitchen counters. I threw the toaster and microwave to the ground and went to the drawers in which I quickly emptied to the floor. I continued on my path of destruction till the sounds drowned out my sobs.

I am not sure how long I continued this, but when I was done, I slumped against the wall opposite of my Dad. I held my swollen-red face in between the palms of my hands and stared at the mess. My breath was now deep, but the tight feeling remained.

I hit the wall behind me with my right fist.

"How could this happen?" I asked myself.

"We warned you of the sight. Unfortunately, we cannot remain here. Come, we must move and fulfill our purpose," the man in my head spoke.

"This is your fault!" I snapped. "I could have helped him. You should have just let me go with the knife. This wouldn't have happened if you had just let me do something!"

There was a pause.

"I did much more than you could have with a knife and it wasn't enough. Do you understand that? If you had left alone then you would be in the same position as Arthur," the man explained.

I looked over at my father with wide eyes.

"How do you know his name?" I asked.

My eyes did not leave what was left of his face.

Again, there was a pause.

"Does it really matter?" Luci questioned.

I was a bit taken back by the question.

"It matters to me, yeah? My Dad was just torn apart by a monster, and now the voices in my head are saying his name. So yes, it matters. I want to know what is going on here. Is that so much to ask?" I huffed in a hoarse tone.

There was a pause.

"Arthur is your father?" the man spoke.

"Of course he is!" I snapped.

There was a long pause that followed. Perhaps it was a few minutes; maybe it was just a few seconds. I'm not sure.

"We need to get going Orion," Luci said.

"I know. They're getting closer," Orion agreed.

"Hey!" I yelled. "That's enough of this bull. Tell me what's going on!"

"Tell me your name," Luci asked.

I hesitated. "Terrance. Terrance Homwell," I answered.

"Do you want to avenge your father, Homwell?" she asked.

I wasn't sure how to answer. I don't know anything about these voices, I could just be dreaming, or maybe it's a hallucination? I can't tell. I have never seen stuff like this before, not even in dreams. Maybe Daisy kicked me, and I'm out cold? There has to some reason all this is happening.

"Kid? Kid! Are you even listening? I'm giving you a once in a lifetime opportunity, and you're not even paying attention," she barked.

"I'm listening, alright?" I sighed.

My eyes looked down at the floor. I looked at my boots with a mindless stare.

Honestly, I don't know what to do.

"Hmm? Well, you must be a pretty bad listener then. Listen up! I'm going to say this once...unless I feel like repeating it. Your father was killed by a minion of demons. It was technically a Leech, but that's not really important, and I don't feel like explaining the difference. Anyway! If you want to get revenge for your father's death, then our goals will line up. Or you know, you can just sit here and do nothing," she exclaimed.

I blinked a few times in silence.

"What?"

A loud exhale sounded from within my head. "Terry...listen, hun, do you or don't you want to avenge your father?" she questioned.

"Terrance," I corrected. "Umm, yes?...No. I'm not really sure what you're asking me to do."

A howl came from outside unlike any I had heard before. It wasn't any animal I could recognize, but the sound itself sent fear through me like a cold chill of the air.

"We have to get moving Terrance. If you want the truth, then it will come with time, for now, we must continue or else those Leeches will come for you," Orion warned.

"Can I bury him?" I asked.

"You know that answer; now we must move," Orion answered.

I forced my way up. My legs shook, but the wall behind me made a good support system. I looked over at the remains and gripped my shirt. With slow and unbalanced steps, I made my way over to the man who gave me everything.

If I only had given him more, but at least now I have the chance to.

I reached down and took the double barrel shotgun from his hands. I paused a moment before standing back up. A few more tears came from my eyes.

I suppose that I had a few more to give after all.

"Dad," I whispered, soft and low against his ear. "Thank you kindly."

I stood up and snapped back the gun. The used shells flew out from the barrel. I reached into the pouch on my side from the cellar box. I pulled out two of the shells and slipped them into the barrel with a slick movement.

"I'm not going to let him die for no reason," I said with the assumption that they heard me.

"Then try not to disappoint us, vessel," Luci said with a cheery tone.

"Same to you," I replied.

I walked out of the white house that was now painted with red and black. I refused to look back as I headed to the garage.

"My Dad fixed up an old truck, I figured it'd be better than walking to wherever you're taking me," I ensured.

I reached the garage and opened up the doors. My body was on autopilot as I moved through the building. I grabbed a few boxes of juice and water that were stored here. Lastly, I walked over to the toolkit. I opened up the metal box and lifted the organizer. Under was a stack of cash Dad had stored for an emergency fund.

This was an emergency if I've ever seen one.

I stuffed everything into a camo duffle bag. With that, I moved to the truck. It was a beat up piece of junk that had no business running. The gray coloring was washed out with a red tint from the years of rust. There was evident damage from the winter salt and from several accidents over the years.

I took the keys from the cupholder and attempted to start the pickup. There was an angered hiss from the engine the first attempt, but I paid it little mind. I twisted the key again and pressed on the gas. The engine hissed once more, but this time it developed into a clunky purr.

"Are you sure this thing won't just break down?" Luci asked.

"No, in fact, I'm pretty sure it will," I answered with an emotionless voice.

"This machine seems to be running. Let us move," he insisted.

"You're a broken record man. I got somewhere to go first. If I can't bury my Dad, I'm going to make sure someone will," I replied.

"Will it take long?" Orion asked.

"It shouldn't. They might be able to help too," I lied.

I didn't even know what these voices wanted from me, but I can't just follow these voices without any explanation. The bonfire would most likely still be going on. I should be able to get to a phone or at least to a charger. Someone's gotta be able to help me, and I figured that Thomas is the first place to try.

I pulled out of my garage and backed out to the road. I turned to head towards Thomas's house and heard another howl. It was still far away, at least that's what it sounded like.

"They will be hunting you. Do not be careless Homwell," Orion warned.

"I got it," I confirmed.

I pressed the gas and sped up to Thomas's.

4
OLD DOGS, NEW TRICKS

Got to find Thomas. I got to call for help. Something...I got to do something.

The old truck, despite the clunks and clangs, managed to get up to a decent speed as I flew down the dirt road towards my friend's house. The sweat on my face took over in the place of my tears. The humid summer night did come early just as predicted and the air in the truck was more of a dust storm than helpful.

When the light from the bonfire came into vision I sped up even more until I was in the packed driveway. I quickly parked and jumped out of the car. I didn't bother to take the keys from the truck, I highly doubt anyone would run off with it, especially right now.

I looked over to the bonfire as people were walking to their rides. I can only imagine the time as everyone seemed to be making their way home.

Marcy Sing walked over to the car next to mine. She was dressed in a swimsuit top and jean shorts. Her tan skin looked even darker in the glow of the fire. I reached out and grabbed her wrist.

I'm not sure if the action was out of fear or what. I just needed answers but I do wish my manners were better here.

"Hey!" she called. She tried to pull back her hand before she looked up at me. I suppose it was my face that changed her expression from anger to worry. "Terrance? What's going on?"

"I need to know where Thomas is. It's an emergency," I pleaded.

Marcy nodded and pointed towards the house. "Thomas went inside about five minutes ago. Do you need help or something? Can I do anything?" she asked.

"Thank you kindly," I said and ran towards the house. I didn't have time to answer her other questions. I needed to get help and right now I needed someone familiar.

I ran into the house whose lights lead my path like a...*I don't have time for this.*

I ran into the house with a pant and shut the door hard behind me. I took a deep breath as for the first time since I last woke up, I felt safe. I looked around the home. Thomas' house was always a mess but I mean I can't blame his family. He has six siblings and two are under five and the house showed that. I walked through the hand-me-down crowded hallway and into Thomas' room.

I saw my friend digging for something under his bed when I walked in. He looked up and smiled.

"Terrance, you made it after all. Sorry to disappoint you man but everyone's going home," he said. Thomas' eyes scanned over me then quickly turned to worry. "What's going on?"

I walked over and plugged my phone into his charger. I knew that I would need it.

I started to pace across the bedroom. I wasn't even sure where to start. I was so quick to rush over here that I didn't even think about what I was going to say.

"Why are you wasting time?" the man in my head asked.

...Man, I'm going crazy.

"Shut it," I snapped, but quietly.

"What?" Thomas asked.

Not quite enough, apparently.

I stopped my pacing and turned to face Thomas directly. "Look, this is going to sound crazy but a lot has happened, like so much that I don't even know where to begin to explain all of this," I said, honestly. I took a deep breath and clapped my hands together in preparation for this insane story. "The cows on my farm got taken over or replaced? Maybe mutated is the better word...Anyway, they ain't cows anymore. I was cleaning out the barn and one attacked me. It looked like something out of a sci-fi movie. I ran back to my house and my Dad was on the porch with a shotgun. He told me to get into the cellar, which I did. Then I started hearing all these voices and they told me to pick up this mirror."

I reached into my pocket and pulled out the mirror to show Thomas before I put it back where it belonged.

"But after I touched it I woke up in so much pain, most of which is gone but like I feel like I was hit by a car on fire. Anyway, I could still hear the two voices and they told me that I had to run cause I was the vessel or-"

"What are you doing!" Orion barked.

I paused. "I'm telling him the truth, that's what I'm doing," I replied in a sour tone.

"You can't tell mortals," Luci added in the same tone as Orion.

"I can tell him, he's my best friend," I argued.

"That's not the point. You cannot give just anyone this knowledge," Orion continued.

I shrugged. "Too late, going to finish," I ensured.

I turned back to Thomas. His teeth were clenched and his eyebrows were dropped. He looked worried and maybe even a bit scared.

"Look, I know it sounds crazy, I promise, it's all true," I said.

Thomas pointed towards my shirt. "You're covered in blood Terrance."

I looked down at the red on my shirt. It was the first time I had noticed it, but I was well aware that it wasn't mine.

"It's not mine," I said with a whisper. The words were sour in my mouth as I tried to tell Thomas just who this belonged to. I didn't even want to admit it myself. "It's my Dad's. He protected me from those things."

"Why don't we sit down for a little bit Terrance?" Thomas suggested. His hands moved to motion me to sit on the bed.

"Right now I can't. Orion says that I have to get going or else those things will come back," I hastily replied.

"Who's Orion? You're talking really weird," Thomas said. There was a pause in his voice. An unsettling pause.

"He's the...actually, I don't know what he is," I admitted.

Thomas paused for a long time. He didn't move or talk. He just stood there for a long time as if he was searching for what to say. After a minute, maybe two, he spoke. "Where's your Dad, Terrance?"

I pushed my hair back. "I already told you, he stopped those things from killing me. He's at the house. Look, I don't want to say it. You know what I'm trying to say, okay? Please...I came here to get some help. I need to keep moving, at least for a bit. I'll come back in a few days but I don't want anything happening to anyone else. I don't know what these things are or why they want me. Please send someone to my house. I gotta get going but I just need someone to help me. I can't do this alone."

"Terrance..." Thomas started.

I narrowed my eyes. I never thought this would happen. Thomas is my best friend, he always has been, and yet, here he was with a scared mug that shuttered at my every word.

"I can't believe it," I said. "You don't believe me."

"No, I mean...Terrance listen to yourself, voices, possessed cows, and you're covered in blood," Thomas sighed.

"I'm not lying," I ensured. "You're my best friend. Shouldn't you of all people believe me?"

"Terrance just tell me what you did to your Dad. I can try and help you but you gotta tell me what happened. Did he get drunk or something? Did you two get in a fight?" he began to ramble.

I shook my head and gritted my teeth. I stormed over to my phone and pulled it from the table with the cellphone charger coming with it.

"I didn't do anything and that's why I'm here and my Dad isn't. Don't you ever try to blame me for this, you know I wouldn't hurt him," I claimed. "Forget it, I thought I could tell you."

I ran out of the room and then out of the house. I jumped into the truck and past Marcy without a word. I left without a single word even as I saw Thomas run out of the house and heard him call out to me.

The dirt of the road flew up as I sped down the dirt road and towards the highway exit ramp. There was a cold and tight grip on my chest as I sat in the hiss of the broken radio's song.

I drove for at least an hour before I noticed how low the needle on the fuel gauge was. I pulled off the highway and onto a lonely exit. It was a rather bare area. Just a few buildings, mainly fast food and the single gas station. I pulled into the station and parked the truck.

I was not quite sure if I turned off this truck if it will ever start again. Then again, this was the only option I had.

If I didn't get gas then I'm pretty sure I wouldn't be getting too much further.

I got out of the truck and turned off the engine. I let out a heavy sigh and leaned against the truck's side.

"You had to have seen that coming," Luci said.

"Shut it," I barked.

There was silence.

I stared out past the pumps of the gas station. The sun was starting to rise across the forest line. The light filled the barren cornfield between the dark green woods and where I stood. The world was quiet here, most likely just from the fact that it was barely dawn.

I let out a deep sigh. I felt like all the air from my body was being pushed out and when I breathed in again it felt like I was breathing in ice.

"Tell me, what are you two?" I asked.

There was a pause.

"If we tell you then you will not be able to avoid the destiny that is laid in front of you. The life you had known will be nothing but a memory and there's a good chance of your life being lost. Are you willing to accept these terms? If you are not then you have no right to hear the truth," Orion claimed.

"I don't have much of a life anymore. My Dad was all I had and now, because he was protecting me, he's dead. I think you know damn well that I'm ready to listen," I answered, coldly.

"Ohh so dark and gloomy," Luci laughed.

"Do you have to do that?" I sighed.

"Of course I do, I'm a demon after all," she hummed.

The name for a moment bounced in my head. I couldn't tell you what I was thinking, I'm not even sure if I can explain it at all.

There was a sinking feeling in my gut and a chill on the back of my neck. With wide eyes and a gaping mouth, I tried to speak but nothing came out.

"Luci, why do you feel the need to scare him?" Orion questioned. "She is not a demon...at least not technically. But if you are willing to listen then we will tell you the truth. Raise the mirror up and look at your face. We will show you our forms. This will soon become your reality as everything you've been told up until this point has been lies."

I pulled out the mirror just as I was told. I looked directly into the pocket glass.

My eyes seemed cold. There was chill around my body and soon the white of eye eyes slowly began to disappear. The pupil also began to change but it didn't hurt. In fact, besides slightly chilly, I didn't feel any different.

The green of my eye pulled out as if it was being stretched across the white until there was nothing left. The green lightened and soon became a dark amber color. The black pupil stretched and narrowed until it looked like that of a cat. Then the image blinked. I watched my reflection blink. I narrowed my brow but the mirror image didn't move.

The skin across my reflection's face began to shift and morph. A dark brown, nearly black color engulfed the tan skin as if a brush was painting the skin. With each stroke of color, the skin dried out more and more till it looked as if my face and neck were made of old bark. The skin shifted and stretched upwards as if there was something pulling at my reflection's face; almost like Playdoh.

I touched my own skin to ensure that it was only the reflection who was changing.

The image looked as if my entire face, neck, and upper shoulders were wearing a mask fashioned from old bark that had been burnt.

There was a bright light of red. It was then that I could see the flames under the wood. Through the cracks between the layers of bark, there was a bright flame that overtook the under color where there was once flesh.

The sound of breaking sticks filled my field of hearing as the empty place where my mouth once was, tore apart. The wood split and pulled as a jagged and startling outline of a mouth formed. It looked like a jack-o-lantern that had been possessed.

The creature in the reflection looked at me and smiled. It turned it's head slightly as smoke rose from the wood.

"My name is Luci," she spoke. Her voice did not match this horrific monster in the reflection. It was almost sweet and very normal sounding. Like I wouldn't be surprised if I ran into a little girl with this exact voice.

"What are you?" I shuttered.

"Well right now I'm a voice in your head my little schizophrenic haha," she laughed. "Actually I'm a little devil on your shoulder so to speak."

"So you're a devil?" I asked.

"A demon," she replied.

I got cold.

I couldn't believe that there was actually a demon in my head. The idea itself sounds crazy. All of this does. In fact, I'm certain this is crazy. I mean just look at Thomas, did you see his face? He really thought I had killed my Dad. Me! I mean I hunt and I've been in a few fights here and there, mostly 'cause they deserved it, but still! I've never hurt a person that bad before. I don't really think I could.

Though if I ever see those things again that attacked my Dad, I'm sure I could.

Ok.

Ok.

I need to get my head on straight. I know this stuff doesn't make sense but if I spend all my time questioning what's going on then I'm going to end up getting killed or arrested, something. It's not like I could explain this to the cops.

Oh F-I didn't think about that! Thomas is gonna call the cops, that much is for sure. Well, there's no way I can explain what's going on. If Thomas didn't believe me then there's no way that the cops will.

I started pumping gas into my truck while my mind raced about everything that has happened.

"So let's just assume for a moment that this doesn't sound crazy. I have a demon in my head who sounds like a little Hispanic girl and then some old dude too? What exactly are you then? The angel?" I asked.

"Yes," Orion answered, bluntly.

"...Ok, umm. I wasn't expecting to be right. I'm not really sure where to go from here," I said.

"For starters, you may want to pay attention to your surroundings. It would seem we're not alone," Orion claimed.

I turned around and moved over to the driver side of the truck glancing over the cornfield in front. I noticed three pairs of red eyes staring back at me.

Probably just some coyotes.

That did not stop me from slowly opening up the driver side door. I grabbed hold of the shotgun without taking my eyes off of the what I hoped was the coyotes' glowing red gaze. I pulled the shotgun out of the truck and the creatures began to make their way out of the cornfields and onto the street. My mouth went dry when they got close enough for the light to make their details visible.

One of the three at least used to be a coyote. Its swollen eyes glowed red as it hungrily stared at me with insane intensity. The skin of coyote's muzzle was pulled back to reveal the muscle beneath and to make way for a host of large razor sharp teeth that oozed bubbling black slime. In fact, it seemed to be the same slime that the cows released as well. Much like the teeth the rest of the creature's body was much larger than a regular coyote seeming to be quite a few inches taller. The skin was ripped in several places along the body releasing more black tar and I swear I could see it bubble from under the intact skin. As I rose my gun up all three dogs growled in unison and I got a look at the other two. They were not coyotes but what seemed to be regular dogs. One looked like it used to be a husky while the other had golden retriever like features except its fur was stained from the constant dripping of black ooze. Both being a bit smaller than the coyote but still large in their own right.

They started moving in a semicircle around me, keeping their distance. It looked like how wolves circle prey to test out which is the best way of attack. I assumed the coyote was the alpha of this hellish pack as the others followed close behind it; they circled me.

I quickly scanned my shotgun between each three to keep them back while I figured out exactly what to do. Since it was a double-barreled shotgun I only had two shots but there were three that needed to be shot.

As I was thinking about this I heard Orion shout in my head, "On your right!"

I looked to my right to see the thing that used to be a husky charging me. I brought around my gun and immediately fired out of panic. The gun thundered but the shot whizzed above the dog's head. This didn't faze it as it continued to close the distance across the road. I quickly fired again, this time aiming, and the shot hit it directly in its head. The husky immediately skidded along the ground and died as the bubbling black slime flowed from its head.

For a moment I felt relieved but then I heard Orion shout, "On your left!"

I reacted too late and felt an intense pain shoot through my arm. I yelled out and looked down to see the golden retriever biting down hard into my left arm. Its black ooze mixed with my blood. I almost could feel the massive sharp teeth grinding into the bone. Tears welled up as the dog started to yank on my arm, keeping it from moving.

"In front of you," I heard Luci yell.

The dog pulled on my arm and growled. I looked up and terror filled my eyes. I saw the coyote leap, its huge mouth opening wide to bite down on my face. I rose my free arm up instinctively and shut my eyes. I felt a burning pain but different from the tearing pain in my other limb. I opened my eyes to see a bright light fading from my arm and with the light fading so did the pain.

My right arm was now covered in a metal gauntlet and armor like someone would see in a museum. The coyote hung from the silver and gold gauntlet but could not bite through. My arm moved on its own towards the dog on my left arm, which carried both the shotgun and coyote with it.

The gauntlet collided with the creature's face; it tried to yelp but was immediately silenced when its eyes bulged out even further as the skull caved in. The coyote slid off the gauntlet sending it scrambling in the remains of what used to be the retriever.

The demon coyote got up after some difficulty and turned to look at me, but it did not make a move to attack. The gauntlet handed the shotgun to my other hand. I grabbed it with hesitation. The weight of the shotgun immediately caused me to cry out in pain. My armored hand, on its own, lifted up and pointed at the demon. It hissed and growled, surprisingly at the same time, before scampering off back towards the cornfield.

My right hand lowered and started to glow. The armor seemed to melt into my skin, but with no pain. I carefully raised my hand to my face and gave it a few test squeezes. It felt like mine again but like I fell asleep on it.

I stared blankly into the field. "...What the heck was that?"

5
LONG WINDED DESCRIPTION THAT I DIDN'T ASK FOR

"Terrance, those things are called Leeches," Luci began. "They are very lowlife demons, actually, I find them rather repulsive to even give them the dignity of calling them demons; it's an insult to me."

"You're not even a full demon yourself Luci," Orion sighed.

"And no one asked your opinion. Anyway, these Leeches have come to your world along with the s-" I cut her off.

"Hold on-" I rose my left arm. "Bleeding."

I ran into the gas station store. I continued to look behind me at every moment that I could. I had no idea if that thing would come back, or how many will come with it. Without hesitation I ran back in the store until I found the first aid section. I pulled ace wraps and medical pads then I ripped open the boxes. The white bandages flew across the tile floor. I fumbled for a moment before getting the material to wrap my left arm.

I used my teeth and good hand to tightly wrap my arm with several layers. With a pant I paused. There was so much going through my mind that I was unsure of what to do next. But, I couldn't think about it too far, after all, I still didn't know if the creature would come back.

The blood was already starting to make its way through the bandages. I continued to wrap the bite mark until there were no more bandages left.

My arm looked like a marshmallow if it was made of cotton and pain.

I let out a heavy sigh as my body relaxed for a moment. Just a moment, my mind was everywhere and nowhere...that sounded pretty good. Truthfully I just felt like I took a four-hour nap but during that nap, I was tied to the back of a startled horse.

I stood and took a deep breath as my breathing slowed down. With my good arm I wiped my forehead and looked out the windows of the gas station. There was nothing new across the empty gas station.

"Thank God," I said, quietly.

The sound of falling change grabbed my attention. I looked over to see a very scared looking man. His hands shook as he held his cellphone with a tight and sweaty grip.

"No," I shouted. I didn't even realize that I had shouted until the store fell silent again.

My eyes were locked with the man across from me. I looked down at the empty boxes of medical wraps and the shotgun in my right hand.

"Look man, I'm not gonna do anything. So why don't we put the phone down and talk about this?" I offered.

I heard the sound of the man's smartphone snap a photo of me. I narrowed my eyes and let out a groan.

"Why can't anything go right today?" I groaned.

I stormed out of the store and ran to my car. I took the pump out of the truck and put it back in the holder. I opened the car door and grabbed the can of cash before heading back inside. The man was holding the phone up to his ear as I assumed he was calling the police.

"How much do I owe you?" I asked and put the can of money on the counter.

He dropped his phone as if from fear and rose his hands high above his head.

"I don't want any trouble," the man claimed.

"I don't either, how much?" I said again.

"T-take! Just don't hurt me!" he begged.

"I'm not going to hurt you," I tried to say calmly. "Why does everyone think-I don't have time for this right now. Here." I pulled out a handful of money and placed in on the counter. "If those things come back, stay inside."

I backed away from the counter and headed back outside. I got halfway out the door before turning back to the cashier. "Thank you kindly," I added.

I left the gas station building and finished filling up the truck before I headed out. I gripped the steering wheel hard before headed back out onto the highway.

"Well, I think that went well," Luci snickered.

"I killed them didn't I? Now, do you want to explain why my arm was covered in armor?" I asked.

There was a pause.

"As Luci was explaining, you are the vessel now Terrance. This means that your body now contains the soul and abilities of Luci and I. This means that your human body will change as we desire in order to fulfill our quest," Orion began.

"So I'm like play-doh?" I asked.

There was a pause.

"How the Hell did you get that? You know, I'm not even going to question it...Actually, I can't help myself. Are you an idiot?" Luci scoffed.

I narrowed my brow. "Why do you have to be so foul?" I asked.

"Did you miss the part when I said I was a demon?" she replied.

I shrugged. "Fair enough. But did you miss the part when I clearly said I don't know what's going on?"

There was a pause.

"Fair enough," she agreed. "Look Trance."

"Terrance," I corrected.

"Does it really matter?" She sighed. "Let me just explain what's going on for you. Orion and I are here to merge with the vessel. Seeing that he's kind of...mincemeat, we're sticking with you."

"That's my Dad, by the way. Maybe be a bit more respectful? I mean he was your vessel," I argued.

"The vessel isn't that special kid. I think you're building this up more than you need to be. You dad was trained to be able to hold angelic souls when needed. That being us. He just practiced suppressing his own mind and being fit enough to maintain our powers without being torn to shreds. He was picked randomly and wasn't even my first choice. Now we're stuck with you; an untrained kid who can barely hold Orion for ten minutes," she explained. "But you're all we got. Once we're in a human's soul, we're stuck till the human dies or until the job is done."

"So you're attached to my soul? Like the actual soul? And I'm basically a meat puppet to help you carry out your job?" I clarified.

"Pretty much," she said. "But you're barely a puppet. I am surprised that Orion was able to take over your arm during the fight. Perhaps you are not hopeless, but we are nowhere near ready to complete the task at hand."

"So that armor was Orion? It looked like something that belongs in a museum but a lot less rusted. It was a weird feeling. It was like my arm was asleep, or something. Where is Orion anyway?" I asked.

"He's working on your arm. You get some benefits for us being around, you know," she revealed. "Orion keeps your endurance up and can use his abilities to heal you at a quicker rate. This does not mean that you're immortal. Far from it. It just means you might survive a hit or two from a demon."

I looked over at my marshmallow arm with interest. "Really?"

"Yes, really," she sighed. "He'll be busy for a while and by then you should be fine, maybe sore, maybe you'll have a scar. I'm not sure how he works, to be honest."

"So you're going to use me to fight those things? Why?" I asked.

"Those things are called Leeches like I already said. They're the least of our worries."

"Then what are we doing? I don't really care for all this explanation. Just tell me what I have to do already," I scoffed.

There was a pause.

"The Horn of Gabriel. It was taken from me and we must find it before one of the Seven Deadly Sins blows it," Luci said, bluntly.

"W-wait. What?" I yelled.

"You said no explanation," she replied.

"Okay, a little more than that! The Seven Deadly Sins? Are they real? I thought that was just something we were told to live better lives or something. And they took the horn from you? Isn't it supposed to be with Gabriel or something?" I rattled off questions.

"There's a lot that is myth and fact within the Human understanding of our world. The horn is real but the Angel of Hell, me, is the keeper of the horn. I have a set date and time when I'm supposed to blow the horn and release the Four Horsemen of the Apocalypse. Now is not the time for this but it would seem that the Sins have gotten the idea into their heads that the blower of the horn will become the fifth horsemen, which I can tell you now is a lie. I don't know how the rumor started but it's gotten out of hand. We have to get the horn before it is blown and prevent the Sins from destroying the world. Enough detail?" Luci explained.

I sat in silence as I drove down the highway.

What was I even supposed to say to that? It was something straight out of a superhero movie.

"Kid? Kid!" Luci called.

"Sorry, it's a lot to take in. So I don't really have a choice in whether I do this or not, do I?" I asked.

"Nope."

"That's what I thought," I added.

I cleared my throat as my thoughts tried to make sense of what was going on.

"So what do I have to do?" I asked.

"That's a loaded question," Orion spoke up.

"Did you finish with his wound?" Luci asked.

"As much as I could. I cannot push his body too far," Orion replied.

"So I'll be okay?" I asked.

"Yes. The bite has been closed. But it will be tender for a while longer. I suggest not moving your arm unless you have to. As for what you must do, well, simply put you must be our vessel. We cannot fully take over your body but it would seem that, for now, we can control portions of you. I can do my best to help guide you in emergency training in the hopes of allowing us to control more of your body at a time. But, I do not know how much help that will be," Orion explained.

"So you have to take over my body to fight the Seven Deadly Sins, right? So we gotta find them too. Anyway, we can do that?" I asked.

"The more Leeches, the closer we are to a Sin," Luci explained. "They do give off a scent but so do we. So we might be able to track them through smell but they can do the same for us. Again, we can try. I can't say that will work."

"Were the cows Leeches?" I asked. My hands tightened on the steering wheel.

"Planning revenge are we?" Luci laughed.

"Do not act on anger," Orion said.

"Don't ruin the fun, old man. If that's what it takes to get what we need then let him be angry. Do you want revenge, Trent?" Luci questioned.

"Terrance, "I corrected. "And if it was a Sin that killed my Dad then yeah, I want revenge. He was the only family I had and he didn't deserve to go out protecting his coward of a son. Just tell me what we have to do to kill that Sin that's responsible."

"Oh, the boy who barely survived the Leeches wants to go to the top of the food chain!" Luci scoffed.

"Hey, you're the one who told me to do it," I replied.

"I think what Luci is trying to say, in her own unique way, is that the Sins are not something to be taken lightly. You are untrained and a child in comparison to the original vessel," Orion said.

"So basically, I'm screwed?" I asked.

"You're not listening. You're untrained which means you need to be trained but we don't have time. We will have to rely on, what's the word for it...field experience, to make up for the lack thereof," Orion added.

"Or you know, we could just find the horn," Luci argued.

"Well, I guess that is an option. Any idea how to?" Orion asked.

"You're the angel, shouldn't you know?" she replied, sharply.

"Aren't you the one who lost it?" Orion said back.

"Stolen and lost are very different birdbrain," she sighed. "Well, I suppose we could track it using the kid."

"What do you mean, use me?" I asked.

"I don't mean it in a bad way. What do you think would happen to a human around the item that is not only holy but has the ability to destroy the world? You'll probably get some strong emotion right? We're already dead. It won't matter what happens to us if the Earth is destroyed. So you'd probably be able to sense something, right?" she suggested.

I paused. "That sounds really stupid," I stated.

"Oh, I'm sorry. What did you have in mind? Since you know so much about ancient relics!" she snapped.

"From how you've been talking, probably as much as you," I replied.

"Why you little-" Luci began.

"Look, it may not be the best method but it is the one we have. We will go and search for the horn while we train your mind and body to maintain our forms. Once you are strong enough we can use Luci's form to travel across the world much easier," Orion explained. "Till then, use your instincts."

I shook my head and let out a long, exhausted sigh. I reached to the back seat of the truck and pulled out one of the juice boxes. I stuck the straw in and took a long sip. "You are the most unhelpful angels I have ever met," I said.

"And how many angels have you met?" Luci scoffed.

"Two, and so far I'm not impressed," I replied. "If this is the best we have then it's the best we have. Arguing ain't going to do anything. So I guess, I should just drive towards where my gut leads me?"

"It's all we have," Orion said.

"Well, alrighty then," I replied.

6
I STILL HAVEN'T PAID THE RESTAURANT BACK

I listened to the voices of the early, and well, sleep-deprived customers. The fry of the grill hissed through the diner as the shuffle of the daily newspapers barely made a sound over the quiet TV. The news talked about this and that, nothing too important or seemingly important. The truck drivers all sat in their special section as they talked about the utter downpour of rain last night.

The muffled conversations continued despite the ringing in my ears. A quiet ring, that much was for certain.

It's like when you're watching the Friday night football game. It's the fourth quarter and the other team has been catching up quickly but were always behind. Well, now they're right there, tied and only a few yards from their goal. We watch with anticipation as our team fights to keep the visitors from winning. Everything is silent in those few moments. Just for a moment, everything is so quiet that you can almost hear the player's breathing. But suddenly, it's no longer quiet.

The sudden cheers from the stands fill your ears as the crowd jumps up. You follow and soon your own voice is joining the cheers. You yell and scream as your players run down the field, seconds are passing by each moment. It's almost over. Just as the clock hits zero your team scores the winning touchdown.

You cheer but there is a ringing, a soft one but just annoying enough for you to pay attention to it. You want it to stop, you even try and pop your ears but nothing seems to work. You didn't think they were going to win, you had given up but not that you'd say that; how could you? They're your team and you didn't believe in them. So you lie and say you knew they would win. Then the ringing gets louder.

"Kid?" a woman's voice called.

I looked up at the middle-aged waitress. Her eyebrows were raised high, it stretched out the dark bags under her eyes. She stood with her weight shifted back and a tray of food in her hand, two eggs scrambled, two slices of bacon, and two slices of toast with jam along with a glass of grape juice.

"Oh, yeah. Sorry, I'm a little tired," I said. "Thank you."

She placed the food down and rolled her eyes just slightly before walking back to the kitchen.

I turned to the food and took a bite of my toast. I chewed and looked out the window of the diner. I stared out at the truck with a bit of discomfort.

I wasn't allowed to bring my gun in, I didn't blame them but I don't want to be without it. I didn't know if those things are everywhere or when they will strike next. It made me uneasy.

"Remind me why we're here?" Luci groaned.

"You said follow my gut," I replied.

"And your gut lead you here? Luci asked.

"I haven't eaten in a while. I'm hungry," I answered. "Leave me alone."

"Do you understand how serious this is Terrance?" Orion asked.

"If I didn't would I be going along with this crazy plan? I'm listening to voices in my head that are telling me to find something that I was sure didn't actually exist. So yeah, I understand this is serious. Look, I've got a lot on my mind and I don't really need two extra voices right now. So unless you have something important to say please just shut up until we go back to the car," I sighed.

There didn't seem to be a reply. I continued to eat and tried to ignore the stares I was getting from those who saw me talking to myself.

"I'm tired," I said.

I hadn't slept since I apparently passed out. Since then I've done enough to be considerably tired. I just want to go to bed.

I pulled out my phone and looked into the camera as a mirror. My hair was a messy, mud-coated, bird's nest. The dirt on my face and clothes showed that I had fallen into the mud a few times. My eyes had bags under them both from the crying and the lack of sleep. Lastly, there were some blood stains coming up from under the white bandages on my left arm.

I sighed and closed the screen. I put my phone on the counter and rubbed my eyes.

"I'm going to clean up in the bathroom before I leave," I said.

I know I told them not to talk to me. I know I said that, but that doesn't mean I couldn't still talk to them. Right then they were the only ones I could really talk too even if I really didn't want to.

Once I was about halfway through the meal, I figured I needed to clean up a little. The diner was getting a bit more crowded as the morning rush was coming in. I was getting sick of the stares. I waved over the waitress and smiled.

"I'm going to go to the restroom real fast, I'll leave my bag here. I'll be right back," I said.

I didn't want anyone to think that I wasn't going to pay for the meal.

She pointed me to the bathroom and went on with her other customers. I left my bag and walked to the restroom. I went into the single stall bathroom and locked the door.

I looked into the mirror to see that the mud did go fully down my back and was splattered onto the front of my shirt and jeans.

I went to the sink and washed the mud off my face and, to the best of my ability, out of my hair. For the first time, I began to get an indication of just how bad I smelled. I knew that this wasn't just mud but I wasn't going to admit that.

I washed my hands and rubbed my eyes. They were sunken from everything. It hurt to see them alone as they reminded me of everything that had happened.

It took a few deep breaths before I was able to leave the bathroom and return to the diner. I noticed that a couple of people looked up at me when I entered back into the main part of the diner. A few looked at their phones and then back to me and then back to their phones. Some did the same thing to the TV.

I rose an eyebrow and looked up at the TV. Up on the screen was my school yearbook photo. The woman on the screen continued the story with a pursed lip and 'serious' expression that made it look as if she had never seen anything like the story.

I looked down and tried my best to avoid eye contact.

The squeak from the counter stools echoed through the nearly dead quiet diner. The only thing that could be clearly distinguished was the voice of the news reporter.

"Authorities are on the lookout today for Terrance Homwell who is wanted in questioning in the death of

Arthur Homwell. Terrance was last seen at the gas station on Mount. Apple Road. He is thought to be armed and possibly dangerous. Police warn not to approach but to rather call the information hotline below…" Her voice was drowned out by the high pitch ringing in my ears.

My feet moved forward. The sound of my boots was drowned out by the ringing. They must have been loud though, everyone was staring.

It was right then that I realized two things. One, these people…and maybe countless others, thought that I had killed my Dad and now I was wanted for his murder. And two, I wouldn't be able to finish my breakfast.

But there was a chance that I could sneak by. I mean, people see the news all of the time and they don't say anything, even if they really saw something wrong; there's a whole TV show about that kind of stuff. I would probably be fine to just get up and leave without a word.

"Hey!" a deep voice called through the ring.

Or not.

Two large men stood from the trucker area. One was round and seemed as if he hadn't had a good sleep in a month. His hair was pulled back into a ponytail and his beard had a braid in it that reached his collarbone. The man next to him was quite taller, taller than me that was for sure. He was bald and had seemingly no facial hair, eyebrows included.

I jumped at the call for action. I didn't give any more time for the men to say a word to me, instead I ran for my bag.

Beach-ball and Eyebrows bolted down the aisle towards me with obvious intent. I cursed under my breath and jumped into the booth on my left. I jumped across the line of booths as the men grasped at my legs.

"Eh…no…no, no, no…ahh," I called out as I ran.

"Terrance," Orion's voice called.

"Finally!" I exclaimed. "I gotta get out of here."

"These are humans, only. You cannot hurt them. We must leave at once before you are caught and more trouble ensues," Orion warned.

"Oh, why didn't I think about that? Hmm, I thought I'd just let them catch me," I spat.

"Crazy kid! Com'ere," Eyebrows ordered.

"I'm not crazy!" I shouted back.

I jumped to the booth behind me to avoid Beach-ball's lunge. When he laid in the booth seat, I jumped forward and off his back to the next table. I reached my table and grabbed my bag. Eyebrows swung his fist towards me. I dropped down on my bottom. I bounced off the booth seat and avoided the attack.

I scrambled out from Eyebrows' reach. I crawled across the diner floor until I could get back to my feet. I ran to the doorway, only to feel my collar be pulled.

"Hey," I called as I was dragged back.

I was turned around and pushed against the window. Beach-ball's hand was on my throat as he held me in place. I stretched out my neck in reaction as if I'd be able to slip through his grasp if I made my neck long enough.

"Orion," I gasped.

My tongue tingled and my throat began to sting. I felt a dry burn come from my eyes. I squinted as my eyes tried to wet themselves but to no help. My mouth opened and a small sound came from my lips with no control.

I felt a deep rumble in my chest and at that moment the world gained a yellow tint.

"Enough!" a voice boomed from my lips. It was cold and calculated. It sounded like a military general but the added rumble seemed like what I always thought the voice of a God would sound like.

The world around me shook and the glass windows and dishes within the diner shattered. The screams from the customers and staff were enough to get the man holding my throat to get distracted and for his grip to loosen.

I pulled away from his hands and backed up against the door. I gripped my throat that felt like it was burning. I coughed a few times and looked at the fearful faces in the restaurant.

"Um." I found it hard to speak. "I'm going to go," I said to the crowd raspy like.

I pulled out some money for my meal and put it on the table nearest to me before running back to my truck. I leaned closer to the wheel as I found my vision to be slightly blurry. My eyes itched to a maddening level, but I had to get moving.

"T-thanks," I coughed out.

"It is far too early to thank me, boy. It seems that our souls are even more incompatible that I had feared," he revealed.

"What does that mean? "I asked.

"It means you're a weak little baby who needs us to fight his battles," Luci sighed.

"H-"

"Save your strength, Terrance. She is right about this. In her own way, she is telling the truth. You are not strong enough to handle our power in your current state," Orion corrected.

"Orion save me," Luci mocked.

I gripped the steering wheel tightly. She was annoying and her mocking was like a toddler, but she had a point. I could have gotten out of that situation on my own. I didn't need Orion, at least I don't think I did. I just got scared. When did I become so helpless?

"You're not helping the situation. We will get nowhere at this rate. Perhaps we need to try and make a plan. Let us move to somewhere secluded. Then we can take more time to think over this unfortunate situation," Orion reasoned.

I nodded.

I had no reason to argue. I had no idea what I was doing. I couldn't even outrun some truckers, I truly didn't think that I'd have a shot at taking down a Sin. Why was I just accepting this? I sounded crazy; fighting a Sin? Not in the state I was, I really don't think that I can do this.

I drove for a while. I didn't want anything to do with this town or the people. Honestly, I just wanted to lay down and pretend none of this was happening. It still felt like a dream, God I hoped it was a dream.

Eventually, I came to a long road that stretched through a very hilly area. I found a dirt trail and pulled off to go down the hidden drive. I continued until I could no longer see the main road. I parked and turned off the car. I let out a long sigh and leaned my head back against the seat.

"Get out of the vehicle. Let's walk," Orion ordered.

I didn't argue. I got out of the truck and walked down through the forest. I kept a close eye on my surroundings so that I was able to find my way back. I continued until Orion told me to stop.

"Sit down. This is your training. As it stands you are not ready to handle our souls. And unfortunately, we don't have the time to get you to the level of your father. So, we will do the best we can," Orion explained.

"Ok?" I replied.

"Basically, this is going to hurt a lot and we're going to try and see how long you can last," Luci cleared up.

"Wait, what?" I said.

"Good luck!" Luci laughed.

Pain filled my face as the skin burned against my skull. I felt like my world was melting. There was a red hue over my vision as a scream filled the air. I pulled at my face as smoke billowed from the holes in my skin. The tears from my eyes fell to the forest floor and burned through the surface as if it were acid.

I fell to the ground as the pain became too much for me to handle.

"S-Stop!" I begged but the voice was not mine. It was feminine and young; it was very odd coming from my eighteen-year-old-southern-boy mouth.

The pain stopped and I panted. I wiped my eyes and felt the skin around them. It felt leathery and dry.

I pulled out my phone, looked at the camera and nearly screamed from the sight. The skin across my face was burned and twisted. It covered my mouth as if I had pulled putty over my lips and nose. It looked like I was a thousand-year-old piece of driftwood with bright eyes filled with red and no pupil.

There was a glowing slit across the putty-like mouth. It was a dark gold color that seemed to move like lava. The slit seemed to curve into a slight V-shape against the long pointed face. It looked as if my face had been covered with a charred-wooden mask with molten liquid within the cracks.

"Ahh!" I screamed. I dropped my phone to the ground. "What the Hell am I?"

"Funny you should mention Hell. That's my face," Luci said, bluntly.

7
I ALMOST CAUSE A WILDFIRE

"So please explain this again," I said.

"That is my face. I thought that was pretty clear," Luci replied.

"Ok, so I got that. But it also feels like I have a thousand ants on my face and I'm this close to freaking out," I added. "So please explain this to me again. Why are you doing this?"

"I thought that was simple. We need to test how much you can take. It would be easier to just do it but if it's too much then I guess we can just take a nap and try again while the Seven Deadly Sins continue to try and bring the apocalypse," Luci snarked.

"Hold on now," I began. To be honest, she is pushing my buttons a bit too much at this point. "I am doing the best I can. Everything just happened and it doesn't help that you're being so...so cruel."

"Cruel? You think I'm being cruel? Oh, I'm sorry let me just tone it down for you. Maybe I can ask the Sins to do the same. Would you like that?" Luci mocked.

"I am trying my best!" I barked.

"Your best isn't good enough. What we need is our best if you even want a chance at being useful then step up and do what we say. This isn't some game boy," Luci added.

I was fuming. My whole body felt like it was going to burst into a fiery fit at any moment. This girl was making me so angry that my thinking was fuzzy. How dare she? After everything that I had been through this was how she decided to act. I was trying my best but there was a lot here to take in. I couldn't just get up and go with the punches right now, and I was pissed that she even wanted me to try.

"Do you even care about what I'm going through right now? All of this was thrown on me. I lost my Dad and now suddenly I'm supposed to save the world? I have two voices in my head that are telling me to fight the demons and there's all this pressure that somehow fell onto me. In the last day I have lost everything and now I'm just trying to understand what's going on but you need to give me some time to take this all in. And you pushing isn't helping!" I yelled.

There was a long pause. I had a very uneasy feeling in my gut. There was something in my throat that seemed caught as if I just couldn't spit out the words.

"You know whose fault this is Terrance. Now how are you going to clean up this mess?" Luci snapped.

I screamed. Everything got hot in an instance. I felt like the world around me was one large fire pit that someone just laced with fireworks and gasoline. There was a rush through every inch of my body. I felt both alive and dead in an instance. The world around me turned to a bright red and orange before dying leaving behind nothing but gray and black.

I took deep breaths and curled over my knees. I felt like I was going to vomit. My heart was pounding a thousand miles an hour. I yelled again and shut my eyes.

I felt something pull on me. I couldn't tell you which direction it came from or how exactly it was pulling me, maybe pulling wasn't the right word. It was like I had just been dragged but I didn't actually feel like I had moved at all.

I opened my eyes, slowly.

The world around me was different than the last time I had closed my eyes. I was still in the forest but in a new area. I turned behind me and saw the path of destruction that followed. The bright colors of the spring leaves were charred and in ashes. The path seemed to go on forever.

"Excellent," Orion said.

"Can someone tell me what just happened?" I asked.

"My power. At the moment that you yelled at me was the moment you allowed your soul to be corrupted. Terrance please understand what it is that I'm trying to tell you," Luci revealed.

"So you were trying to get me to yell at you?" I asked.

"So you aren't hopeless. I know your soul isn't strong enough to handle me, willingly. I am an angel of Hell. I am not a demon but that doesn't mean that I can't possess you," Luci explained. She took a deep breath. "This isn't ideal Terry. But we need you to be able to handle our souls."

"You got my name right literally five minutes ago. And, so you were making me mad to possess me?" I clarified.

"I was playing on your wrath and pride. I have to use your sins enough to feed off them. However sinful you are is how long I am able to control you but you have little or no control. But this was all that I am able to give you," Luci explained.

Orion cleared his throat. "But be warned, the more sinful you are the less control I have over you."

"So I have to be sinful to use Luci's powers but not sinful to use yours Orion?" I repeated. "Anything else? Or should I add juggling onto that?"

"This isn't going to be something that will come easy," Orion said. "But look at what you've done. This power is worth it."

I looked at the path of burned trees and ashy grounds.

"I did that?" I asked.

"Well, I did but it was your body, so we did it. We're about a mile away from where we first arrived from," Luci pointed out.

"What?!" A mile? A mile! That's insane. It felt like I had blinked and then I was that far away. It was absurd, unreal, crazy, and so cool! "I'm like a superhero!" I exclaimed.

"If that's what it takes to get you on board then so be it. Now let's get serious," Luci said.

"Agreed. Terrance, you have to calm your mind in order to block out Luci. She has a hand on your soul and if you allow her to remain too long...well perhaps we shouldn't let it get that far," Orion warned.

"Wait, no. If this is something that I'm going to have to avoid then I need to know why I am exactly avoiding it. Why can't you guys just possess me or whatever like Luci is doing now?"

"Haven't you noticed that there are a few things missing?" Luci began." Your face and voice are the only things to change. If I had fully taken over you would look much different, not to mention you'd have wings. In order to take you over completely, you must be either extremely passive or you must be so full of sin that I can control your spirit freely, but that would also mean our enemy could control you as well. Basically, your soul would be in a tug-a-war."

I guess I did forget that angels had wings, then again this face didn't look anything like an angel.

"Was my Dad like that?" I asked absent-mindedly.

"Your father was trained from the time he was young. Each generation has a handful of vessels that can be used by angels to come to earth. These vessels are trained to suppress themselves. Their mind, body, and souls are strong and able to ignore those influences around them," Orion explained.

"Why can't I do that?" I asked.

"Currently, you have too many feelings and care about what others think of you," he answered.

I blushed, at least I felt like I did. I'm not sure if this face is able to blush. "I mean. I could try not to care."

"But you care for your father. You will not be able to do this with such a short amount of time so instead, we will need you to focus on your emotions and expand them. You need to be able to control what you feel and when in order to allow us to possess you," Orion added.

"Did my Dad not care?"

"I cannot tell you certainly but what I can say is that it is possible for the vessels to be able to turn this control off and on when they have enough practice," he replied. "Terrance. This is the best method we can think of to get you ready to take on the Sins."

"Then can't you use those other vessels?"

"It's too late for that. Big guy here, decided to jump into you and now we're stuck till the council releases us or you die," Luci revealed.

"You're stuck in my head till I die?" I exclaimed.

"No, if you die then we will be released back to our bodies or the council will release us. But in this current situation I highly doubt we will," Luci answered.

"Why wouldn't they change? I mean this is a pretty big deal," I said.

"That maybe, might be, kind of is my fault. So the goals of the Sins is to blow the Horn of Gabriel, which they currently have. But, they think they can't blow it till October 30th," Luci explained.

"The Horn of Gabriel? Why the 30th of October?" I asked.

"Because I made it up."

"And they are listening to you because?" I added.

"Because...I'm the guardian of the Horn. But I didn't mean to let it out of my sight! Look when I went to Hell my eternal punishment was to know one day I would end Humanity but it was the Sins' punishment that they had to answer to someone who was once mortal. They didn't like this and eventually they somehow got the idea into their heads that if they blew the Horn of Gabriel then they would become the fifth Horseman of the Apocalypse," Luci explained. She sighed and growled a bit. "I have no idea how they got that idea. But they sure are convinced of this! The Horn isn't supposed to be blown at this time so, it's our job to stop them."

I nodded like I understood. This only confirmed the insanity that I was going through and how unlikely that any of this was true. But, it's not like I had much of a choice.

"So basically, I have to save the world?" I said.

"We have to, you're just the body," Luci corrected.

"Thanks. I'm so honored," I replied. "But how am I supposed to be sinful and not while making sure no one else can take over me?"

"Pain," Orion said.

"Excuse me?"

"Pain," he repeated.

"I got that. But...How? Why? Explain?" I asked.

"When you're in pain, what do you think about?" Luci asked.

I thought for a moment. It took me a bit of time before I had an answer. "Nothing really. I guess I just want it to stop," I answered.

"Exactly. When you're in pain all you have is wants. You want it to stop, you want to feel okay again. This prevents your mind from thinking about anything else," Luci added.

"So you're hurting me to make it easier to take over?" I clarified.

"The pain is a side effect from your body morphing into our forms. It just also happens to clear your mind. Just a happy coincidence," Orion claimed.

"What about this is happy?" I asked.

"We have a fighting chance," Orion said.

"So I have to be angry, or rather sinful, and in pain?" I said.

"Yes," both exclaimed.

"Alrighty then," I sighed.

I pushed back my hair and let out a long, potentially, overly dramatic sigh. *There is honestly way too much here to unpack, just try to imagine that you have to save the world right out of high school with a magical gift that you got by stumbling into the wrong situation at the wrong time and the only person who could tell you what's going on has been killed by the bad guy before you could get a proper explanation for what's going on. Oh wait, I just described every teen movie ever, but this isn't the movies. This is my life and my story, even if I have no control over it.*

I threw up my arms and screamed into the air with no regret. I can't say how long I did this but it was well needed, I think that was why Luci and Orion didn't say anything to stop me. When my scream came down, my throat hurt and my tongue felt numb but it seemed my voice had returned to my own, instead of Luci's. I took several deep breaths before trying to say anything else.

"Alrighty then," I repeated. "Let's get a move on. What do I have to do?"

"You currently have a stronger connection to Luci, try to summon a part of her to take over your body," Orion instructed.

I thought about the offer for a moment. I already have Luci's face which is creepy in itself. I can honestly say I have no interest in seeing the rest of her body any time soon. Not to mention there's something wrong about my body transforming into hers. It just doesn't feel right. But I can't really argue, I am supposed to save the world and I kind of need all the help I can get.

I guess I could start with the wings. I mean she's some type of angel right? "Okay, so how do I get wings? I mean you have wings, right?" I ask.

"Of course I have wings." Luci replied, "Anyway, the best way would be to cross your arms, bow your head, and then shout, 'Wings activate!'"

"...Really?" I said raising an eyebrow.

"Hey who's the angel here?" She replied, sounding almost insulted.

"Alright, alright." I closed my eyes, crossed my arms, and bowed my head. "Wings activate!" I shouted to the forest scaring a few birds in the tree. I slowly opened my eyes and turned my head trying to see my wings, but there was nothing there. "Did I do it wrong?" I asked.

Luci in my head began laughing like crazy. I swore I could feel her actually rolling in my head with laughter. "I can't believe you fell for that." She replied in between a series of laughter.

I will admit I was quite embarrassed and if my face was my own I would probably have been as red as a... um...

thing that is very red. "Is this really the time to mess around?" I said frustrated with falling for it.

"Aw, come on lighten up a little," she said still giggling.

"Come on Luci, let's proceed" Orion ordered, but even he couldn't hold back a small laugh.

"Fine, fine." She sighed "Okay, Terr bear. What you need to do is just focus on your back, right below the shoulder plates, imagine something growing from it, and just think about how much you want to kill the sin that killed your father."

"Okay, I'll give it a shot," I said slightly weary that she was tricking me again. I finally started by taking a deep breath and thinking about something forming from my back. I was also thinking about how much I wanted to see that sin dead to get revenge for my father's death. After about probably ten seconds I felt sharp pains shooting through two parts of my back. I let out a gasp as the pain transformed from a sharp pain to an intense burning. I fell to my knees as I could feel my skin popping and smell what I can only imagine was burning flesh. I let out a yell as I felt something pushing straight out of the bubbling burning skin. It hurt like someone was pulling out long glowing hot metal rods through the small spots below my shoulder plates.

I began sweating profusely as it felt like it was stuck in my back. "You gotta push Terri. Come on push." Luci cheered. At least she is having fun, I had time to think before the searing pain brought back my attention. I took a deep breath and then began to push the muscles in my back. The burning pain increased but I felt the rods moving again. The front of my shirt was soaked with sweat. "Almost there," Luci said.

I got the strength to look back and my eyes went wide with what I was seeing. A pair of long bones had literally burned their way from my back and shirt. They were glistening with what looked like blood as they finally seemed to have stopped growing from my back. After a couple seconds of me panting, I saw bones grow out of the long main stem as they began to take the shape of bat wings. *Now there are phantom pains, when there is a pain for a limb no longer there, but I was experiencing new limb pain.* It was cool though as I could feel the bones growing and new limbs form. Looking back again I saw a black leather drape down and meld over the bones. Heat waves radiated down the wings and I could feel the heat from them.

"See was that so hard" Luci observed. I just took a few deep breaths and then got up from my knees. I immediately almost fell over as I didn't expect the weight the wings added to my back. After a few wobbles, I got my feet beneath me. "Now move them" Luci commanded with a giddy tone. I focused on the new sensation of the wings. I felt the cool wind push against them and how warm they were. Finally, I thought about moving them and after a few seconds of straining my brain, they twitched. I took another breath and focused harder and the wings moved down quickly. I then began having the feeling of control as I flapped them slowly.

"Okay... this is so damn cool" I said as a smile spread across my face.

8

BAMBI'S REVENGE

After marveling at the wings for a time, snapping my neck back and forth to get a good look at them it finally came to my attention that it was getting to evening time and I have a mile walk back to the truck. Oh wait, I guess I could fly, I thought excitedly. "So how do I fly?" I asked.

"Well I am not sure you are strong enough for that yet but you can attempt to flap them quickly to get you off the ground," Luci said thoughtfully. I thought about the wings again and strained the new found muscles. The wings obeyed and began to flap up and down quickly. With each flap, I felt my feet lift off the ground slightly.

"I did it!" I exclaimed, excited. I felt tired though as if it was sapping my energy from moving them.

"Yes, you managed to lift a few inches off the ground. I am sure the sins will be quaking in their boots" Luci laughed. "Though it is a start." She added.

"Darn, I was hoping these could help me make the trek back a bit faster" I absentmindedly said.

"Well walking with them will help train your body to be used to having them out and train the muscles and your balance" Orion replied. At that time I heard some rustling in the bushes around me.

"Wait, what was that?" Luci asked suddenly curious.

"Probably just some deer or squirrels" I replied dismissing it.

"No, I sense demons around us, three or four of them" Luci warned. I quickly swiveled around looking at the locations where the sound came from, and though I could see movement I could not figure out what was moving.

I instinctively looked around for my shotgun. Then it hit me, the shotgun was in the truck… a mile away. "Terrance your body won't be able to survive us taking over for battle. We need to get out of here" Orion remarked. *Didn't have to tell me twice.* I began to back away from the bushes towards the burnt out path I had carved. I did not want to immediately turn my back on them and be surprised when they came out. Though I was still surprised at what came out of the bushes.

One creature pushed its way through the brush, and I saw Bambi on steroids. It was a deer but like the other Leeches before was disfigured. Its face was melted away revealing the bone beneath and it had no eyes. In those eye sockets though were two glowing red dots that stared right at me. Out of its boney mouth steam came out as if it were cold out, but it was a warm summer evening. It was taller than a normal deer at about five feet. It still had skin along its neck and body that boiled with the same black ooze which came out of multiple cuts and holes. Its most impressive feature had to be its horns. They were charred black and huge with multiple points in all directions. I knew for sure that those horns could gore straight through me.

I had seen enough. I began to sprint down the charred path back towards the truck. My feet crunched the burnt leaves and twigs as I ran and I could hear them hot on my tail. The weight of the wings was really pulling down my back and made me slower than usual, and against creatures, with four legs I needed all the speed I could get. I felt a horn poke me in the back as the deer caught up. I took a swift turn into the woods ducking under a tree. I heard something slam into the tree as I came back up and took the time to look behind me. One of the deer had slammed its horns into the tree and was now struggling to pull its horns out. Two more were behind it though and not stopping so I kept running.

"Luci is there a way I could use these wings to go more than an inch off the ground?" I asked huffing as I took another sharp turn around a tree, carefully making sure not to get my new wings caught. A deer flew by where I was and almost slammed into another tree but stopped in time, sadly. If I did not have these wings I probably could make it away from these guys easier, but I was getting winded with all the weight.

"I can make you go very fast but I am not sure if you can handle it at the moment" Luci replied.

"I don't have time to think about that" I yelled almost tripping over a root as I turned by a tree. "I just need to get out of here."

"Fine, but don't say I didn't warn you. Okay I need you to feel mad again, I need you to feel like you just want to tear something apart" Luci told. "These small demons should do fine. Imagine how much you would love to shoot them and get them to stop chasing you."

I pictured what she suggested. It was not hard for me to feel a lot of anger. I did not ask for all this. I did not ask to be chased by steroid Bambi through the forest or forced to apparently fight the Seven Sins of Hell. I felt a strong burn in my gut. It felt like a... very hot... rock in my stomach. *Hey, I'm getting better at these.* Anyway, the burning moved through my stomach and into my back. It was hard to dodge the branches and antlers while this was going on. I dodged around a tree a moment too late and one of the demon deer's antlers scratched across my arm leaving a good size cut.

I yelled out in pain but kept running. The pain from the burning became intense before I finally felt a pulse of heat shoot through Luci's wings. I heard a hissing noise, as I ran, like steam shooting out of a pipe. "Hold on" I heard Luci say in my head. With that, the hissing became a roar and I was launched forward at an incredible speed. I couldn't help but scream a little as a tree came rushing up to me, but then I dodged around it quickly like it was nothing.

"Wow, I am good at this" I cheered as I flew around each tree low to the ground heading back for the originally burnt path.

"You're not the one flying." My mouth moved by itself as Luci's voice came out. It felt great flying and the speed was addictive. I almost found myself wishing for her to go faster. I busted out of the brush and landed on the ground as my feet slid along the ground before coming to a stop. I had a moment to look at where I came and saw many burnt and broken limbs. I also sadly saw three of the deer charging toward me but they were much more distant than before.

I felt my feet start to run forward as I was launched into the air. The wings did not even flap in the open area but instead worked like jet engines as their flames and heat pushed me forward. After a little bit of flying, we began to approach the truck. "So how long can we keep this going for?" I asked feeling sweat drip down my face.

"Up until right now" Luci replied in a strained voice.

"Wait. What?" I asked. I felt my new limbs recede into my back and the burning subside as the ground quickly approached. I barely had time to protect my face before I slammed into the ground and began to roll and slide towards the truck. I could not stop myself in time and slid straight into the truck's front wheel. The air got immediately knocked out of my lungs and I swear I could feel the truck slide slightly from the collision.

I got up onto my arms and knees as I coughed and saw stars. "Terrance get to your feet" Orion called. I snakingly held one finger up to ask for a moment. I took a few shaky breaths before attempting to get to my feet. I used the truck as support and pulled myself up.

I glanced up towards the path as my vision cleared and noticed almost too late the demon deer charging to gore me. My eyes went wide as I attempted to dodge to the right of the attacker. I got my body out of the way but my arm got pinned by the horns as it slammed into the truck. I luckily did not get my arm stabbed through by the antlers but I was completely locked. The deer stared at me now stuck in the truck door with pure hatred and hunger. It was breathing heavily so Luci really gave them a run for their money. I tore my eyes away to see another deer charging towards. There was no way for me to dodge with my arm locked. "Luci, can you help again?" I asked desperately.

"It's going to hurt but yeah" Luci answered breathing a little heavy. It seemed like taking over was putting some strain on her. I felt the familiar anger in my gut but this time the heat quickly traveled to my arms. The deer was about ten feet away when I felt my right arm spin around quickly towards the antlers of the deer locking me in. In one foul swoop, my new hand cut straight through the horns.

Once my left arm was free it moved in a blur and grabbed a broken antler shoving it back into the neck of the first deer. It let out a squeal and my head quickly snapped towards the second deer. It had traveled about half the distance closer to me. The second deer lowered its head for a charge but as it got close to me I expertly dodged around it dragging my hand along its neck and body. It slammed into my truck dead with five long and deep cuts traveling its neck and side flowing with black tar.

The last deer moved its way down the path towards me but more cautiously. It seemed to be wary of my new found powers and so was I. I stole a glance at one my hands as they rose in a defensive position. They were now black with soot with much longer fingers. They looked as if the skin was gone with nothing but hard bone leftover. The fingers ended in points and looked incredibly sharp, and based on the damage the hands did to the first two deer they were quite sharp. I could see my hands shake slightly though and it began to feel like they were falling asleep.

"Terrance I need you to slowly back to the car and grab your gun. I won't be able to hold this form for much longer." Luci warned. I did as she said and backed up to the truck and came up to the driver side door. "Good. Now I am going to give you your hands and it will charge immediately. You need to either drive away quickly or deal with it."

Steam rose from my hands as I could see skin grow back over my hands as they dropped to my sides feeling like TV static. That was the monster and I's cue. It charged forward as I turned around and fumbled with the handle. I got the door open and jumped into the seat on my stomach reaching for the shotgun. I got a hold of it and quickly twisted onto my back to take aim. The deer had already cleared the distance and I quickly threw my legs up as it slammed into the seat. I spread my legs and shouted, "Stop putting holes in my dad's truck!" I fired two shots into its head as it desperately tried to get free of the seat. Its head disappeared into mist and brains as my ears rang.

S.G. BURSON

I dropped the shotgun below the steering wheel,
laid back, and screamed to no one.

9
MIXED EMOTIONS

Breathe.

Last year my Dad took us out to Chickamauga Lake in Tennessee. It was a surprise trip. He told me I was looking too stressed out with school. So we took a long weekend in May, right before finals. I remember thinking it was weird how he just decided to go one day. I woke up to go to school and he said we were going down to Tennessee instead. I didn't argue much, I would have been crazy to. But, there was something in his voice, something that let me know that we had to go.

He had packed all the supplies while I was sleeping and that morning we set out. I didn't think of it being that weird back then, just slightly off. But I was glad to be out of school and to relax one weekend.

We went down to the lake and got a tent site for a few days. Dad left me to set up the tent and said he'd be right back, that he had to run to the store for some more supplies. He was gone for six hours. I made myself busy of course. I assumed he ran into some friends. We came down to this area a lot, at least once a summer. He just got caught up talking, at least that's what I had to tell myself.

The rest of the week was nice. We woke up early and went down to the lake. We fished all day. I remember just how warm the air felt. The sound of the water against my boots. The birds were singing all day and the sky was a perfect blue.

I never felt so relaxed. Dad seemed to have calmed down a lot after that first night. I think he was glad that I didn't ask where he had been. I just assumed he had a reason; Dad always had a reason. I just learned to assume that if it was that important then he would have told me. But I never expected him to keep something like this from me.

"Angry."

How could he keep something like this from me? How could he! Better yet, how dare he. I always trusted him. I never dug too deep if he told me to stop. I wasn't a perfect kid by any means but I tried my best. I really did.

I always said 'yes sir' to any request. I did my chores without too much arguing. I even tried to get good grades, although I could never seem to get past average. I always got the exact middle grade in my class. I have no idea why, but I did. That doesn't matter! None of that mattered. It didn't matter that I was polite or smart. Now I was alone. God! I'm alone, I'm really alone.

"Sad."

How can I do this? Save the world? Defeat the Seven Deadly Sins, get the horn of Gabriel, and just hope I'm not torn apart in the process. Seriously? I'm a kid. I'm just nineteen. Not to mention that my Dad just died. He was ripped to shreds by those things, those evil things!

"Terrance, focus," Orion warned. "Sad, not angry."

I let out a long sigh. I sat up from the bed of the truck and took the old towel off of my face. The morning light shined through the tree levels. The birds sang their songs and the sun gleamed overhead. It was getting hot. I was sweating from being in the heat for so long. But this is what Orion wanted me to do.

It had been two weeks since I last checked in with you guys. During that time I had been traveling around the Appalachian area. Mainly hiding in the woods and avoiding the police as I could. I was full on wanted at this point. So I did my best to stay out of sight. I stopped by truck stops from time to time for food and to shower.

I tried not to stay anywhere too long. The ground in dirt and blood in my clothes didn't make that too hard. I ended up buying a few shirts from a bin at a gas station a few cities over. But the smell, Oh the smell was gag-worthy when enough sun hits it. I've been trying to clean it out but Luci told me that it helps cover my scent from demons. I was not sure that I believe her if I'm being honest but it's not like I can afford not to.

"Terrance," Orion called again.

"Yeah. Yeah. I get it. Sorry Orion, but I think I'm a little drained for right now. We've been at this for weeks now and we're no closer to finding any of the Sins," I replied.

"We have till October, you know" Luci reminded.

"Which is a limited time. Terrance the mastery of your emotions is hard work. But you need to be able to call upon them at a moment's notice. We have been working on your training and it isn't ideal to be in our position but we don't have much of a choice," Orion said. "We just need to keep working till something clicks inside of you."

"I can get parts of you out. Isn't that enough? We just have to find the horn right?" I asked.

"You can get parts out, sure. But you have limited control. None of your skills are constant enough to face a Sin head on" Orion said.

"And we have to find the blessed thing to begin with," Luci scoffed.

"I thought you said to follow the demons?" I asked.

I have been tracking demonic deer for the last two weeks. Occasionally I had to kill them and wait for new ones to surface but they are not trying too hard to hide. It's been rather easy to track them.

"Follow the Leeches and you'll find a Sin. However, I can't say if we will find the horn or not. The horn itself is a powerful item but it's dormant right now. It's not meant to be blown during this time. It would be much easier to find if that were the case. I predict one of the Sins already has the horn. It was taken from me and they were the only ones who had access to me. If I had to guess I'd say Gluttony, Envy, or Greed has it" Luci revealed.

"Why one of those?"

"I'm curious myself, dear" Orion added.

Luci was quiet for a moment. She sighed and mumbled a bit under her breath. "To be honest, I don't see them as much of a threat. They could have snuck past me. I know that they are Sins and all but some are just more powerful than others. I always keep a close eye on Wrath and Pride. Sloth would have had someone else do the deed for him, and Lust is more interested in other matters."

"Why are you even in charge of this? I mean I get it you're a demon and all and the horn brings the apocalypse. But why you? I mean shouldn't that be the Devil or Gabriel?"

"Humans believe far too much of their own writings," Luci grumbled. "Look Tracy. It may be Gabriel's horn but he doesn't blow it. I do. And I'm not a demon, I'm an angel. Get that through your soft skull kid. As for why it's my job, well it's because I'm the angel of Hell. It's just in the job description just like keeping the Sins in line," Luci explained.

"Which you failed at," I replied.

"Look, I'd love to count all the mistakes you've made but we're on a time crunch. We're seeing a lot more demonic animals around here. I say we're getting closer. Which means you need to focus."

"I agree with Luci," Orion added. "Let's prepare ourselves. The best thing we can do with your current strength is to avoid a fight at all costs. We need to see if the Sin has the horn or not. If they don't then we need to move on. If they do, then we will work out a plan."

I nodded and laid my head back against the bed of my truck. My mind was racing. Everything that could go right or wrong filled my thoughts. Anything could happen. More than likely I was going to die but if I didn't...if I didn't then I could be the hero that saved the world. I would be like a comic book hero, I might even get my own movie deal!

I wondered if I was just crazy. I probably was. *Still, probably am.* Man, if I was then I've killed a lot of animals for no good reason; and burned the corpses, but that wasn't my choice. Luci took over my hands and burned them to an appetizing barbecue. Something about the demonic presence spreading. Honestly, I was not sure. I had just been going along with the flow for a while. I'd honestly like to relax for a few hours or something. Every waking hour has been these two bickering in my head. It has been annoying.

I got up and scooted my way out of the bed of the truck. I walked over to the driver's seat of the car. When I opened it empty juice boxes and hamburger wrappers spilled out. I sighed and picked up everything. To be honest I wasn't in the mood for any of this. I was beyond scared and sad because of where we were.

I missed my Dad. I missed him more than I could say. I thought about him every day. It didn't feel like this was even happening. So I pretended that it wasn't. It was one thing to throw me into this crazy saving the world thing but it was another thing to do it right after my

Dad...after he left. I wanted him to be waiting at home for me when this is all over. I wanted to go home so badly.

I shook my head.

"It's happening again," I said.

"What specifically?" Orion asked.

A lot had been happening. *Actually, that's an understatement. In fact, that's an understatement of an understatement.*

"I keep switching between excited and upset. I thought you said this training was supposed to help me control my feelings," I replied. "I was just excited to be a real hero and now I feel like I need to lay down."

My head was silent. I wasn't used to this anymore. It was off-putting now.

"Terrance, you need to focus on your breathing. The feeling will pass," Orion said.

"Orion," Luci scolded. "You're going to mess him up."

"We don't have time for this. We have to get the horn back," Orion bellowed.

"He's a kid Orion. You're going to mess him up and after all this-" Luci stopped speaking as if she didn't want me to hear the next part.

There was a long pause this time. Orion cleared his throat and spoke in a stern tone. "We don't have a choice, Luci."

"You know if you two are going to talk about me, you should maybe include me in the conversation or better yet, GET OUT OF MY HEAD," I yelled. I breathed heavily for a few moments as I calmed myself down. "I'm sorry. There's just a lot going on. I'm stressed out and scared out of my mind. I just really want my Dad to be here and to tell me what to do."

"You lost someone you loved. There isn't anything wrong with that. But right now we need to focus. You're going to have your off days; some days will be easier than others. However, the most important thing right now is to get that horn and stop a lot of people from losing a lot of loved ones," Luci encouraged.

"But what if I can't?"

"Then we cross that bridge when we get to it. Right now let's just focus on one thing at a time. Right now that's finding the cheeky bastard that keeps infecting all these animals. Now, be warned. As we get closer to the Sin's lair, more things will be infected with leeches or by the influence of the Sin's themselves. We have to watch out for any humans that might be infected," Luci exclaimed.

I didn't reply right away. I took a few moments to try and wrap my head around what she was telling me. "These things can take over humans?"

"Yes, Terrance. Anything can be possessed. You cannot trust anyone from here on out however, you are protected because of us," Orion added.

I swallowed, dryly.

"Anyone?" I asked.

"We don't have time to walk you through everything. You said your Dad took you down here? Where did he take you?" Luci barked.

"Ow, fine. We went to Chickamauga Lake. Well, a campsite near there. Why is this important?"

"Your father knew much more than he let on, Lawrence. I believe he knew where the horn was," Luci clarified.

"I thought you said you were watching the horn?" I questioned.

Luci was quiet. There was a pause. Orion cleared his throat and the silence continued. "Luci," Orion scolded.

"Fine," Luci exclaimed. "I am in charge of the horn and I may have taken a bit of a vacation up to the surface. And since the horn has to come with me it well, it went missing."

"You mean you lost it?" Orion corrected.

"Listen...I just misplaced it."

"You brought the Horn of Gabriel to the surface and lost it?!" I yelled. "Because you wanted a vacation?...because you wanted a vacation the apocalypse might come?"

My head suddenly felt hot, like it was boiling. I grabbed my temple and bit my lip. "I know I messed up. At least I'm trying to clean up my mess. Now you can blame me all you want but that doesn't change the fact that we need to find this damn horn." The words flew from my mouth, I could taste the heat that spewed from my lips.

The headache disappeared and I let go of my head. I took a deep breath through my nose. I looked up at the sky as I released the tense air. "Let's just head to the campsite and see what we can find. I mean we made it this far, so why not," I reasoned.

I started up the truck and drove. I had been dragged around by these two bickering voices for the last two weeks. I could have honestly used an hour to myself where I didn't have these voices in my head. I really could use a break.

Wait, what was that smell?

10
AT LEAST IT WAS FREE

I drove down the highway only for a short time. I was following my nose. Something smelled amazing, sweet, and delicious. I felt my mouth watering. Right then my stomach was driving the truck and my mind was completely ignoring the voices that barked at me to explain myself.

"I'm hungry. Let me at least get something to eat before we go off. It won't hurt if I stop for ten minutes," I argued.

It didn't take long for me to find the source of the smell. A carnival was in the distance. I looked as the rides moved and the smell became intoxicating.

"We need to move," Orion argued.

"Come on, what's the harm? Ten minutes, I promise. I could use some corn on the cob. I'm pretty sick of burgers too," I said. I licked my lips and pulled off the exit. "God it smells good."

"Terrance," Orion barked.

"Ah," Luci began. "What's the harm? Ten minutes won't kill anyone."

"Thank you!" I exclaimed.

"The horn!" Orion yelled.

"Ten minutes, in and out. Boy's got to eat," Luci purred.

"Ok, why are you on my side?" I asked.

"What? We get hungry too you know. Well, it's not that we need to eat but that we want to and I haven't had a funnel cake in decades."

I shrugged. "Fair enough."

It took ten minutes to get to the fair from the exit ramp. I parked the truck and got out. I nearly ran to the fair but I stopped myself. I grabbed some cash from the coffee tin and stuffed it into my wallet. I then took my shotgun and harness. Orion had drilled into my head over the last two weeks that I needed to carry my gun everywhere and after a few 'lessons' I got the message.

I threw the strap of the harness over my shoulder and walked to the entrance of the fairgrounds. The whole lot was filled with people of all ages. The screams from the rides and the sweet smells of carnival food filled my senses. A large smile painted its way onto my lips and I took a deep breath.

"Oh I needed this," I said.

"Everyone deserves to have a little fun every now and then," Luci agreed.

Orion cleared his throat. "Not during times of war. Humanity lies upon a dinner plate."

"Orion, sweety. Ten-minutes in and out. Remember?" Luci mewed.

I walked up to the nearest food stand. The smell was driving me up a wall. I felt like I was starving. To be honest I didn't remember the last time I didn't just eat out of my car.

I pulled out my wallet and ordered a funnel cake with everything on it. My sweet tooth was really acting up today and who was I to deny it. I only had ten minutes to enjoy myself after all. I was going to make the best of my limited window.

As I took out the six dollars the teenage boy at the window shook his head. "You're new in town, huh?"

I rose an eyebrow. "How did you know?"

"Because on the last day of the fair, all food is free," the boy said so a-matter-of-fact like.

"Uhh, what?"

He laughed. "I know it's weird. We don't get a lot of out of towners. Almost everything here is local. This year we all decided to give food away for free on the last day of the fair. That way people pay more for the raffles and rides."

I was visibly confused but eventually, I shrugged. "That seems nice. Thank you kindly."

I took the funnel cake and walked over to a table. I looked around the fairgrounds. People were going over to food booths and just got food without paying. It was odd, I didn't think too much of it. The people seemed nice and the idea made some sense. Plus, free food.

I cut off a piece of the strawberry, chocolate, and whipped cream covered mess of goodness. I took my first bite and moaned out with satisfaction. My eyes went wide and my lips curled up. I let out a long moan and sucked against the fork. I didn't want to let go.

What? It was really, really good.

I swallowed and the food went down smoothly. The warmth of the sugar filled me. I closed my eyes and hummed. "God, how I have missed this."

I started to eat quicker. This might have been the best funnel cake I had ever had. I continued to scarf down the food until my plastic fork went through the plate. I was still hungry. I honestly wanted another but there was so much more here to eat.

I got up without hesitation. I walked up to another booth and ordered more food than the last. I returned to the same table with three pulled pork sandwiches, two ears of corn, and a fried pickle on a stick.

I started to chow down on the food. I filled my mouth with the enticing food. Each bite was better than the last. I couldn't stop, I didn't want to. Something about eating this food made me feel at home again.

"Terrance."

I got three pieces of fried chicken and two corn muffins.

"Terrance."

Nine fried Oreos, two ice cream cones, and a chocolate banana.

"Terrance."

Candied apples, cotton candy, and chocolate covered hot dogs.

Chips, burgers, and cake.

Chicken wings ah, why spit out the bones? It was all good anyway.

Apples, cores, yes.

More, more, more.

More, more, more.

More, more, more!

My head forced its way up. I noticed that the table I had been sitting at was no longer empty. The remains of my feast and the feasts of those around me cluttered the table. There were at least six people around me. Their clothes were torn and dirty. Their bodies were bloated and there was a thick sludge around their mouths. The people moved animalistic like as they devoured whatever was in front of them.

The rotting remains, of whatever the pile was, was creating this sickly sweet stench, laid across the table. Insects had been well integrated into the mix, it looked like a breeding ground. Some of the sludge had recognizable parts such as a chicken bone here and there or the fuzzy remains of a strawberry.

I felt my stomach twist as I stared out at the mess. Despite the grossness of the "food" the people kept eating, even fighting over what was on the table.

My eyes widened and my mouth hung open, letting the remains of what I had been chewing fall out and land in the heap of slop that would even make a pig's belly turn. I looked down at the monstrosity that I had been eating.

My stomach jumped and vomit spilled from my lips. I felt my stomach tighten and the vomit spilled all across the table. I gasped in between gags until the last of the contents of my stomach was on the park table.

I felt weak and exhausted. My body forced a few more gags but nothing came out. The smell somehow wasn't even affected by my sudden sickness. I groaned and looked at the people who were eating all around me...still eating.

I turned my head and closed my eyes tightly in fear of getting sick again.

"What the Hell," I gasped.

"Hell is an understatement." Luci's voice came to mind.

I perked up. "What? Why didn't you tell me what I was eating?" I barked.

"We called out to you for hours. I have been waiting for a moment when your body was accessible to take control," Orion explained.

"Hours?"

"Days actually," Luci chimed in.

"Days?!"

I gasped and tried to get up from the table, I fell over my seat and landed on the dirt ground. I crawled a few feet away before I opened my eyes again. I looked around, the fair seemed much more distorted than I remembered.

Marching in between the tables, and keeping an eye on the crowd eating, were what looked like people. These people were horribly disfigured each one a little different from the other. One turned down my aisle and began to approach. It had a bulbous torso that dragged along the floor like a dress of horrors. The skin was stretched and ripped in some placed, out of these rips flowed the familiar black blood of the leeches. I assumed there were legs under the flesh skirt since it was steadily making its ways towards me. A mouth was open in the center of its chest, drooling and chomping hungrily at the air. Two flabby arms hung from its shoulders, but at the end, long stained claws came off each pudgy finger. Its face was the stuff of nightmares, as if the rest wasn't. The skin from its chin had sunk down it no visible neck. Its eyes seemed to be small as the fat suffocated it but a red glow came from them. Its mouth was open and just like its chest mouth drooled constantly. It scanned the crowd almost like it was a prison warden watching them eat.

I covered my mouth as the fumes, of what I was just eating, filled my senses. My tongue was catching up with the realization of what my hands had been doing. I felt the vomit come up but I didn't taste any difference as it spilled across the ground. I continue to vomit for a solid two minutes before I was able to sit up. I wiped my mouth. My body was shaking.

"Terrance. We are in Gluttony's lair. They have to be close. Don't make yourself stick out," Orion warned. "If we stick to our wits then we can get out of here before we are spotted."

I scanned over the other victims of the feast. They were stuffing their faces with anything within arm's reach.

Their bodies were bloated and many seemed as if they hadn't bathed in days. I looked over to the other food stalls. People were scattered across the area. Some continued to eat despite not being able to stand. Some... weren't moving at all.

I watched a boy, a bit younger than me, crawl over to my vomit. His body was twitching and his face was covered with a thick layer of rotting food. He didn't look up. He crawled with gaping mouth and jagged strides.

"What's happening to these people?" I whispered.

"They're barely considered people anymore," Luci revealed. "This is the influence of the Sins. He's not even at full power either. If Gluttony is allowed to roam free, the whole world will be like this and when there's no more food-"

"You don't mean!"

"I do," she continued.

"We have to help them. I broke free so we should be able to get them to see what's happening, right?" I asked.

"It's not that simple. You have us. In order to break someone else we'd need something big enough to take their attention away from their desire to eat," Orion explained. "But that is none of our concern at the moment. The most important thing that we can do right now is to get out of here."

"But-"

"Terrance. You cannot defeat a Sin at your level. We can barely take down a small hoard. The best thing we can do for these people is to get out of here and find the Horn," Orion's voice echoed in my mind to the point of a headache.

I honestly didn't want to go. This place was a Hell on Earth. I was supposed to be some vessel, or something.

Shouldn't I be saving people? This didn't seem fair. The only reason I was not exactly like these guys was because of the blasted angels in my ear.

One of the mutant creatures made a hiss like sound and turned towards me. My face went white. The soulless eye sockets of the beast glared through me. I felt as if my blood had stopped cold in its tracks.

I turned to see the people I had been eating with, also staring at me. They had stopped their feast and were glaring. I looked back at the boy who had been dragging himself through the muddy fairgrounds. His gaping mouth and smell were similar to that of a starving dog. The want in his eyes was haunting. He didn't look human.

I gritted my teeth and looked up. The guard creature was now within a foot of my face. It tilted its large, unhinged jaw at me and gave out another hiss. This time I felt its spit hit against my face. The vile smell from the open mouth was that of rot.

The guard stood there as it waited for me to do something. I knew what it wanted, there was no mistaking it.

I looked down at the pile of mush against the soiled table. I swallowed dryly and stuck my hand into the substance.

Now, I know this may not have been my brightest plan. In fact, looking back I can stay it was probably in the top ten dumbest decisions had ever made. But I never regretted it.

You are strong. You are brave. You can do it. You can protect these people. See?

They need you.

They need you.

They need you!

My back jolted and forced my shoulders up. I squinted my eyes in pain as the sound of ripping fabric filled my ears. I screamed and within an instant, the large white feathers burst from my back like water out from a hose. The first pair of wings stretched the length of my body, long enough to push back the monster that was in my face. The second set of wings were about a foot shorter and remained closer to the sides of my body. Their color was more of an off yellow than white and more of the feathers were missing. The second pair faced downwards more, almost like those of a moth.

Orion had said he had one more set but that I wouldn't be able to handle them without a full transformation. Still, this should be plenty to get their attention.

I flew up from the table and heard a scream as the monster belted out a horrible sound. The scream was ear piercing to the point that my teeth hurt just from the sound. I pulled my shotgun from my bag and fired into the mouth of the screeching creature till it died.

The people around me began to blink and rub their eyes. Several screamed and vomited as they looked at what they had been eating. Others looked to be in shock. Their eyes were wide and spacey as they locked on to me. It didn't take long until the crowded table disbursed. The people scattered like ants as they ran back towards the parking lot.

I couldn't help but smile.

"Do you realize what you've done?" Orion barked.

"I broke all those people free. You said something shocking, right? It's what I could think of on the fly," I answered.

Orion grunted and let out an angered huff. "You've let Gluttony know we're here. Now we have no chance of getting out of here unseen. Do you understand the danger you've put us in?"

"I got those people out. You didn't feel that. I didn't think that I could stop. No one deserves that," I replied.

I didn't think that I was ever going to stop eating. I probably wouldn't have, either. This was the best thing I could think of and it worked.

"You've let Gluttony know right where you are!"

"I saved those people!" I shot right back.

"Alright boys, that's enough," Luci chimed in. Her voice was strangely calm. "Ah." It sounded like she stretched and the noise was the result of it. "Let's get down to business, shall we?"

"How can you be so calm?" Orion asked.

"I knew that Gluttony was here the moment that Terrance saw the fair," she revealed.

"And you didn't say anything, because?" I asked.

"Because we needed to know how the Sins would affect you," Luci explained. "I needed to know if you could even get near the Sins without being taken over. If we couldn't break you through, well you would have died and we would have moved onto the next vessel."

"You just tried to see if I was going to die? That's what you're saying?" I spat. "This is unbelievable."

I narrowed my eyes and started to fly off. I flew only a few feet from the ground. Orion's wings could keep me up a lot better than Luci's. I was more used to using them too. Though this was only the third, or so, time that I had control. Still, I did my best and made sure I didn't make quick turns. I did my best to take it slow and to go over the most people I could.

"So you're just waiting for me to die then? Is that it?" I asked. When I flew over large crowds I yelled down to them to draw as much attention to myself as I could.

"It's not that we want you to pass, Terrance. You were not one of the chosen vessels. You had no training. But this is our situation now. It would take too long for us to be able to enter into the next vessel as well. For now, we need to focus. What exactly are you doing?" Orion questioned. I didn't care how well he tried to explain things. It didn't matter. It didn't matter if I argued either. Orion would just make some excuse or claim that I didn't have a choice now. Which I didn't. "Terrance."

"I'm getting people out of here."

11
GLUTTONY

I kept flying around the park shouting to people to try and break there trance. It seemed some people were more hooked than others and would not respond to my calls. It became harder and harder the further I flew into the festival for me to wake people. The place became more broken down and disgusting. Piles of what used to be food were stacked on the ground as people shoved their faces into them. Even worse was that the body count started to rise. As I flew around and glanced at the carnage I noticed more people laying on the ground not moving. They were dirty with extended bellies.

I honestly hoped that they were just unconscious, but I feared the worse.

The whole time I was flying Orion and Luci were arguing telling me to back off or keep going. It wasn't too hard to ignore them. I have gotten rather good at ignoring the voices in my head since apparently angels don't need to sleep but they often forget that I do.

I began to get a headache but I was determined to save these people. For the first time since all this insanity began, I felt like I was doing what I had decided rather than following what the two angels wanted. Besides, if I am just a meat suit then I wasn't going to make this easy. If I had to save the whole world then I was dang well going to do it my way.

Orion attempt to wrestle for control of the wings but I was able to resist him every time and keep commanding them to drive me forward. He was deeply annoyed by this.

As time went on, panic filled me. I couldn't get some people to move at all and more of the disgusting guards began to appear and make it hard to land long enough to help people. Their bodies were beginning to look more and more grotesque as I went deeper into the fairgrounds.

"They ain't listening," I said to no one in particular.

I flew low enough to be able to touch the scrambling people. I shook a man's shoulder. He shoved my hand off continuing to eat.

"He's close. I know that smell anywhere. Be on your guard Garry," Luci replied, sounding almost excited. It was true though I felt myself gravitating towards the food as I flew by. It flashed from looking like vomit to ice cream.

I was flying low, scanning the crowd and shouting. My heart was racing and Orion's wings began to feel heavy; more than heavy, they were feather boulders wrapped in skin bags, that popped out of my back.

My eyes locked onto the gathering of four of the skin creatures below. I narrowed my eyes. Something wasn't right here.

"Hey does something seem of-Oof!"

I fell down to the fairground as my face met with the sign for the ring toss game. I slid down to the ground, luckily the stuffed animals and my wings dampened the fall. I stood up huffing and puffing from using the wings so long and wiped my hand under my sore nose.

I looked at my hand and saw blood smeared on it. The pain from my face was minor, at least minor to all the pain that I had felt over the last two weeks. I could feel Orion's energy already working to heal the small bones as an automatic response. I have gotten too used to this already.

I picked up my shotgun off the ground and cracked it open.

"Okay so I have two shots in here and-" I reached into the shot bag on my hip. "-two in the bag... not good" I mumbled, worried.

I closed the breach and immediately heard four hellish screams. I snapped my head up, shotgun at the ready to see four of the guards slowly approaching from about ten yards. I could take them out if I was a perfect shot but then I would have no ammo if Gluttony showed up. Plus, I don't even know how many shots it would take to take a Sin down. I scanned my shotgun across the four of them slowly backing up till my back was to the stall.

Suddenly the guards stopped moving about eight yards away and everything was silent other than my breathing. Orion's wings were aching and I wasn't too sure how much longer I could keep them out. In the distance, I saw a man approach he was pretty fat but looked strong. Built kind of like a sumo he slowly approached. The guards paid no heed to him and stood silent. He wore a loose fitting t-shirt and shorts that were on the brink of disappearing. His skin was pale with red splotches. He had a large double chin that seemed to have a layer of filth on it. The moment I met his eyes I felt an insatiable hunger. I looked to my side and grabbed the nearest thing to me, and shoved it into my mouth.

"Terrance stop!" Orion shouted in my head. I snapped to my senses and spit the poor innocent Teddy Bear out of my mouth with a squeak.

My hands were shaking as I looked back towards the strange man. I had a deep feeling of fear and that I should be running right now. Though, as I glanced around I noticed that the guards would be too close to get out quickly. "That must be Gluttony, Terrance. Be on your guard." Orion warned.

"I think he got that, Metal Head. Let me talk with him Terry," Luci said with anger in her voice. I mean I can understand why she'd be mad at Gluttony, it was her job to keep him in line anyway.

So you see at this time I saw only one option. There were probably other smarter options but I always tend to act before thinking too much.

I raised up my shotgun and immediately shot at Gluttony. The pellets hit his right shoulder and made him flinch back. Three shells left. I fired the second shell and it hit home in his other shoulder making him flinch the other way. Two shells left. The guards still did not move or react to their leader being hit twice with a shotgun.

"Maybe this will be easier than we thought," I said to Orion and Luci. I then heard laughter come from Gluttony. "Or maybe not," I corrected.

Gluttony looked back my way and I saw a torrent of leech blood flow from the holes I put in his shoulders. He smiled wide, much too wide for a normal person's mouth.

"Well it has been a long time since I have had an angel to eat," he hissed through his growing teeth. "Especially one that tries to fight back."

He bent over as his body bubbled and black goo continued to flow from his wounds. Suddenly his body erupted into a blob of leech blood. This blob grew as the liquid seemed to gain a more thick consistency. He looked like a popped kiddy pool that had been filled with black swamp water with a smell that matched.

Also, yes, this is when I realized I screwed up.

Gluttony's form elongated into the shape of a Twinkie, the liquid bubbled and turned like boiling cheese paste. Six legs sprouted from the sides lifting him up. The legs were somewhat humanoid. I say somewhat because it looked like someone took an overly obese leg and stuffed it into a pastry bag and squeezed, oh and it was like the size of a bus. I was about as tall as his knee. His mouth was like a Pitbull's but split from cheek to cheek. Drool and puss fell from the salivating lips, soaking the ground below him. Two sets of teeth filled the mouth to what appeared to be a dentist's worst nightmare. The wiry texture of the teeth looked similar to a whale's but as sharp as a dog's.

Horror movies did not prepare me for how disgusting this thing looked.

The insect-like body was almost see through. The black substance that made up the figure showed the outline of everything inside of Gluttony. From animals to tractors and even...remains, filled him.

I gripped my gun tightly in my hand. My body was shaking. Everything in me was telling me to run but my legs wouldn't move. I didn't even know if that was because of me or Luci and Orion.

The final horror in the monster that laid before me was the face, *or rather a mask of the face? I'm not sure.* I couldn't even tell where the man stopped and the monster began but one thing was clear, I was terrified.

The faceless mask was at one point the face of the human version of Gluttony. But now, I would call it anything but human. The eyes and mouth were missing and there was no sign of hair on the stretched skin. It was like the face of a doll after they had been cleaned with rubbing alcohol. Everything was just gone.

Gluttony's shoulder jolted forward as an arm bubbled out and exploded from the blob. The arm crashed down on top of one of the skin bag guards. It crushed the smaller monster between its mucky fingers as the ground shook.

"I will feast on your entrails!" Gluttony snarled. His voice boomed louder than a tornado siren.

I covered my ears and looked up at the monster in fear. My heart was pounding out of my chest and I was breathing so hard that it hurt.

Come on, legs move!

"Terrance!" Orion's voice boomed like a- *it doesn't matter. I've never been so happy to hear him yell at me.*

I felt my body push back. The powerful gust of Orion's wings blew from behind me and towards Gluttony. I flew backward faster than I had ever gone with Orion's wings. The blast sent me through the fair stand and back at least a football field length.

The Sin hissed as the wind hit its face. It covered the nonexistent eyes with its arm.

The weight of Orion's wings was really starting to hit me as the large wings drooped down. I didn't stop to see what Gluttony did next. I turned and started to sprint towards the exit, a path of feathers fell behind me with each step.

The pound of the earth drew my attention back. I turned my head just enough to see Gluttony running on all eight limbs towards me, catching up quick.

"Guys!?" I yelled.

"I told you," Orion replied just as sharply as I had yelled.

"Is it really the time for this?" I replied.

I shook my head and saw an overturned food cart. I figured that if I could take off I would have a better chance of getting away. Gluttony was fast but he didn't have wings under all that fat; at least he didn't have any wings I could see.

I ran towards the cart and narrowed my eyes, my mind cleared, as much as it could, in preparation to take off.

"Terrance no!" Orion yelled but I had already made it up the cart and jumped. I went to flap my wings but fell to the ground, rolling over several times till my momentum stopped.

I looked back to see the wingless stumps on my back and the large trail of feathers that lead to me.

"Damn."

I felt the blood in my hands boil. I closed my eyes tight and clenched my fists as the skin molded to Orion's gauntlets.

"Left!" Luci yelled.

I rolled left and barely avoided becoming a pizza. I made my way to my feet and turned to bolt. A skin guard stood directly in front of me. I swung my right fist into the bridge of its nose and sent it into the ground. It felt like I just threw a cinder block into the monster and looked like a meteor smashed his face. I didn't have time to marvel at my work. I continued my sprint before Gluttony could get in another attack.

I needed to get out, but what about the people? Though if seeing something like this didn't snap them out, nothing would. Still, if I could avoid Gluttony squishing them, it would be ideal. Alright, so that was the plan. Lead Gluttony (without getting hit), use him to snap people out of his influence (without letting them get hit), and then escape (without dying). Simple.

"Right!" Luci shouted. I jumped to the right between two stalls into the open. I heard a large crash and pieces of cheap plywood flew past me. I looked behind me and was able to see Gluttony shifting out of the ruined stalls. It would probably only buy me a few seconds. I saw the picnic tables far in the distance with a large crowd still around it. They weren't eating anymore though. Instead, they stared with wide eyes and open mouths at Gluttony and me. I swear I even saw a camera flash.

"Run! Get out of here!" I shouted at the top of my lungs. Some snapped out of it and ran screaming towards the exit. This helped as I had no idea which way the exit was anymore. Problem is many of them still stayed, probably stuck with fear. I was in the open and didn't think I would be able to turn fast enough to not get smacked by Big Boy's stretchy arms, or he would not be able to turn fast and barrel into the crowd.

"Orion, Luci we are going to have to make a stand." I declared.

"Terrance we will more than likely die. Leave these people we have a more important-" Orion started.

"I will not leave them behind. We will protect them" I forcefully said even though I had no idea how we would protect them. Gluttony roared behind me, the moment I stopped and turned he would be close enough to attack pretty quickly. Well, here went nothing.

I spun around about ten yards from the people. They were still petrified by the giant monstrosity barreling down on us.

Focus Terrance. I will protect them. I can protect them. "Orion, we have to do this." I quietly said. He said nothing but I felt a refreshed feeling within me. I hoped that means he was ready. Gluttony quickly approached slobbering everywhere. He raised his gelatinous arm back ready for a punch. I raised my gauntlet covered arms up. The silver shined in the sun but I swear they had their own glow. I also felt my legs start burning and aching. I felt the bottom of my jeans and boots get covered by metal.

The fist hit me in my hands. I skidded backward as I felt the force resonate through my body. I let out a yell as my arms screamed and I swear my shoulders were almost popped out of socket. My feet, as I skidded, got pushed deeper into the ground. The gelatinous fist squished in my fingers as I attempted to grip it. The skidding eventually stopped and I was actually holding my ground. I opened my eyes to see a fist larger than me being held as my arms struggled. I heard some gasps from behind me and even a small cheer. I was amazed I had actually blocked that.

Wait… didn't he have two arms? I looked to my right just in time to see the fist careening towards me. It slammed into my side and sent me flying.

I flew like a doll until I crashed into the empty picnic tables beside me. I gasped as I tried to breath as it felt like a million nails in my chest. It took me a few moments before I could even will myself to look up. Orion was trying his hardest to mend my countless broken bones.

I watched as the grotesque Sin stalked his way over to me. The people around us had all fled or gotten far enough away where they could still see but weren't in immediate reach.

I gritted my teeth when I saw people recording on their phones. "Get out of here!" I pleaded.

My attention was forced back to Gluttony as he prowled over me. I felt the hairs on my arm stick up as he sniffed me with his non-existent nose.

"Guys?" I whispered.

"I need more time," Orion called.

"That's not exactly something we have right now," I replied as some drool hit my face.

"Then I'll make it," Luci ensured. I heard the woman clear her throat and then I lost vision in my right eye.

"Gluttony," her voice was powerful, demanding, and from my lips.

The blob hissed and pulled back, just slightly. "Lucccci," he hissed in return.

"Don't 'Luccci' me. You knew I'd be coming. Don't act so surprised. Now, why don't you be a good little monstrosity and go back to Hell where you belong. You know just as well as I do that it isn't time for you to return yet," Luci scolded.

"And since when did I have to take orders from some mortal?" Gluttony scoffed. He dragged himself sluggishly around me. His body looked like it was going to pop and let out all the waste across the fairgrounds.

"You're still going on about that?" She moaned. "Look piggy, this isn't ideal for me either. But I am no mortal now. So unless you want me mad I suggest you listen up and do what I say."

Gluttony let out a belly laugh that shook the surrounding area. "Listen to you? No. We have all had enough listening to you. What a mockery! To have us, the Seven Deadly Sins, take orders from a human is insulting. We are done with your orders. We are done with your time. Now we will rule."

"Oh, you're going to regret that big boy. But I'm feeling nice. So I'll give you one last chance," she said aloud.

There was an echo in my head as Luci's voice returned to being internal. "Orion, please tell me you got something."

Orion replied. "Stall just a little longer. I am doing my best."

"Well, work faster," she scolded.

"It looks like I get a two for one deal. I am too hungry to listen to your nagging anymore." Gluttony sneered. He reached down towards me, and I couldn't move a muscle. My body screamed and it felt like I had glass shards in my sides making it hard to breathe.

"We have to do it now Orion," Luci said.

"Just one more moment," Orion replied sounding like he was slightly out of breath. Gluttony grabbed me with gooey hands pulling me towards his giant maw. It looked like this was the end. My bones were broken and I did not even have my shotgun to fire off one last shot. I also felt an intense burning growing from my chest. "I'm sorry Terrance, but what I am about to do is going to really hurt," Orion spoke softly.

I couldn't even reply as the burning was growing to be unbearable and Gluttony was crushing what was left of my ribs. I looked towards the mouth that spelled my doom. Just as I reached the entrance my entire body felt like it was erupting into flame. A bright white light glowed around me. It was so intense that I could not even make out any details around me. I quickly shut my eyes and heard Gluttony shout. I felt his grip loosen and I fell to the ground with a thump. I tried to yelp but it felt like my entire body was made of fire and TV static.

The light died down as quickly as it came and I saw Gluttony backing up with his hands in front of his face. Smoke radiated off both our bodies. I could not move at all. I could not even turn my head while I laid in a heap on the ground. As Gluttony backed away a little more I heard what sounded like a gunshot. Gluttony shuttered and started swaying side to side on his six legs. "Impossible." I heard him mutter out before he collapsed to the ground unmoving.

THE THREE ANGELS AND THE SEVEN DEADLY SINS

I saw a pair of human legs walk up to me. I tried to look up but with the exertion of moving my head and the pain that screamed through me, I immediately passed out.

12

A ONE-SIGHTED INTERVIEW

The elevator doors opened in front of me. I looked out at the high-end office complex in front of me. The fancy stuff made it look like one of those offices from one of those soap operas Mrs. Fickle watches. I looked over the weird black and white art that hung on the wall. It looked like a toddler got into paint if I was being honest. But it was hanging right over the large marble desk. I took a step out of the elevator and heard the click of my boots on the hard floors. I looked around and scratched my head.

"Where are we?" I asked.

There was no reply. My head was empty. *I'm not saying I'm stupid I mean- you know what I meant.*

This kind of felt like a dream. I mean I didn't remember how I got into this place and I didn't really feel that scared either. It was strange but I felt comfortable here. It wasn't like I had been here before but it was more like I knew the things that were here. I didn't recognize any of this fancy stuff but I felt like I did. *I'm not sure, to be honest.*

I continued to walk through the office. It was just as fancy as the entrance as I moved through. There was no one to be seen. I rose an eyebrow and started to walk through the rows of cubicles for any sign of someone who could tell me what was going on.

"This is impossible," I huffed.

There was still no reply. I hated to admit it but I had gotten really used to having those voices in my head. *Man, I feel like a nut.*

[111]

"What is?" A voice called. It was unfamiliar. The voice was deep and relaxing. The voice was clearly a man's and clearly an adult's. It felt like it came from my core but it sounded like it also came from behind me.

I quickly turned around but was only met with the emptiness of the office.

"Who's there?" I barked. I felt kind of bad. I was used to things just attacking me without warning. But this voice seemed friendly. I don't know why it seemed nice, but it did. I think I knew it.

"Sorry, what was the question again?" He asked. The voice was coming from the left side now.

"Who are you?" I repeated.

"Actually the question was," he cleared his throat, "What is?" The voice was on my left side now.

I stopped and tried to think about what this voice was saying.

I put my hands out in front of me and began to gesture as I tried to make sense of everything being said. "Wait. You asked 'what is' and I asked 'who's there' then you asked me what I said and then replied to what you said."

"Did I? Well, what is?" He asked.

"What is what?" I replied.

"Who's asking the questions?" He replied.

I went to reply but stopped and left my mouth hung open. I shook my head and tried to get my bearings. "Ok, let's start with my question. Then yours. Okay?"

"That's fine," the voice answered.

"Wh-" I was cut off.

"What is?" He asked.

I let out a long groan and rubbed my face. "I said I ask first!"

"You did. You asked if I was okay with the plan, look let's get to business. We've played enough," he ensured.

I felt a strong hand on my right shoulder. I turned around and saw a towering black man behind me. He was dressed in a nice suit. His whole outfit was black. The button-up shirt, the jacket, the pants, and the shoes. He even had on black leather gloves. His jaw was very defined and covered in a clean stubble that made him look very intimidating. His hair was long dreads that were tied back. They went down to his mid-back and were the darkest black I had ever seen.

"Let's go to my office," he said with a smile.

I noticed the glaze over his eyes. The green color was so faded that it looked nearly white. I was pretty sure he was blind, at least he looked like he was. I looked down to see a cane with a metal hawk head on the top in his hand and a white tip on the bottom. Overall, he was very well put together and quite scary. I feel like I should be bowing or something.

The man pulled me through the complex office. The click of his dress shoes made me feel extremely underdressed. This all felt like a dream. It would make sense if it was. Dreams sometimes start in the middle and this definitely started in the middle. I was not even sure I knew where the beginning was.

The man led me to a corner office. He opened the door and showed me an office scattered with papers and empty paper coffee cups. Unlike the rest of the office, this place looked like it was in use.

There were three chairs seated on one side of the desk. Two people were already seated and facing away from the door and towards the wooden desk. I stepped in as the man motioned me to. I took a few steps and looked back at the man like a child would to their mother. He motioned me to sit.

I turned to see the people who were sitting in the other seats. The one closer to me was a woman, she looked the youngest out of all of them, around thirty. Her hair was up in a neat way, it kind of looked like a cinnamon roll on her head. Like most office women on TV. Her skin was pale and had very few wrinkles. The most notable thing was a burn around her mouth. It looked like her mouth had been burned off and stretched back on. I didn't think that was the nicest way to describe it but I couldn't think of another way. She obviously had some type of accident and had a skin graph on her face.

She wore a white blouse and a black pencil skirt that went to her knees. Under she had on tights and black flats. She sat with her hands folded in her lap and her eyes facing forward.

The second person sitting was an older man. He looked to be around his mid-fifties. His hair was a graying blonde and short. He was a more built man, he obviously kept himself healthy. He looked like a lot of the guys around the farm. He was tanned and scarred. His face was well wrinkled but it was still clear about how old he was. He had a well-kept beard and mustache that went about two inches off his chin.

He wore a white button-up shirt, black tie, and black dress pants and shoes. Overall there wasn't anything too noticeable about him. He just seemed like a normal, dime a dozen, office worker.

My guide walked around the desk and sat across from the three chairs. I sat on the end chair and waited for him to talk again. I had no idea where I was or what I was doing here but there was a feeling deep in my gut saying to listen.

The blind man folded his hands on the desk and leaned forward. He had a gentle smile on his face. "So Terrance," he began. "Tell me about yourself. What makes you qualified for this position?"

I rose an eyebrow. "Umm, what?" I asked.

"The job," he replied so matter-of-factly like. "What makes you the right candidate?"

So this really is a dream. But it feels weirdly real. Almost more real than real. "I'm not...?"

He clapped and let out a raspy laugh. "Honesty, that's a good quality to have. Tell you what, why don't you see how our other team members got here. Then maybe you'll have a better answer."

He dug into his desk and pulled out a card. It was bigger than a playing card and had a black back with detailed line art in a shiny black throughout it.

He smiled and showed me the card. I had seen some of these before when I went to the fair growing up. It was a tarot card. This one had the symbol of the devil but it was upside down. He handed me the card. I took it and suddenly the woman came to life. Her eyes were a deep red color but flashed to green for a moment before closing. She slumped forward and took the card from my hand.

The moment she touched the card, everything went black. I felt like I was falling but I wasn't moving at all. I could feel the chair still under me. It was steady and unmoving.

There was a flash of green light and suddenly I was in a living room. Unlike the office, the living room was dirty and looked like it hadn't been cleaned in a long time. The room smelled of smoke and cheap cleaner.

The furniture was covered in plastic but there were still stains under. I looked around and noticed a small and very old TV that was on. The TV had been flipped on its side but was still playing a Coke commercial through the static. It was black and white and the actors were in 70's style clothes.

I narrowed my brows and stood up. My first instinct was to reach for my shotgun but I didn't have it. I didn't have anything but the clothes on my back.

So instead I wandered a bit around the house. The place was trashed. There was furniture spilled everywhere and broken glass across the ground from plates and cups. I didn't see anyone in the house and the only sound was coming from the creek of the ceiling fan and the TV.

After a while, I made my way into the kitchen. There was blood spilled across the floor. It looked like a bucket had been dropped because there was so much. I bit my lip and looked around. The back door was slightly open. There was a trail of blood out of the back door. It looked like something had been dragged across the checkered tiled floor.

I swallowed dryly and walked to the back. I felt like my body was being moved forward. It was like Luci or Orion was controlling me but it felt like I was still somewhat in charge. It was more like leading than full-blown control.

I walked into the backyard. It was a small backyard that was met with a deep forest line. I saw the blood trail go on into through the woods. So I began to follow it. I walked for about thirty minutes or so until I heard voices.

I quickly hid behind a fallen tree and looked over at a strange and horrifying sight. There was a large clearing. About the size of the living room I was just in. A man in his forties was wearing a pair of slacks and a white, bloodstained tank top. He was stubbly and his hair was half slicked back. It looked greasy and somewhat wet. He was panting and yelling words I would not repeat.

There were symbols written in the dirt and rocks scattered in varying places but they look to be there on purpose. In the center was a large pile of wood, newspapers, leaves, and a woman. She looked to be in her thirties. Her black hair had been ripped out of her up-do. She was in a plaid dress that had been torn at the bottom. She was shoeless and face down. The trail of blood seemed to be coming from her.

I felt my stomach turn. I watched for several minutes but she didn't move. I think she was dead. I couldn't see her breathing at all. My guess was that was the woman in the office. But I couldn't see her face.

"Get off!" I heard a young girl scream.

I looked over to see that the man was pulling a younger girl over to the pile. She was about thirteen or twelve with long black hair. Her skin was very pale to the point that I could see bruising from here because of how well it stuck out on her skin. She wore a pair of bell-bottom jeans and an orange t-shirt. Overall she still looked young but she was tall.

I watched the man pull her by the hair over to where the dead woman was. She was clawing at his hand but it didn't seem to affect him. I did notice that her hands were tied together with rope. The girl was thrown down next to the woman. Her face was red and stained with tears.

My fist was clenched tightly. I went to stand but felt a hand on my back. I looked behind me to see the mysterious man from before. He put his finger in front of his mouth and smiled.

"We're just observing cowboy. We couldn't change anything if we wanted to but unfortunately, this is her fate. These were the cards she drew," the man ensured.

"But-"

He shh'd me and shook his head.

I looked back at the sight with defeat. Everything in me was screaming to go and punch that guy in the face. I bit my lip so hard that it bled. It was not fair, we're here.

"Fate-shmate," I whispered.

I pushed past his hand and jumped over the tree. I sprinted towards the circle with rage in my eyes. "HEY ASSHOLE!"

I was yanked backward and fell hard against the forest floor. "Oof."

I looked back to see the man in the suit, still in the same place, but now he was holding a chain. I followed the chain to see it leading into my back. I reached back to feel the cold metal merged into the crook of my back. There was a seamless attachment, the heat was the best way to determine where the chain ended and where I began. But I didn't feel it at all.

He shh'd me again and pointed to the opening. My eyes were drawn to the disaster in front of me. The first thing that hit me was the smell. It was a smell that you can't mistake no matter how much you try too: Gas.

The man was pouring gas over the girl and her mother. He was shouting nonsense and more profanity. The girl was screaming for help and her crying had turned into sobbing. He had broken her leg. I got up and tried to run towards the circle again but the chain kept me planted. I began to pull and scream, anything I could think of to get their attention, but they never looked.

Tears fell down my face as I watched. This was torture, absolute torture! I was so close. If I could just get a little closer I could save her. *Goddamnit! I could save her.*

I was starting to slow down but I still tried to fight against the chain. The moment that the match was lit, I felt the world turn cold. It was like everything was in slow motion. I felt my mouth open as if to scream, but no noise escaped. I turned away from the horror and bolted towards the fancy man. I moved faster than I ever thought I could without Luci. My body was moving on instinct.

I needed to use my head.

I bent over, slightly and headbutted the fancy man. The moment he dropped the chain everything sped up. I didn't waste a second as I ran towards the circle. I made it right to the edge when the pile went up in flames.

The scream of the girl bellowed through the air. I felt my heart crack as the laugh of the man rubbed it in. It didn't take that long before the screams stopped and I fell to my knees. Just like before I was in a black room. I couldn't see anything. There was a flash of green light and I was seated again next to the two office workers and across from the fancy man.

"Why didn't you let me help her?!" I screamed.

The man was quiet for a moment before he crossed his knee over the other and leaned back in his chair. "Because it was only a memory. You couldn't have changed anything even if I let you try," he answered.

"Why would you even show me something like that?" I spat. I wiped my eyes with my shirt and did my best to catch my breath. My heart was beating out of my chest. I felt like I was going to vomit. I've seen some messed up stuff in the last two weeks but that was a human doing that to another human. It was horrible. "What was your point?"

The woman sat back up and looked forward again. There was something about her that looked like a doll, especially with the way she sat. It was like she was placed there. The life seemed to drain from her the moment she sat back up and now she was only hollow.

"My point was to show you the truth, no matter how painful it is," he answered.

The man cleared his throat and pointed to a TV set that hadn't been in the room before. It was a modern TV and on it was the face of the little girl, with a burn across her mouth just like the woman who sat next to me. She was clearly talking to someone but to who, I couldn't see.

The fancy man turned up the volume.

"You wish to give up your paradise?" an off-screen voice asked.

The girl nodded. She had such a serious expression, it was clear that she meant what she was saying. "He deserves to pay." Those words were odd hearing from such a young girl but after what I saw, I didn't blame her.

"You are giving up your eternal rest. Once you choose this path, you will not be able to come back here. Do you understand what I'm saying?" The voice asked.

She nodded again. "I don't care what happens to me. I want him to pay for what he did. Let me do this," she ensured.

There was a long silence.

"April Lucinda, Fletcher. Do you give up your immortal happiness for revenge?"

"I do," the girl answered with a strong voice.

The video paused. The fancy man looked at me. I rose an eyebrow and scratched my head. I wasn't sure what the point of this was. I mean, I got that the woman sitting next to me was April but that was about it. I felt like a child.

"What was the point of that?" I questioned.

The fancy man sighed and shuffled some paper on his desk. "It's for the job. You've already asked that question once, you know? If you don't intend on listening I can give you the printed version."

I stood and slammed my hands on his table. "I have no idea what you're talking about! All I know is that I just watched a girl die because some crazy guy decided to set her on fire and now you're telling me she gave up Heaven for revenge? What does this even mean?" I barked. I panted for a few moments. I was getting more and more angry and with it, the temperature was rising.

The man looked at me and blinked a few times. He took out a piece of paper and a pen. He pretended to write but never actually put the pen onto the paper. "Not a good listener..."

I groaned and pulled down on my cheeks. "It's like talking to a brick wall," I sighed.

"I wouldn't say you were that bad. Would you like to hear Mr. Ward's origin story?" he asked.

"Do I have a choice?" I questioned.

"No."

13
SOMETHING SURE DID HAPPEN

The fancy man reached back into his desk and pulled out another tarot card. He turned it to face me. It was the Hermit card but like the Devil card, it was upside down. I took it again and watched as the other office man slumped forward with life and took the card.

Just like before I was taken to a black room. I could only feel the seat below me before the green flash took me to the next location.

The world around me was very different than the last one. Actually, it wasn't much of anything. I was expecting something, anything really but this was just black. It was like the moment before the flash but this time I had a better sense of my body. I couldn't see a thing but I could feel myself. I knew I was standing this time. I knew I had my arms down at my side and I knew that my feet were cold.

There was a slight noise that happened every few seconds. A *blop.* It sounded like when a drop of rain falls into a bucket. It just continued to drip but there was no sign of the source.

After a while in the dark, I decided to move forward. With my first step, I found half of my source. The splash of water came from below. I still couldn't see so I bent down and put my hand into the water. It was only a few inches deep. Nothing too noticeable but that begs the question: where am I?

"Hello?" I called out. There was no reply. Not even an echo. "Fancy Man? Anyone?"

Still nothing.

I can't tell you how long I wandered around in that nothingness but after a while I stopped talking and focused on finding a way out. I couldn't see and no matter how far I ran I never seemed to get anywhere. Slowly but surely I felt myself getting lost in the invisible maze.

This had to be Hell. I had to be in Hell right now.

....

How long has it been?

I never knew that feeling nothing could feel so horrible. Every fiber of my being is begging for any source of feeling. I think I've scratched my arms raw. Even the pain feels. It just feels which was enough for me.

Scratch, scratch. And for a moment I could feel again.

....

The voices mocked me. They were just out of my range of hearing. But I knew they could hear me. I knew they are laughing at me. Oh, I knew they were just having a party at my expense.

"I can hear you!" I called out into the dark.

Of course, I was lying but they don't know that. I had to make them think that I had the upper hand.

....

"I am convinced that I'm blind. I'm convinced of it. It's the only explanation."

I continued to sprint.

"I know the entrance is around here. I came in I have to go out now...I'm not really paying attention to my surroundings. I'm just focusing on my feet. I have to keep them moving."

I stopped to catch my breath. I leaned on my knees and coughed a few times.

"I don't get hungry or thirsty here. But I'm sure that I've been here for days."

I rested a few minutes, "maybe a few weeks" and then I started to run again.

....

"Light!" I yelled.

After what seemed like a lifetime I finally spotted my salvation. There was light, actual light coming from a path in front of me.

I sprinted towards the light and eventually I managed to go through the portal. When I entered the next room I had to shield my eyes. The light was so bright that it was making my eyes burn. I rubbed my eyes and peaked from time to time until my eyes were used to the light.

I looked around my new surroundings. It was a library. It kind of looked like the library in my hometown but the rows of shelves seemed to go on forever. I looked around and took in the sight. I was finally able to see. God, it felt like it had been forever.

"Hello?" I called. I couldn't help but get a little giddy when I heard the echo. My voice was finally carrying again.

"Shh," came a familiar voice.

I turned to see the fancy man reading at a table. The table had been where I had come in from the blackness but there was no darkness there. Just a normal looking table.

I peeked at the book he was reading. It was a red covered book with no other features. It looks thick. Maybe like three-hundred to four-hundred pages. The most notable thing about it was that the book was upside down and the reader was blind. I wasn't sure what was going on. But that wasn't the most pressing issue on hand.

"Don't Shh me. What was that?" I barked.

The fancy man looked up at me and tsk'd. "You really should keep quiet in a library."

I groaned. It was like I just couldn't have a straight conversation with this guy. So I guess the best thing to do was to play his game.

"Ok," I whispered. "Where was I a few seconds ago? In the black room. Where was the black room?"

He put down his book and smiled. He motioned to the seat across from him. I sat down and he put the book down so that the pages were the correct way for me to read.

"Can I tell you a story?" He asked.

He flipped the pages of the book and landed on a picture. The picture was of the man I had seen in the office but his beard was longer and not as well maintained. The man was dressed in medieval armor and looked to be studying a map that was sprawled across a wooden table.

I was about to ask what the picture was but it began to move. The image changed and moved like a movie. The man was looking over the map and giving directions to the others in the room. I wasn't sure exactly what they were talking about but it sounded like a war was going on and this was the strategy plan. The man was well collected and calculated. It was as if every move and every word was thought out and planned years in advance.

"He looks like he really knows what he's doing," I commented.

"That he does. Orion Ward was one of the most brilliant strategists during his era," the fancy man revealed.

"Wait." I looked up at the strange man to see if he was indeed serious. When his face didn't waver I slumped back down in my chair. My head was swirling with a million questions. I carefully tried to figure out which I should ask first. Or rather, which he would answer.

"Would you like to hear more?" The fancy man asked.

I nodded. We sat in silence for several minutes. "Oh! I mean yes," I added. I may have forgotten he couldn't see.

"Good. Like I said this is the story of Orion before death. He was a great leader in battle. He proved himself over a lifetime of service. It would be hard to show you a single moment to indicate his sacrifices. Unlike April, or rather Luci, it is not as simple as one major action that led Orion to his path," he explained.

I looked down at the table as my mind desperately tried to wrap itself around what was happening.

"Ter-"

"Shh. I need a moment," I cut off.

I sat in silence until I was sure that everything was in order. Orion and Luci were once humans. I got that. Luci was burned to death by who I guess was her father. She then gave up her heaven for revenge. And Orion was a knight who led armies and was a great strategist. I can't say I was too surprised at Orion. If I had to guess that would have been what I pictured him doing as a human.

But I'm surprised they were once human. Neither of them acted like it. They just seemed to treat me like a puppet which got really old, really fast.

"Okay. Okay," I took a deep breath and calmed myself down. "Continue."

The fancy man motioned back to the book and I started to watch the story that was being told.

A man walked into the scene. He was dressed in armor just like Orion but he wasn't wearing any type of fabric prints like Orion.

He started to speak to Orion in a language that I couldn't understand. I turned to the fancy man with a confused expression.

"It's Saxon. I wouldn't expect you to understand. Let me explain," he began. The fancy listened for a moment before he started to speak again. He pointed to the other man. "He is informing Orion of the current standings of their forces. He does warn that they had lost a major battle and many men with it. Orion is now giving the directions for their next move. However, he only mentions this."

I continued to listen as the fancy man gave me the translation of the battle. The story went on for what felt like hours but honestly, I was so into it. Orion was amazing! Even when it seemed like they were in a corner he always found a way out. It was like when we read the Odyssey in school. The epicness of his leadership was like something out of a movie. I was so excited to hear the next part but the fancy man stopped translating.

"W-what? What happens next?" I asked. I sounded like an excited child. I needed to know what came next. I honestly didn't want it to end.

"Next? It continues the same way it always has," he said.

I rose an eyebrow. "Huh?"

"Tell me, what do you know about the life of Orion? Outside of his work?" he asked.

I went to talk but then I stopped short. I had to think about this. Honestly, I had no idea. "I guess nothing. Oh wait, he mentioned his son," I said.

The fancy man nodded. "That's correct. He has three children and a wife. But they are not a part of this life that he has chosen."

"But he mentioned his son. I mean yeah he didn't mention them but you only showed me his time in battle."

"I only showed you his life," the fancy man replied. "This was the life he chose to live. He was in constant sacrifice for his mind. He was brilliant for his time but he did not address his life outside of his duty. Thus the sacrifice wasn't his own."

"What do you mean?" I asked.

"This is not something that is mine to tell. I believe that you have seen enough for my intended purpose. Now I will ask you again. He closed the book and turned to me. "What makes you qualified for this position?"

I furrowed my eyebrows and frowned. "What? Are you still on that? I don't understand much, but you don't make any sense."

He was silent for a few moments. He pulled out a tape recorder from his pocket. The fancy man clicked a button and put the recorder back into his pocket. I blinked and suddenly we were back in the office. There was no black room or green light. We were just there. I jumped in my seat and looked around to see that he and I were the only ones still in the room. Luci and Orion were gone.

I looked back at the man and rubbed my eyes. "Stop doing that!" I barked.

"That's the first time I did that," he clarified.

"Well, stop it."

He let out a deep and raspy laugh. "Alright. Well, since I have you here. Let's go over your resume." He pulled a paper from the pile on the desk. "You are resourceful and have a desire to save those in danger. In a situation when you can't move forward you use your head. Even in a situation with no perceivable end in sight, you do not give up and you continued to move forward. These are very good qualities to have," he ensured.

"Umm, thanks?" I replied.

"However, you tend to miss the point even when the situation is obvious. You do not think about the picture in front of you but you instead try to act on impulse," he continued. "I have to say, you show promise but I do not believe you are ready for what this position would entail. Still, if you wouldn't mind I would like to keep your contact information in case you are able to overcome your weaknesses."

I had been through so much today. I didn't even know where I was or who this was. But he did know about Luci and Orion so maybe he really was trying to help. I guess it wouldn't hurt to take what he said to heart.

"Sir, I know I don't think all the time but I am doing my best. I don't know what this job is you're telling me about but I guess I can understand that I'm not ready. If you want to help then I don't mind if you come to me again but if you're just trying to play around with me then I don't have the time," I replied.

It was in this moment that I could hear a ticking. I looked around the room as the walls were now covered in clocks. They were all different sizes, shapes, and patterns.

The ticking became louder and louder. I looked at the fancy man and noticed the large grin on his face. He pointed towards his wristwatch. It was simple but I hadn't noticed it before. It was gold with a black leather band. I was about to say something when the watch went off.

"It's time to go Terrance. But before you do, pick a card," he instructed. The fancy man pulled out about ten tarot cards from the pile on the desk. He held them out and tilted his head.

I took a deep breath and shook my head. This is the craziest thing I had ever done, dream or not. My brain was tired from all of the thinking. But if it was time to go, then it was time and I doubt he would let me go without doing what he asked.

I drew a card.

14
IN A STRANGER'S RV
WITHOUT CANDY

I woke up with a start. I sat up quickly and immediately regretted the decision as a pounding headache nearly made me lie down again. I was thirsty, extremely thirsty. I glanced to my right and saw a cup on the table near my bed. I quickly grabbed it and poured its contents into my mouth.

I immediately spat it out. It was horribly salty water. I coughed and sputtered as I tried to clear the liquid from my throat. I felt like I was going to vomit. I took my hands and began to scrub my tongue with the blanket that was on top of me. When the taste was out of my mouth I looked around and noticed that I was somewhere new.

I was getting really sick of this whole, waking up somewhere else bull.

I looked around the moving room. It looked like the inside of an RV. I looked out the window and saw the passing countryside. The rest of the room was clearly a bedroom. The area was outdated but not as much as Luci's home from my vision.

I wiped my mouth and looked around as I took a tally of my surroundings. I had no idea if I was still asleep or awake. I grabbed my head and groaned. My body hurt like hell. It felt like I had been kicked by a horse like six times and then run over.

"What the hell?" I whispered.

"He's awake!" Luci gasped.

I let out another groan. "Morning to you too..."

"Do you have any idea how worried we were?" Luci asked.

I rubbed my eyes and cracked my back. "No. Why?" I was tired and it showed. My voice was groggy and my body was so heavy. Though I had expected it to hurt a lot more, I mean I did get thrown like a rag doll... and stepped on and... wait a second.

I bolted up in the bed and made myself attempt to get up. Well, I attempted to get up but ended up landing right on my face.

I pushed myself up and groaned. I sat up and rubbed my head.

"I actually thought I died," I said.

Orion cleared his throat and began to speak. "We weren't sure if you were still with us either," he spoke with a sluggish voice.

"You thought I was dead?" I asked.

So I really was in Hell.

"Indeed," he replied. Orion sounded like he was exhausted.

"Orion has been waking up your body. We've made sure that you've been fed, hydrated, and everything else. You've been asleep for three days. But not exactly asleep," Luci explained.

"What do you mean not exactly asleep?" I asked.

"So while we're in your head we can see your soul, your consciousness. But while you were out your soul was muted. It was like you were brain-dead but a bit more active. We were just concerned that you weren't going to wake up," Luci admitted.

I rubbed my head and sighed. I wasn't actually that surprised. After all, I'm pretty sure I was in Hell for that time.

"It felt a lot longer than three days," I admitted.

"What do you mean?" Orion asked.

I pulled myself up and shook my head. I feel like I didn't sleep a wink.

"I'm pretty sure I was in Hell," I admitted.

The pair was silent. I took the time to get my bearings and could still feel the world around me moving. I had to be in an RV or at least something similar. I gazed out the window and watched the highway fly past.

"What do you mean you were in Hell?" Luci asked.

"I mean that I was in Hell. God, it felt like a week, maybe two. I was just in this office building. There was this weird guy in a really nice suit. He had a raspy voice and some kind of accent, maybe African? Honestly, I don't know. But I ended up applying for a job and I ran around a pitch black room for what felt like two weeks," I explained. I didn't feel like I should tell them what else I saw. I'm pretty sure that Luci and Orion wouldn't be happy. But I also didn't even know if it was real.

"That's not Hell. I don't actually know what that is," Luci ensured.

"Not Heaven either. Not that, that was a thought. But I can say I also don't know where that is," Orion added. "Are you sure that wasn't a dream?"

"It wasn't. Trust me," I said. "Where am I? What happened to Gluttony?"

Before either of them could answer I pulled out my phone from my back pocket. The screen was cracked in several new places, along with old markings. I turned it on and went to my browser. I typed in the name of the festival and long behold I got my answer.

Videos, new arrivals, witness accounts, support groups, memes, and everything under the sun appeared in my feed. I clicked on the first video and watched.

A news reporter for one of the major news channels appeared on the screen. "Reports are coming in of, and I'm not pulling your leg Jim, an angel has appeared in Dayton, Tennessee. From eyewitness accounts to live video, people all over the nation are beginning to believe in miracles. But don't take our word for it, here's one of the many videos shot during the events," she reported.

The screen switched to a cellphone recording of me flying with Orion's wings. I was yelling at the crowd and avoiding Gluttony's swings. The video ended with my gauntlets coming out and me being batted like a doll.

I mean they could have cut that part out, that's all I'm saying.

"Still no word on the whereabouts of this angelic man. Perhaps this is a blessing or our warning, America. More on this breaking story when it happens. Back to you Jim," she finished.

As the video ended I wasted no time in turning off my phone again. I tried my hardest but I couldn't hide what was creeping onto my face. A smile bigger than a kid's on Christmas was on my face.

"Ter-"

I cut Orion off. "I'm like a real superhero!"

I felt the room turn to the right before coming to a stop. I looked out the window to see a rest stop. There was some noise out of the room, sounded like a person was walking around. The door slid open and a middle age man stood in the doorway.

He was a black man with clearly defined muscles. He was fit but still had a bit of a stomach behind his gray t-shirt. His jeans were dark as well. His head was shaved and his eyes were brown. His eyes felt like they were glaring holes through my very body. I honestly I thought I was going to be burned from the power behind them. He looked to be about my Dad's age, maybe a little older but not by much. He leaned in the doorway with a bitter expression.

"Is that what you think, now?" He asked with a deep southern accent that made mine sound like I was British. I didn't get a chance to reply before he walked fully into the bedroom. I noticed he was carrying my shotgun in the sling. I was thankful to see her. "You don't even begin to understand the trouble you've brewed up," he added.

"What do you mean?" I asked. I saw no point in pretending I had a lick of understanding.

"What I mean is those videos. News, radio, the internet. You're an overnight celebrity. The whole world is wondering who or rather what the hell you are," the man explained.

I didn't see that as a horrible thing. At least with this fame, I might not be wanted for my Dad's murder. But I didn't say anything.

"You don't get it, do you? Alright, listen up." The man sat down on the foot of the bed and cleared his throat. He unsheathed my shotgun and pointed to a small logo carved into the gun. It looked like one big cross with four little ones surrounding it. "This is the symbol of the Crusaders. I'm sure you heard about them in school. Well, we are a faction of that society. Of course, we don't force religious beliefs, rape, pillage, or any of that bull anymore. Now we're the protectors of what the Crusaders knew very well. We protect the secrets of angels. Specifically angels on Earth, meaning those nats buzzing around in that head of yours, Vessel."

"Wait," I interrupted. "So people have known for years that angels are real. And that they really walk among us? And people keeping calling me this vessel but I honestly have no idea what that means."

The man let out a long sigh. He seemed very tired. He moved and acted much older than his actual age. I wondered how long he had been driving. I wondered what his name was too, maybe should have started with that one.

"Mankind has known about angels from the beginning. But people are fickle and tend to forget that angels indeed exist. As for a vessel, your father was one of them. He had trained his entire adult life to allow an angel to enter him and take control of his body without the loss of his soul or mind. There are many vessels that exist and have existed. These are people touched by angels at one point or another in their lives. That and they must choose this path. Your father was one of these men," he explained.

"My Dad? You knew my Dad?" I asked.

He nodded.

"And you knew that he knew all this stuff?"

He nodded again.

I have no idea why I was so mad but I honestly felt like steam was coming from my ears. He knew all of this and didn't tell me. He told this random guy, sure, but not his son.

"Now, I heard about your father and for that, I am greatly sorry. But we don't have time to waste. Now the whole country knows your face including the other six Sins. We need to be smart about our next move," he began to explain.

I shook my head and put out my hand. "Wait. Wait. I have a lot of stuff happening all at once here. So I already knew that there were other vessels and that we can't trade off unless I kick the bucket. But I'm not a vessel. I haven't seen no angel before and I surely haven't been touched by one. Well except these two who insisted that I touch some weird mirror in my Dad's cellar. And now-"

He cut me off. "The mirror is a transfer device. It's an object that has been both in Hell and Heaven. This is needed to transfer the Angel of Heaven and Angel of Hell into the chosen vessel."

"Ok...I also know that recently I was in a fight with Gluttony. But I have no idea how it ended or who you are or how I got here," I finished.

The man sat still for a moment, just blinking at me with what looked like bewilderment. Honestly, I should be the one that looks like that. After an eternity wrapped up in a few seconds, he started to laugh. He hit his knee a few times and wiped a tear from his eye.

"You certainly isn't a bright kid, are you?" He laughed.

I puckered my lips and bit the inside of my mouth not to say anything. *Dad always said to bite your lip if ever someone hit a nerve so you don't hit their face.* "These are fair questions," I mumbled.

"Oh, no, they are. But you've just been going along with all this without a lick of understanding," he continued. He took a few moments to calm down before he stuck out his hand to me. "Let's start with hello. I'm Frank."

I took his hand and shook firmly.

"Terrance," I replied.

"Didn't your old man teach you no manners?" He prodded.

"I'm Terrance, Sir," I corrected.

"Nice meeting you. Now, let's get down to the work," Frank said. He held up my shotgun again and then handed it to me. "There ain't nothing special about this gun, other than that she's a beaut. You wouldn't kill a Sin with just this thing. It was a good way to die, seeing as you tried."

"Hey, I didn't try to fight Gluttony head on. Well, I mean I did. But not on purpose. I got trapped with those people too. I couldn't just leave them there. Luci and Orion said that it would take something shocking. So I gave them shocking," I argued.

The man covered his eyes with his hand and rubbed them with a groan. "You are that bastard's son."

"Hey!"

"I don't mean no offense. Your father was a stubborn man and it looks like the apple doesn't fall far from the tree. I appreciate your guts kid, but if I hadn't stepped in to save you, them guts would be smeared against the ground," Frank replied.

"What do you mean?" I asked.

"Well, how do you think you beat a Sin?" He asked. I thought for a while and ended up shrugging. I figured that you'd just shoot it till it died but I'm guessing that was not the right answer. "A Sin is an idea. It's a feeling. To kill a feeling you have to overcome it."

I still had no idea what he was talking about. I pressed my lips together and thought. I tried to not make eye contact so it looked like I was thinking. "So when you're hungry, you eat?"

"You can't be sinful and kill a Sin," he stated, bluntly.

"Ohh," I said.

"You still don't get it, do you?" Orion asked.

"Nope," I replied.

"To kill the Sins you must be free of that temptation. So in order to defeat Gluttony, you cannot be gluttonous," Orion clarified.

"Ohh! So I just can't be what their name is. Otherwise I get in that head fog again!" I exclaimed as it clicked.

Frank sighed and rubbed his eyes again. "You know, you look mighty funny when you is talking to yourself."

"What? Oh sorry, I forget other people can't hear them," I apologized.

"Well, all that matters now is that you got me and those angels. Now we got to find that horn and then the rest of the Crusaders can deal with the other Sins," Frank ensured.

"Wait, if you can deal with the Sins yourself, then why do you even need me or these guys?" I asked and pointed towards my head.

"Because, these Sins is no pushovers. It will take an army of us to even banish them back to Hell. It would only take one you. That, and the Angel of Heaven and the Angel of Hell can tell the danger of the Sins better than any man. I only won because Gluttony was staring at you," Frank explained. He stood up and cracked his back. He seemed tired.

"Where are we?" I questioned.

"Near Dallas, Texas," he answered.

"And what are we doing here?"

"I got a tip on where that horn may be," he replied.

I sprung off the bed. "You do!" Just as I spoke my legs went weak and I fell to the ground.

He offered his hand. "Easy there. You're still weak."

I took his hand and sat back on the bed. I was a bit red from the fall. I must have looked like a baby deer to this guy.

"There has been a lot of activity around this city. Lot of people have been going missing, just up and vanished. Then I started looking into it along with a few buddies of mine. Turns out a major...get together has been going on for the last five days. My buddy's daughter said these Con-things are normal and often go on for three days. But no one has seen a person leave, only enter. Odds are a Sin is near," he explained.

"And why does he think the horn is there?" Luci asked.

"Why do you think the horn is there?" I repeated.

Frank cleared his throat and stood. "Here," he pulled out a folded up flyer from his jean pocket.

I looked at a flyer for a dance music convention. It had a list of bands and an advertisement for a brand new instrument that had never been seen before.

"Well, that would do it," I said. "So what are we supposed to do?"

"That's where you come in. Look a guy like me would stick out in this place. The Sin would know I was there before I even set foot in the building. But you, you're young enough not to raise suspicion," he revealed.

"So you're sending me in before you go in? You are coming right?" I asked.

"Damn right I am. This is big kid. And from the looks of things, your old man did not train you to be a vessel," he said. "You will make the distraction and I'll take her down."

"And if you can't take it down?" I asked.

"Then you take it down," Orion answered. "You have to be free from their sin. Just think pure thoughts."

"Blah, or you could just beat them till they can't move," Luci countered.

"With how the last fight went, I'm thinking I will go with Orion's plan," I answered.

"They done explaining to you?" Frank asked.

I nodded.

"Good. Now get that gun loaded and get yourself up, we got leeches," he called. Frank moved to the dresser in the room. It looked like it was bolted to the wall, or at least held in place with cables. He removed a cable and opened a drawer to take out a scoped hunting rifle. He grabbed some ammo and then dug around a bit to throw some to me. I watched nine shotgun shells fall onto the bed. "Then let's go."

15
GUESS WHAT, MORE TRAINING

Frank kicked open the door to his RV like something out of an action movie. There was an immediate screech. I saw a sickly looking squirrel, with perfectly clean fangs jump towards the man through the entrance. Frank shot the animal dead without even flinching.

"Wow," I whispered.

Frank looked back at me and motioned for me to come. I followed along without a word. I peeked out the RV to see the unholy pack of animals that looked like a Disney song waiting to happen. They were almost all pure black with perfectly sculpted teeth while still looking like the grotesque spawns of Hell they were.

Frank looked back at me and threw me a hunting knife from his pocket. "Catch. Leeches will die like any other animal, they might just put up more of a fight," he warned.

I picked up the knife and headed outside with Frank. We quickly and cleanly took out the hoard. I had gotten pretty good at taking out Leeches. But I was nowhere near as good as he was. His movements were so precise and well planned. It was like i was watching an action movie.

Now, I'll admit it. I was distracted. While I was watching Frank, a mutant badger managed to get behind me. It would have had me too if it hadn't hissed.

As I heard the monstrous hiss I jumped forward and felt a rush of energy pump through my veins. It felt like I had just gone down the biggest roller coaster in the world.

My hands burst into flames and I quickly slashed the little thing. When it was finally dead, and it stopped its blood curdling scream, the flames died down. I looked over my hands. They looked like they were made of charred wood. Like they were the end of a bonfire. The skin was cracked like bark, with a molten liquid moving under the surface. The fingers were longer and much sharper than even Orion's hands. They looked like knives and were just as sharp.

Smoke rose from my hands and I smiled. Luci's powers always made me feel so cool. My heart was still pounding a mile a minute. I looked over at Frank who seemed to have backed off.

"Boy that better still be fully you. That smile of yours is giving me the creeps," he claimed.

My smile was stretched from ear to ear. I ran my tongue across my teeth to feel that they were jagged and sharp. Luci's powers were never that pretty on my face.

"Sorry," I said.

"What does he know? That smile suits you," Luci hummed. She seemed really happy right now.

"Kid. Let me ask, can you switch between them yet?" Frank questioned.

I shook my head.

"Then I think I know our next step," Frank suggested. I nodded. Orion has been telling me that I needed to be able to switch on command. I still haven't gotten that far. But maybe this guy knows more than me. "Any ideas?" He added.

I stand corrected.

"To switch between us, you must be able to fully control your emotions and deep desires," Orion answered.

"Oh you know, easy stuff," I sassed back.

"People spend their whole lives training for this Tara. Nothing about it is easy," Luci claimed.

"Well, I don't have all that time. Luci I switched to you fast. How did I do that?" I asked.

"You got scared and your emotional desire was to kill it," she bluntly answered.

"Ok...I don't think I was exactly feeling that-"

"I'm in your head. You can't lie to me," Luci cut off.

"Fine. Orion, I switched easy at the fairgrounds," I said.

"You wanted to protect those around you. Your desires were not for yourself," he answered.

"So I have to want to kill things and want to help people?" I asked. "Then why didn't Luci come out when I was fighting Gluttony?"

"Your desire to save those around you out weighed your personal desires," Orion revealed.

"So Luci is what I want selfishly and Orion is what I want to do to help people?" I tried to clarify. I don't know why all this stuff needs to be that complicated. I mean I'm using it all for the same reason. Why can't it just be easy?

"We can try to simplify it, sure," Luci agreed.

"Alright. I'm going with that then," I said.

I tried to clear my mind the best I could. Orion had drilled into my head the proper breathing techniques and the "easiest" way to clear my head. Honestly I didn't listen to a word he said. Instead, I thought about happy things and tried to let myself get lost. Now, I didn't think about my Dad or friends. That always made me sad in the end, so I tried cartoons. Just mindless cartoons. I would start at the beginning of the episode and by the time I got to the first commercial, Orion or Luci could take over. So I focused on an old episode of Spongebob. You know, the one with the pizza? Da Da Da-ta is the pizza~

I felt my back begin to burn again as the white wings burst from my back. I grunted but did my best to keep my mouth shut. In all honesty, I didn't want to look like a kid in front of this guy. *He was like a secret agent, I mean, he kinda was. Not the point, the point was that he was super cool and I didn't want to seem like I couldn't handle this.*

I felt my hands begin to burn and cramp. It felt like the sun just got a Charlie-horse. I cried out and fell to my knees as my hands were smoking even more. The tears that fell down my face were evaporating before they even could travel halfway down my cheeks. Everything was so hot right now. I'm pretty sure I started to sweat too.

"Terrance that's enough," Orion and Frank said.

"A l-little longer," I stuttered.

I tried my best to focus through the pain. The wings were draped over me like a blanket, lifeless. I felt like something in my back was going to burst through my skin and go flying into space.

I cried out and suddenly there was no noise. I closed my eyes and when I opened them the world looked different. Everything was a muted gray. I looked around the rest stop. I could still see everything just as it was before. I could see Frank and all of the dead Leeches. Then I noticed something. In the muted reality there was a pinkish-redish glow. I squinted my eyes and realized something I wish I could unsee. I noticed myself. I was laying on the ground with a concentrated expression on my face. I couldn't hear anything. I looked over my body that was coated in the odd color. I then noticed something forming. I saw the same woman I had seen in the office holding my hands and the same blond business man with his hands on my back. The woman was coated in red and the man in blue.

I closed my eyes and when I opened them again, I was back. I looked around with fear in my eyes. But I didn't hurt anymore. I looked down at my hands as they were peeling. The soot was falling off them to reveal my normal hands below. With a gust of wind, the feathers from my back began to blow away. I looked up at Frank with sweat dripping down my face. I panted for a few moments before I forced myself to stand.

I walked away from the pile of Leeches and towards the welcome center. I didn't say a word as I stumbled into the building. I walked up to a drink snack dispenser. I reached into my pocket and pulled out the last of my singles. I put them into the machine and selected my number. I watched my snack fall and I selected the next number.

When both fell I reached down and took my chocolate bar and juice box from the machine. They were both warm, but right now I don't care. I opened the juice first and took a long sip and then a bite of the candy.

Frank came running in after a few moments and looked at me with a raised eyebrow. I didn't say a word. The room was awkwardly silent. The only sound was me finishing my snack and the hiss of the nearly empty juice box as I tried to get the last of the warm apple juice. When I was done I threw away the trash and looked at Frank.

"Is he tuning us out?!" Luci barked.

"Yup," I said. I saw Frank jump at the sudden burst of voice.

"You okay, kid?" Frank asked.

I shrugged. "Honestly, probably not. But hey, I just saw myself in third person. So there's that. Also, I think I just saw my soul. Although, I have no idea if that's true. I don't know if anything is true anymore! I just want to go back to bed," I laughed.

Frank looked at me for several moments without speaking. Luci and Orion were also silent. I sighed and sat on the ground. I gripped my head and pulled at my hair. I'm just insane, none of this can really be happening.

"You actually did it," Orion and Frank said.

"What?" I asked and looked up.

"You don't understand what this here means, Terrance. But this is a very good thing," Frank assured.

"You have gone one step closer in your training as the Vessel," Orion added.

"You're going to kill yourself if you keep doing this. Don't push yourself like that again," Luci scolded.

"What's going on?" I barked.

"What you just experienced is one of the things that Vessels are trained to do. By seeing yourself in third person, you were able to see the souls around you. This is amazing news!" Frank cheered.

"What?"

"It means you can see the souls, or rather the lack of soul, of the Sins," Luci clarified.

"Really?" I asked, my face lightened. "Wait, how does that help me?"

"If you can see the soul of a Sin, you can kill it," Frank clarified.

"So I can kill a Sin? How?" I asked.

"I killed Gluttony 'cause I have got no gluttony in me. That and my training, I can see the weak spot. Even a Sin can be killed by a bullet if you know the right place to shoot," Frank cheered.

I was beginning to understand. I smiled and stood up from the ground. "I can really do this now?" I questioned.

"We're a lot better off than we were," Luci said. It honestly felt like she was smiling at me.

"Hell yeah!" I cheered.

Frank laughed and smiled. "Now we've got ourselves a fight'n chance. Remember that feeling, boy. We will need it to fight Lust."

"We're fighting Lust?" I asked. Frank nodded. "Alrighty then. I'm pumped now."

"Don't get ahead of yourself, this is still a Sin," Orion warned.

"I got this," I said, happily.

"Here's the plan. We will drive into Dallas' convention center and I'll drop you off. You'll have an easier time to sneak in. I'll go around the back and see if I can get the jump on Lust. I'm not going to go in till she is focused on you," Frank warned. "You need to be careful and remember, no matter how hard it may be, no lust-filled thoughts. Keep it in your pants, kid," Frank added.

I slightly blushed and shook my head, it's fine. It's not like I'm a hornball or anything. Just a teenager...this may be harder than I thought.

16
I BLEND IN MORE WITH THE WINGS

Frank and I drove up to the Dallas Convention center the next day. I was still feeling a bit tired but after a hot shower and a good breakfast, I was honestly ready for this. I spent most of the morning looking through news articles about this place and some about me, ok, mostly about me. How could I not? It's like I was a real superhero! People were already giving me hero names and asking about my next move and who I was! It was like something out of a comic book. I couldn't help but be pumped. But I did try my best to keep a level head. This was a Sin, and I didn't do so well the last time I fought one. Now, I really got to be on my A-game.

Orion and Luci made me practice that weird head thing for hours yesterday but after a while I got so nauseous that I threw up. Still, this is our best weapon against the Sins. I just unlocked some kind of new power and it's kind of the only thing giving me any sense of hope at the moment so I won't let an upset stomach stop me! Hopefully.

I got out of Frank's RV and looked up at the center. People were going in by the truckload. Most of them looked pretty normal but there was a handful from time to time who were dressed in odd and very flashy clothing. They look like if a glow stick grew legs and went to Hot Topic. But no one else seemed to mind, so I did my best not to stare.

I walked into the front with the others, Luci and Orion were both emitting a feeling of nervousness. I had no idea why, we took down- Frank took down Gluttony with no issue. I figured that I could do the same. I took a deep breath and headed in. Right inside the door was a security check. People were putting tags on their bags and any prop-like weapons. I tightened my hand on the strap of my carrying case.

"I don't know how I'm supposed to get this in," I whispered.

"It would best not to draw attention to yourself right now," Orion answered.

I swallowed, dryly.

I continued to walk forward like I belonged there. I noticed that there was a mindless glare in some of the eyes of the people, I did my best to copy that look. I continued to walk forward until I was stopped by a security guard. The guard's eyes were all black. There was black drool spilling from their mouths. The guard made a few noises and pointed at my back. I tried to keep walking forward, paying them little attention.

I had never seen a Leech take over a person, but I recognize that black goo anywhere.

I was stopped again. I bit my lip. I didn't know what to do. I felt my hand raise on its own. A heavy blush came to my face and my head looked down. I felt my hand take off the gun strap and drop it to the ground. I moved forward and this time I was allowed to pass, but my gun had to stay behind.

The moment I got control of my body back, I turned to look back at the weapon now on the back of one of the guards. I hit my head and frowned.

"What was that? I need that shotgun," I angrily whispered.

"You couldn't get through," Luci began. "I had to do something. Lust is probably watching."

"But what am I supposed to do without it? I still need to take down Lust," I barked.

"Maybe here is not the right place," Orion added.

I felt my body turn towards the men's restroom. I let out a sigh and walked into the restroom. I looked around and I didn't see anyone. I leaned against the counter and pushed back my hair. The light from the window felt nice. It was very comforting.

"So now what am I supposed to do?" I asked.

"Frank will be the one who is giving the final strike. I say do your best to distract Lust and if it comes down to it, we will take over," Luci said.

"But won't I pass out?" I asked.

"I'll get you out of here if I have to and Orion can shield you. We're not going to let you die, Tommy," Luci assured.

"Real reassuring," I sighed.

I heard a small grunt. I jumped and turned towards the now open window. A girl started to climb through the window. She was short and it looked like she was struggling to get in. She had dark brown hair, down to her shoulders with some natural red mixed in. Her eyes were a deep brown that almost looked black in the right light but like syrup in another. Her face, arms, and legs were covered in the cutest darn freckles I had ever seen. She wore a black tank top and short denim shorts. Her feet were bare and muddy and in her hands was a pair of black sandals.

She looked at me and jumped, her hand to her chest in surprise. "Dang it, don't just sneak up on a girl like that," she scolded. Her accent had a sweet southern ring to it. But it wasn't Southern Ohio, more like Texan. "Well? Aren't you gonna say sorry?"

"You just climbed into the boy's bathroom," I finally managed to say.

"And? Aren't you gonna say sorry?" She asked again.

She was cute. The way she was asserting herself did send a chill down my spine though. She was like Ms. Patterson whenever we kids were playing too close to her wild berry bushes. I didn't think she would relent either.

"Sorry Ma'am," I apologized.

"Now that's more like it. Name's Elysia," she greeted.

"Terrance," I replied. "What are you doing here?" I pointed to the open window.

She snorted and smirked. "They wouldn't let me in again."

"Again?"

"Hey, I'm not all sunshine and rainbows, you know? I rejected some guy who kept grinding up against me. Made me uncomfortable so I told a guard and they kicked me out! Weirdest place ever, am I right? Anyway, I wasn't going to take that laying down so I snuck back in. I paid like fifty bucks for this weekend too. But they just started letting people in for free. I don't know what's going on but I'd love to find out. What about you? Did you sneak in too?" She explained. Her nose crinkled at the last part.

"No. I just walked in. They wouldn't let me bring my stuff though," I answered.

"They're weird here. I want to try and figure out what's going on- Hey! You're that guy from all the YouTube videos. It was funny when you flew into that sign. It was like something from an old cartoon," she giggled before becoming serious again. "Wait! If you're that guy then what're you doing here? You're like some kind of superhero?"

That's right! I was a superhero. I mean, I was trying to save the world and stuff. The least I can get for all this work was to be able to revel in some of the superhero perks. *I know, definitely one of my more shallow moments.*

"Terrance, be careful. Don't allow Lust to cloud your judgment," Orion warned.

"Lust doesn't know we are here yet. Don't let him," Luci chimed in.

They both had a point. I took a moment and collected myself before speaking again. "No, I'm not that guy. He's super cool though."

Smooth.

"Really?" She shrugged. "You look just like 'em."

"Do I? I didn't really think I did. Hey, do you want to go dance some?" I asked. I had two reasons for doing this, one, I wanted to go and look for the Horn and two, she was very cute. I didn't see an issue with it if I did my work.

"And if someone tries to bother you again, you can pretend you're with me. If you wanna," I inserted. It would look less suspicious if I was with someone else and I wanted to let Orion and Luci know that but I didn't want to look like a psycho who talks to himself. *Which I was.* I hope they got the hint.

Elysia hummed and shifted her weight on her feet. "Sure, but you get handsy and I'll knock your lights out, cowboy," she warned.

"Noted," I replied.

Elysia and I went into the main dance hall. People of all different kinds were in the room. It was basically packed from wall to wall with more people coming in.

I hadn't really felt it too much before but the smell of sex filled the room. I can't really tell you how I know the smell but somehow it's unmistakable. I watched people grind on each other and strip too. I swear I even saw more X-rated actions too. The feeling in the room was making me nauseous. The smell along with the blasting techno music was giving me a terrible headache. I felt like I was going to throw up.

"Guys?" I said. I didn't care if I looked crazy. Right now, I needed to talk to them.

"Ter-" Orion began.

"Come on, let's dance!" Elysia cut in. She pulled me out to the dance floor and started to dance among the crowd. The girl smiled and clapped her hands. She started to speak but I couldn't hear her. Everything was getting drowned out.

I figured there wasn't much of a reason to fight this. I was honestly having a lot of fun. The music was pretty good and Elysia was a pretty good dancer. I laughed and joked with her but overall we danced. But I didn't forget what I was doing here. I did my best to move us up through the crowd. I wanted a good look at the stage but I seemed to always get dragged back.

After a bit, I took a few songs to enjoy myself. At first, I thought the people dressed in the bright clothing were weird but they looked really cool in the dark. They were calling out and dancing with the best. A few even danced with me. I was getting a little tired.

"The horn?" Luci asked.

"Yeah. Yeah, I'm working on it," I said. That was all she seemed to talk about. It was kind of annoying. I mean I was working after all, what was the harm in dancing.

After a bit though, the people around me were getting closer and closer. I was being grinded on in every direction and even a few people tried to tear at my clothes. It was making me super uncomfortable. I looked around for Elysia but I didn't see her anywhere.

Slowly but surely I forced my way through the crowd until I could see Elysia again.

"Hey!" I called out over the bass of a cartoon theme song, remix.

"Hey," she called back. I couldn't help but notice that she wasn't looking directly at me. She looked really sad like she had been crying.

"Are you okay?" I asked.

She let out a forced laugh and wiped her eyes. "Yeah, I'm fine. It's just...do you like me?"

I didn't understand. "I mean you're a nice girl an' I think you've been pretty fun to hang out with," I replied.

"That's not-" she began. Elysia put her hand on my chest and came close to me. "That's not what I meant."

I stepped away from her. Even if I liked her, this was just Lust's doing. This isn't fair to her, or any of the people here. "Elysia. I think you're a nice girl. But I don't know what you want from me."

Now I'll admit it, here in front of everyone. I don't understand girls or flirting. I'm probably denser than a block of wood. But even I knew what she wanted.

Elysia loomed over me with fallen eyes. But slowly her expression changed. At first sad, she now looked overjoyed, demented even.

"Are you rejecting me, Cowboy?"

17

LUST

The girl's face began to change and twist. The once sweet smile became an evil grin that stretched across her face. The perfect teeth grew into fangs but were still pearly white. I began to back up but was still blocked in by the crowd that did not notice this transformation. She still had a humanoid face but now the mouth was stretched from ear to ear. She giggled at me as her arms became longer claws formed at the end of the fingers. The skin grew hard dark and spiky. It looked like rubbing your hand on her would give you horrible splinters.

She met my eyes and yelled over the music, "Let's dance cowboy."

She looked like black smoke as she drifted through the crowd away from me. Some dancers coughed as she shadowed through them but otherwise paid no notice to her. Her eyes remained locked on to me as she moved away. If I had my shotgun I could have fired in the air and caught the attention of the people in front of me but I didn't. So, I only had one idea.

Dance my way through.

I began to dance in the crowd as I tried to make my way in the general direction of where Lust went. I lost sight of her so I had to hope she was still heading in a straight line. I did my best attempt at dancing and started wedging my way through the crowd. It was working okay but was still pretty slow. Not to mention the number of men and women who attempted to grind up on me. I tried to politely decline as I danced past them.

This was too slow though I knew Lust was going to either get away or find some way to get the drop on me. I suddenly felt Luci about to say something in my head. "...You remember that you can fly right?" I stopped dancing for a moment. *Yes, I had forgotten.*

"Okay, but Luci if I bring your wings out you will burn all the people around us," I reminded her. One plus about them being in my head was that I did not have to shout over the music. "Orion, can we get your's out?" I asked.

"Not right now Terrance. There is a lot of concentrated sin around us. If I bring out the wings and with it holy light it may burn them all just as bad as Luci's fire but not just those around us," Orion answered. So, I needed to get to a clearing or find a way to get a clearing to form around me.

"I have an idea," I replied to the angels. I began tapping on people around me and shouting. "Dance circle!" People seemed to love the idea and began forming a circle clearing around me. I kept dancing so that they would be convinced that it was an actual dance circle. "How much room do I need?" I asked Luci.

"At least ten feet," she quickly answered realizing what I was doing. I don't think she will admit it but I think she was impressed. I kept pushing people back until I had a large circle about ten feet across. The crowd started to get hyped about what I was needing so much room to do. The circle was complete. I spun around finishing a dance move as everyone cheered.

"Now Luci," I ordered.

The familiar burn concentrated on my back as her flaming leathery wings ripped from my shirt and back. Flame formed around me and got dangerously close to the crowd. They screamed out but they should be far enough away not to be seriously burnt. I jetted up above the crowd. Luckily, the ceiling was quite high so I could comfortably stay above the crowd at a safe height.

I glanced back down to the crowd. Those who formed the circle were looking around confused and scared. They immediately started making their way to the exit obviously terrified. So at least hellish fire will snap them out of their lust. I returned my attention to the rest of the crowd, scanning for Lust. I didn't see any sign of her. I suddenly saw a flash of movement from near the punch table. It finally hit me what I saw. Well, it literally hit me. A glass cup flew and slammed into my forehead with expert precision. It cracked and left a nasty gash on my head. I pressed my hand on it as I felt the blood seep out of the wound.

I looked back to the table and saw nothing there other than people moving about and... other things. I flew towards it. The room was rather large but it only took me a few seconds with Luci's wings. I could feel my anger burning and powering Luci. With all the sin around I did not feel the usual intense burning from Luci's wings but instead they felt natural.

I glanced by the table. I did not understand how she can hide so easily. Just a few moments ago I could not take my eyes off her and now it is like she is not even in this room. Though my throbbing forehead said otherwise.

"Terri, behind you," Luci said quickly. I spun around to have another cup slam into the same spot on my head. The cut on my head got bigger and the blood started to drip near my eyes. So, there were two punch tables. Now I have a combined headache from both the music and cups.

I wiped the blood away and kept pressure on the wound. My eyes were stinging and I started to cough. Confused, I looked around me for the source. Then I noticed the smoke that was beginning to fill the ceiling with me.

"Lust has lit a fire in the room," I said to Luci and Orion. I tried to quickly find the source but couldn't.

"Um, Travis honey, Lust didn't start the fire. You are the fire," Luci replied, stifling a laugh. I looked back towards the wings. *Oh yeah, those are on fire aren't they.* So, now on top of looking for an invisible cup wielding lunatic, I was also making it hard to breathe. I didn't want to land though because then Lust could get the pounce on me even easier.

I looked towards the exit and saw people scrambling to it. They must have noticed the smoke and were now trying to escape the fire. That or they saw me, a flaming winged man floating above them and were afraid. Either one made sense. I noticed that they were struggling with the doors. They started panicking and banging on the sealed exit. They must have been locked but I just entered a moment ago. Lust must have moved and sealed the doorways.

I felt myself begin to panic with them. I now had a large scared crowd, a demon who wanted me dead, and suffocating smoke. Not so good for my first official mission working with the Crusaders. I lowered myself below the smoke but still a good height away from the floor. No more cups came so I figured Lust must be waiting to see what I would do.

I took a deep breath and focused my mind. I needed to get the smoke an easier way to ventilate and the crowd to calm down. I had an idea to deal with the smoke. I will worry about the crowd later.

"Luci are you able to cut through the ceiling?" I asked, "I want to make a hole so that the smoke will billow out." It was a blunt plan but an effective one.

"I don't think I could get through the metal and it would take a while to make sizable enough hole to make it through." Luci replied, "Plus we have to worry about Lust stopping us the whole time we would be doing it."

"I can do it," Orion chimed in. "But I need some way for you to clear your mind. Your panic and slight Lust are keeping me from being able to take form."

He was right that I was panicked. The people screaming and banging on the door kept me from focusing very hard. I felt their fear and confusion and it was affecting me. If I could get them calmed down then maybe I could focus enough for Orion to take over.

So, let's recap. I, a flaming winged man, who was causing the smoke that was making people freak out was going to attempt to calm them down. You know, simple stuff.

The stage was a good place to start. I flew over and landed on the stage. It was weird that Lust had not made an appearance yet but I shrugged it off as I needed to get this smoke out. Also if I got things to calm down it may force her to come out.

"Hey!" I shouted. No one heard me. They still were banging and pushing themselves on the doors. I was starting to worry that they were going to crush each other. I needed some way to project my voice. I glanced across the stage and saw the DJ booth. I immediately rushed over to the table and found the DJ himself cowering beneath the bench. He was a skinny pale man with half of his hair long and the other half shaved to a buzzcut. He looked up at me and immediately screamed. Probably because he saw a man with demonic wings. I focused on my back and tried to push the wings back in. They certainly weren't going to help me convince the crowd that everything was okay.

"Terrance what are you doing?" Luci asked.

"I need the wings away so that I can get the crowd to calm down, but I am struggling," I replied. I clenched my back as hard as I could and could only feel the bones slightly slip back into me. They would not go any further though.

"Remember how I said the more sinful you are the more easily I can come back? Well, it also inversely affects how easy it is for you to put me back in," Luci answered.

So, I need to be not filled with sin in a room with a Sin. I took a deep breath and used my brief training with Frank to help. I felt my mind slowly clear and it felt like I was looking at myself from third person. I put all my energy into putting the wings away. After about ten seconds they were about halfway through. Then my worst enemy flew from the crowd. The glass cup hit me in the cheek cutting me slightly again. Worse it took my attention away from the wings.

I felt the wings stuck halfway in my back. It hurt, but as I wiped the blood from my cheek I realized I could work with this. I peeked back over at the scared DJ. He was still hiding in the booth. I shouted at him and he looked up at me. I could see in his face the confusion of why my wings had shrunk but he also seemed more willing to not scream immediately.

"Calm down," I started, "I am the good guy here and I need you to follow my lead. Do you have a mic?" He looked around and nodded nervously as he grabbed it and turned it on. He looked up and handed it over to me.

"Thank you kindly," I mustered up a smile, "We both need to be brave for this." I turned away from him and towards the crowd. They were still at the door. Some were still working tirelessly to open but others seemed to have given up. They cowered against the walls some looking at the ceiling and the smoke others looked at me and my half wings. Luckily the half wings were slightly less intimidating than in their full form.

I took a deep breath. I knew Luci was going to make fun of me forever for doing this but in the stress of the moment, this was the best I could come up with. I looked back to the crowd and raised the mic to my mouth.

"Everyone, I need you to calm down. To help I came up with an idea but I need you to work with me on it," my voice boomed over the mic. Everyone turned to look at me with fear in their eyes. *Well here goes nothing.*

"S-Silent night. Holy night. All is -" I began to sing. To be accurate I began to sing Silent Night. *Listen, Christmas songs always made me feel calm and I could not come up with anything else. Now I am not the best singer, in fact, I am completely average.* My voice carried through the whole room. Everyone in the room was staring and I am sure Lust was staring in confusion as well. Slowly though I heard a couple voices join in. Then more and more joined in. People looked around confused but slowly felt compelled to sing along. The DJ started playing a quiet background dubstep version of the song. *I guess that was the closest he had to the original.*

Soon enough everyone in the crowd was singing. I turned my focus to my back and attempted to move the wings back in. They quickly moved back in though my shirt was ripped once again.

"You made them sing Christmas songs," Luci grudgingly spoke up, "That was idiotic but effective."

"Great job Terrance," Orion piped up sounding energized, "Now let's get to work on that roof." I focused and Orion's wings exploded from my back in a plume of feathers. The crowd cheered. I scanned their faces and they seemed so excited to see me. I looked up and shot towards the roof with a flap of my wings. I approached the ceiling and felt Orion's gauntlets cover my fists. *At this moment I truly felt like a superhero*. I stopped just before the roof inside the cloud of smoke. It made my eyes water but I pulled back Orion's fist and then slammed it into the roof.

The metal bent in a satisfying way. I pulled back and punched it again I could see a crack of light. I punched one last time with my other fist and a hole broke through to the fresh air. The smoke then began to billow out of it. I spent a couple more punches making the hole bigger before coming back out of the smoke. I coughed and my eyes stung but I felt successful.

"Duck!" Orion yelled. I immediately ducked down back to the stage as a table flew over me and embedded itself into the ceiling. I heard the crowd gasp as I narrowly dodged it. I guess I made Lust angry. I landed on the stage. Orion's wings felt heavy but they were not sapping my strength as fast as with Gluttony. I heard a slow clap and looked out from the stage. Lust was walking out being the one slow clapping. She was in her full demonic form but this one was much prettier than Gluttony's.

Her hourglass figure flowed with black shadow that cascaded to the ground. She was very fit and taller than anyone in the room by at least a head. Her skin was a dark obsidian black and shined like the stone as well. In fact, her skin seemed hard like a rock. The people closest to her looked at her with lust in their eyes. It seemed her beauty ended at her face. Her mouth was past her cheeks now with black teeth that hung out like fangs. She had six eyes all different colors that stared at me with hatred. She had long claws and sharp feet.

"He always was the prettiest demon," Luci said.

"He?" I asked confused. Then it hit me. Lust must match the type you are most likely to be, well, lustful for. Though I guess by making her mad she is showing me more of what she truly looks like.

I needed to focus. I jumped off the stage and ran at her. I took off in flight when I got close to her to do a flying punch. I pulled back my arm and punched for her face. She dodged it at lightning speed and returned with a punch to my side as I was still in the air. The force of the punch made me launch through the air and skid on the ground. I was able to spin around by pushing myself off the ground with my wings. I stopped on all fours and was able to get up. Luckily the crowd was smart and stayed up against the walls so I was not close to hitting them.

"You can do it angel man!" I heard someone shout. I stood back up and stared at Lust while holding a hand on my side. It was tender to the touch but I could not let that distract me right now. Man, I really wished I had my gun. I raised my gauntlets ready to fight.

Lust seemed unimpressed with me and said, "You will die in front of all these people so that I may become the horseman and let lust run rampant through this world."

"Sorry I can't let that happen," I replied. I jumped towards her again but my gauntlet missed. This time I was prepared for her counter and blocked it with my other hand. The gauntlet absorbed the blow but it felt like when you try and hit a baseball without gloves and a metal bat. Orion was helping my movements by making me more tactical, but I could tell our training had helped some.

I spun around from the block and was able to land a punch on her side. Orion's gauntlets were able to crack her stone body slightly and send her skidding to the side.

"Where is the horn?" I forcefully asked.

She laughed, "Why, it is backstage waiting for the finale of course. Too bad you will not be around to see it blown." It felt like I was talking to a supervillain. The crowd was eating it up too. I glanced and saw them enthralled by this fight.

"Terrance, focus" Orion called. I turned my head just in time to see Lust launching herself towards me. I crossed my arms in front of my face and blocked the shot. It sent me skidding backward. Blow after blow came from her. I was successfully blocking them but had no time to throw a shot of my own and I was getting tired from Orion's form already.

She punched to my right and I went for the block but she fainted and clawed my other side. I yelled out in pain as three wounds were shredded into my side. I grabbed my side. She was too fast and Orion was too slow. I needed to mix things up but I don't know how easily I could change to Luci.

I whispered to the angels. "Orion I am going to need you to fully armor myself for this next move and to trust me. Luci, I am pretty dang mad so get ready to come out."

"Terrance, a switch like that could tear you apart," Orion warned.

"No time to discuss possible side effects. Let's go." I answered back. I spun back towards Lust, she seemed to be enjoying this fight. I saw my blood drip from her right hand. I felt a burning in my chest. I focused on Lust and felt that third person feeling that Frank taught me to achieve. It was hard to focus but I faintly saw a red gem in the front of her throat beneath the shadow. That was it, that must be her weak spot.

I flapped Orion's wings and flew towards her with the gauntlets again. I saw her smirk as she prepared to finish this fight. As I came close I let the gauntlets fade and switched his armor to my sides. I felt a burning as the silver armor covered my wounds on my sides. Lust did not seem to notice though. My punch missed as she dodged. I landed and she sped towards me to counter. I dodged to the side and her claws scratched across the armor. It made a horrible noise but did not cause me pain. Lust was surprised by my trick and skidded to a stop. That skid was all I needed.

I yelled as I let my wrath flow through me. Orion's wings disappeared in a poof of feathers as Luci's wings erupted out in a ball of fire. The crowd gasped at the sudden transformation. My back was numb and it felt like my spine was going to snap. I flew towards Lust at an incredible speed with Luci's wings at full throttle. I held my hands out and willed Luci's arms to appear. My skin burned away into claws just as I reached her. I slashed towards her stomach and she dodged back out of the way. But, that was the plan.

I changed the direction of Luci's wings to make me full stop and spin. The world became a blur and I hoped my hand was in the right place. I let the claws out at full length and heard a screech as I passed through a stone surface. The world came back into focus as I finished spinning. I looked at Lust to see her clutching at her throat. She looked at me and opened her mouth to say something, but only black bubbling tar fell out. Her eyes rolled into the back of her head and she fell face down on the ground unmoving.

I had actually done it.

Luci's form quickly disappeared and I fell to my knees. I coughed into my hand and saw blood but I had won. I shakily got to my feet and looked over to the crowd. They stared at me with huge eyes and open mouths.

Then, they erupted into a cheer.

18
THE NEW HERO STEALS A CAR

I could not feel my arms, could not straighten my back fully, and I just coughed up blood. But I felt great. The crowd cheered again and ran up to me. A couple of the guys propped me up on their shoulders. I had to put most of my weight on them. The crowd surrounded me, which made me a bit nervous, and they began to thank me and talk over themselves.

A lot of comics having the hero loving the attention but to be honest it is really awkward to have so many people thanking you. Though I'd be lying to say I didn't enjoy it in that moment.

I waved at them as I put almost my full weight onto the two guys holding me up. These people were dressed real strange and some had binkies , but I was glad to see they were alright. I nudged one of the guys holding me up and nodded towards the stage. I was finding it hard to speak as it felt like all my energy had shot out of my body. The guy understood and got the attention of the other one carrying me. They began to drag me back towards the stage. I could help walk some as my legs were not too exhausted but I do not think I could have made it back on my own.

"You did it Terrance," Luci congratulated me with sincerity.

"Yes," Orion cut in, with strain in his voice. "Though we will need to work on how to avoid injuries. I glanced down and saw streams of blood flowing from the three deep cuts on my side. A parting gift from Lust. There was a faint glow to the wounds as Orion worked hard to close them.

"I'll try and work on that," I laughed. I knew I should take it serious but right now I was just so over the moon. I actually took down a Sin, by myself no less.

As if I'm cue, I saw Frank running up through the crowd and to the stage. The doors had all been open and people were running out, well some were while others stayed to gawk at me. A good amount of them were singing Silent Night now.

Frank hopped up on stage. He had my shotgun in his hand. "What on Earth is going on in here?" He asked.

"I did it!" I had no issue in boasting. "I did what you said and found Lust's weak spot."

"And you took it down without this?" I asked. Frank held up my gun.

I laughed and nodded. "I'm surprised too. I'm also feeling exhausted." With my words I fell to my knees. My body was so tired. I felt like everything in me was burning, it probably was. I looked up and let out a long, exhausted sigh.

"Did you find the horn?" Frank asked.

"Not yet. But there's a lot of cases and instruments over there," I called. I pointed towards the storage area on the stage and tried to get my legs to work. They had other plans, however.

I crawled over to Frank and started to go through the cases of instruments. Some people wanted to help but Frank said no. I don't blame him, I didn't even know the Sins could look like people in the way that Elysia did. This was really making me question who I wanted to trust.

"Luci," I whispered. "Do you feel anything?"

"I am still smelling Lust. I can tell he's gone. But I can't see much more. His haze is still here and may very well still be affecting people. Be careful," she warned.

I nodded and continued searching. After a while I came down to the last case. It was an odd shaped case. It was long and narrow. I opened it to see the oddest looking horn I had ever seen. It looked like something you took to a football game. It was a long brass horn. Skinny at one end and wide at the other. Just a brass triangle cylinder. Frank looked up at me and quickly got up. He rushed to my side and looked at the instrument in the case. He picked up the axe with the instrument still inside. He looked over the horn and rose an eyebrow.

"Is this it?" He asked me.

"I have no idea. Luci? Orion?" I asked.

"I haven't seen the Horn before. I believe this is Luci's department," Orion said.

Luci was quiet for a few seconds. "It looked different in Hell, but very similar. I don't know if it was just the atmosphere," Luci answered.

"Better safe than sorry," I said and closed the case. I locked the outside of it and did my best to try and stand.

Frank helped me up and looked around. There were still a decent amount of people. Somewhere on the phone, some crying, some running, and some still gawking at me. Frank cleared his throat and put his hand on my shoulder.

"I don't think it's safe to stay here too much longer. Listen to me close," Frank began. He pulled me close and got real personal with my ear. "We need to take down the next Sin. An old friend of mine thinks there may be a couple out in the desert, a day's drive or so, maybe two, out near El Paso. That horn is safer with you than anyone else. Send it back to where it belongs and meet me out there," Frank instructed.

"Can I send it back?" I asked.

Luci made a small sound before speaking. "Yes, but with me. Your job as a Vessel will be done once we return the horn. I'll teach you the ritual. But we need to get away from anything that may stop us," she warned.

"Wait. Really? It's all over?" I asked.

It's really already over? I was just starting to get used to this. But if it's going to be over, what am I going to do? I don't have my Dad and I think I'm wanted for a lot. And for saving the world, it didn't go on very long. I'm thankful that I didn't die or anything. But, I don't know...I was expecting more. Still, if it's all over, I guess that's a good thing.

"O-ok."

Frank looked at me before smiling. "Don't worry kid, our work ain't over yet. Let's just get that horn out of the Sins' reach."

I sighed and nodded. He handed me a piece of scrap paper. "Here. It's my cell number. When you get near El Paso give me a call. I'll be in undisclosed location. Keep those Simms scratching their heads and hopefully work on plans to give us the upper hand. You won't have them angels with you no more. But we can still take these bastards down," Frank ensured.

I took the paper and put it in my pants' pocket. This was really happening. Luci and Orion were going to be gone. It felt like we just started this and now they were going away. I felt a tight grab in my chest. There was so many unanswered questions still in my head. This couldn't be the end. But it needed to be.

"Got it. I'll call when I get close," I answered.

"Terrance," Luci began.

"I'm okay, really. I'm glad this is all over," I replied with a warm smile. "Things are going to feel a lot better when none of us have to worry about the end of the world."

I took the stairs down off the stage and held the case to the Horn, right in my hand. I wasn't going to let anyone get their hands on this. I went through the stage doors and out the back of the room. I did my best to avoid people. I honestly didn't want to be around anyone right now. I know I should be happy, but I'm really not.

I took a deep breath and focused. I don't have the time to feel sorry for myself. Right now my focus was on this Horn. No matter how I feel or what I think, this is the most important thing I can do.

I walked out to the parking lot and took inventory of myself. I was tired and honestly my mind was fighting me but the adrenaline that Luci gives off had me wired. I looked around the parking lot as my mind took a moment to catch up to my body.

"Ok. Let's get my truck and we can get somewhere hidden. Luci what all do I need for the ritual?" I asked.

"Nothing you can't eat at a grocery store. Come on, let's move. Lust's scent is stinking up this place," she gagged.

I nodded and went to find my tru-where is my truck?

"Hey guys? Where is my truck?" I asked. Now that I was thinking about it, I didn't drive here. Frank brought me. "It's still at the fair!"

Orion let out a laugh. I hadn't heard him laugh much. It sounded like the kind of laugh you would expect from an old man: gritty and dry.

"Hey, I was passed out," I said.

"That doesn't help you," he continued.

His laugh was somewhat contagious. I couldn't help but let out a laugh myself. "This whole thing was so crazy but now, now it's over!" I laughed. "It's over. You will go back to Heaven and Hell and I'll...Everything can be normal again."

Orion's laughter stopped. Everything was quiet again. I don't like this sound anymore.

"Hey Thomas, I think I can help you get a car. We need a lot of space. That shouldn't be too hard to find. But we can't walk, not to mention those boys in blue may not be too happy with you," Luci warned.

"Well, I'm happy to hear what you got in mind," I said.

Now, I think I'm good person. I try to pay for everything and I don't lie but with angel who calls Hell, home sweet home in your head, you're bound to do some bad stuff. Please remember that when Luci or Orion is in charge, I can't say no, easy.

My eyes flashed red and the world gain a haze over it. My body moved without my consent. I watched myself move over to a parked, black convertible with the top down.

"Luci? Luci what are you doing?" I asked.

I felt myself get into the car by sliding over the door. I sat down in the driver's seat and buckled myself in.

"Luci," Orion called.

"You got a better plan, winged wonder? Besides, whoever this is, we just saved their life from a Sin. This is a nice thank you," Luci relied.

"No, no, no! Luci give me back my body, we are not doing this!" I barked but my hands didn't stop moving.

Luci changed the finger next to my pinky into one of her thin and long claws. I had no idea what this girl was planning, but I was doing everything in my power to stop it, which was basically nothing.

Luci stuck the claw into the Ignition. She fiddled around with the lock.

"This can't not work. This cannot work!" I repeated. The car started. "There's no way this should have worked…"

"Ta-da," Luci sang.

"Please don't make me do this," I whined.

"I'll give you control when we get on the highway and far enough I know you won't turn around," Luci ensured.

"Orion, do something," I demanded.

"I can't with all of the sin in this place. But if this is the best way to get the Horn back to where it belongs…"

"You're a real good angel, aren't yah?" I spat. Why did she make me steal a really nice car? I wouldn't have felt as bad if it was something like my truck. I want that truck back too. If it hasn't been sold for scrap. After all, it was my car and my Dad worked damn hard on it.

I sighed and let Luci do what she was going to do. I didn't think I could fight it, so I didn't. I was tired. At least I could take the situation to relax and take a breather.

"Oh, one more thing," Luci began. I felt my hand whip down with inhuman strength and a loud snap. I screamed and looked down at my hand. I was now missing the top half of my right ring finger. "There. Don't worry, it will grow back."

"Woman!" I barked. I wanted to hold my hand but my body wasn't listening. Though I was glad to see that there wasn't any blood. I guess Luci doesn't bleed. "That doesn't make it better!"

Orion cleared his throat and I forced my eyes to stare into the rear view mirror. I stared down the voices in my head and gritted my teeth. "What are you trying to say?"

"I can't actually do much here," Orion said.

"Luci!"

"Wait, you can grow wings but not a finger?" Luci asked.

"I cannot grow anything human. I can speed Terrance's natural human healing along but human limbs don't grow back like ours," Orion clarified.

"You didn't check with him before!?"

"He can repair every rib in your body in a day, sorry for believing in him," Luci snarked.

I grind my teeth and bit my cheek. My body was already driving out of the arena's parking lot.

Oh, I thought I was mad before, but this takes the cake. "Our Father who art in heaven, hallowed be thy name. Thy kingdom come. Thy will be done, on earth as it is in hea-"

"What are you doing?" Luci sighed.

"You're a demon. So I'm praying," I replied. The pain was lessening.

"I'm an angel, you dense boy," Luci barked.

"Ok, one, you broke off my finger because you thought Orion could heal it, without asking. Two, you broke my finger off because you thought Orion could heal it, without asking! Excuse me if I forgot your holy-ness," I spat.

"Terrance, take a deep breath," Orion warned.

I took a big gulp of air and began to scream/sing "this is the song that never ends!"

"What are you doing?!" Luci yelled over me.

"You broke off my finger and a prayer doesn't work. But you're in my head. You have to deal with everything I do. That means I can at least annoy the Hell out of you," I ensured.

We drove for a while before Luci gave me back control. I guess she thought that I would turn around, which I would have. I did have to admit, if she had to steal any car that this one was rather fun to take such a long drive in. Oh, I never stopped singing. My throat was raw and I gave myself a headache but at least those two were just as annoyed. It may have been a bit childish but Luci is like thirteen years old. Well, I guess she is. She died when she was so technically, she's still thirteen.

"T-this is the song that ne-ver-r ends..." I continued to mutter. "Ok." I paused and cleared my sore throat. "I'm done."

"Finally," Luci whined out.

"Indeed," Orion agreed.

I was getting tired. After a while you can even annoy yourself, I mean that was the point but...well never mind.

"I'm surprised you lasted as long as you did to be honest," Orion added.

"I have a lot of practice with pain," I replied, sourly.

"Do you smell that?" Luci asked.

"What?" I replied. "Is it the rotting flesh in a car?"

"Do you want me to say sorry? Would that make you feel better?" She sighed.

"Actually, yeah, it would. Neither of you have said sorry once for any of this. I was perfectly fine with my life before you two came around," I barked.

Orion cleared his throat. "We saved your life. I apologize for what happened to your father but we truly thought you were him."

"Would you have saved me if you didn't think I was my Dad?"

They were silent. I rolled my eyes and huffed. "Here I thought angels were supposed to be helpful." I bit my lip. "Am I not good enough? I'm just as good as my Dad. I mean we did it. We killed two Sins already! I'm just as good, I'm better!"

I covered my mouth. Did I really say that? How could I say that?

"Terrance-"Luci began. The sound of police sirens cut her off.

I looked behind me and saw a police car on the otherwise empty highway. I cursed under my breath and pulled over.

"Don't pull over. Did you forget you're a wanted man?" Luci warned.

"I also have wings that can shoot out of my back on command. Besides, it's one car. I'll probably get a warning for speeding and can go on my way," I explained. I really didn't care. It was a cop. I could easily get pass him when I needed to. But right now I needed to pull over anyway. My head was pounding and I was so shaken up that I just needed to take a moment.

The police cruiser parked behind me and an officer got out. I noticed that there was already a person in the back of the cruiser as well. But I didn't pay too much attention to her as the officer came up.

A man approached the driver side of the stolen car. He took his time coming up as he looked over the convertible. He looked the stereotypical cop with sunglasses and mustache. If felt like something out of a movie.

"Do you know why I pulled you over this evening?" He asked. His eyes were locked on the car as he looked up and down the interior.

"No officer. Is there an issue?" I asked. There are a lot of reasons that he could have pulled me over but since his gun isn't aimed at my head, I'm assuming he doesn't know who I am.

"This is a nice car you got here. It looks mighty expensive. Mind telling me what you did to deserve something like this?" He asked.

So he knows it's stolen. Great.

"I didn't really do anything to deserve it," I lead on. I'm not exactly saying I stole it. But I'm not lying.

"Tuni, please just drive off," Luci sighed.

"Guys like you never do anything to deserve anything. Handsome, strong, and you got that southern charm that turns nice ladies into nothing but wild animals. But that doesn't matter to you. Everything just gets handed to guys like you. You never work hard for anything," the cop spat.

"What are you talking about?"

The man's hand shot out and grabbed onto my neck with inhuman like force. I gagged and tried to peel the man's hands off of my throat.

"Guys like you don't deserve to even live," he growled. Black was dripping down his chin from the corners of his eyes.

"It's a Leech!" Orion exclaimed.

My right hand went back and punched the man in the gut. Orion's gauntlet formed in the air and sent the body of the cop flying a good twenty feet into the desert road.

I jumped from the car and grabbed my shotgun. I aimed it at the man and walked over to him with caution.

Please don't be dead.

I walked over to the man who laid still in the dirt. I bit my lip and judged him with my shoe. He didn't move.

"Oh crap," I said.

CRACK.

I fell to the dirt as something hard hit the back of my head. Pain filled my skull as my vision crossed. I groaned out and turned my head the best i could to look up.

The criminal in the backseat of the cop car was now standing to the left of me. She was dressed in sweats and a Cookie Monster tank top. Her red hair was a rat's nest of a mess and her makeup was smeared down her cheeks. But the most important thing was that she was holding the Horn's case in her right hand.

I watched the fat officer jump back to his feet like a pro athlete. He cracked his neck and went over to the girl and smirked.

"Well done sister, I could have done better myself," he said.

"But you didn't. I obviously did better," she replied.

"Better in what way? You merely did as you were told?"

"And as did you, brother."

"Then let's agree," the cop said.

"Agree to agree or agree to disagree?" She replied.

"Agree that one is wrong and one is right," he said.

"You can agree to that."

"But don't you agree that one is wrong?"

"But not in the same way as you. So I cannot possibly agree to a statement that is wrong."

"But you do agree."

"Agree to disagree."

"Agreed."

I already had a pounding headache. This wasn't making it any better. I thought I was annoying but this is nonsense. It's just stupid really. They just keep saying the same thing as each other. Not to mention, I had no idea what's going on!

"Guys?" I whispered.

"Shh, quiet you."

"Quiet you, shh."

"Meet Envy," Luci whispered back to me.

This is bad. I didn't even need to say a thing for Orion and Luci to know the same thing. I was exhausted. We just defeated Lust a few hours ago and already another Sin had appeared, rather two appeared and they now had the Horn.

Fu-

19
ENVY

I had no idea what to do. My head was killing me, I was exhausted, and I was really pissed off. Honestly, I just wanted to rip the heads of those Sins and then Luci and Orion. I'm sick of them. They always tell me what to do or make jabs at me. They don't care at all and to think I was upset that they would be gone. Boy, was I wrong.

So not on top of Orion and Luci arguing in my head, I had these two saying the same damn thing over and over. If I hadn't already lost my mind I was about to. I rubbed the back of my head as I forced my way back up. I wobbled some but I got stable enough to pull out my shotgun. I aimed it at the male Envy.

I looked around the cop's body and bit the inside of my cheek. This was still a person. It wasn't their fault they were taken over by a supernatural voice. They were probably just minding their own business and now they are being forced to find the Horn of Gabriel. They didn't get a choice. They didn't get a say. They didn't deserve this. It's not fair.

I lowered my gun.

"What are you doing? Shoot!" Luci ordered.

"Why? They didn't do anything," I spat.

"Terrance, you are under the control of Envy. You need to breathe and think-" Orion began.

"No," I cut off. "You know, I don't want to kill an innocent person. It's not their fault that something jumped into them."

"They are not human. This is the best way to kill-" Orion began again.

"What part of no, don't you understand?" I barked.

"Listen here kid, we don't have time for this. They have the Horn. Get your mind together and find their weak point," Luci demanded.

"And why don't you do it?" I sassed.

"My, my, what do we have here?" the cop said.

"An internal struggle, I would assume," the criminal replied.

"More of conflicting dialogue."

"Is there a difference?"

"Only to those with a thought."

"Are you saying that I do not think?"

"I'm not saying, you are assuming."

"And you are bumbling."

"That would be what it sounds like to you."

"And that would be what it sounds like to you."

"Ter-" Luci began.

"That's enough," Orion cut off. "Terrance is right."

"That's right...I-I am?" I asked.

"Yes. We've been taking advantage of you. But right now someone else is taking advantage of you too," he said.

"What? The Hell they are," I said. "Who is?"

"Envy. They think they can take your Horn. They're taking your belongs Terrance. The thing you worked hard for," he lead.

"You're right. Hey!" I directed my attention to the Sin. "That's mine!" I pointed at the Horn case and rose my shotgun again.

The two Envys looked at me. They tilted their heads and a wide, unnatural smile came to their faces.

"I believe we have a challenge, dear sister."

"Indeed. What a challenge it is."

"Do these angels really think they can defeat us?"

"You're forgetting yourself, brother."

"I forget?"

"We have what we want. Why fight?"

"Because there's always more."

"He does have a nice car."

"Nice gun."

"Nice eyes."

"Nice hair."

"Let's take it all."

The skin on the two began to peel away like a… it looked like a banana being peeled. The skin fell piece by piece onto the ground revealing the Sin's true form underneath.

The female Envy was an unearthly skinny. She still maintained a female body shape but her pitch black body looked like it was being held by a corset that was way too tight. She wore a flowing green skirt but nothing on her top. Not that there was anything to cover, her top was completely smooth. Her legs were long and perfectly sculpted. She looked like a Barbie doll, but instead of a face she wore a large, white mask. The mask looked fox-like with two green stripes down the center of the eye slits.

The male Envy was just as skinny as his sister. But his body was much more bony and yet, muscular. He had long claw like fingers and a tall figure. He wore a green sash over his shadowy body. His head was that of a dead crane's skull. There was a green line down the center of the skull that seemed to drip down his boney beak.

The Sins stepped out of their meat suits and locked their attention on me. I tried my best to focus on leaving my body and finding their weak point, but to my surprise, I couldn't focus.

"What's going on?" I grumbled.

"They are taking advantage of you. As long as you're under their power, you cannot find their weakness," Orion revealed.

"How do I get out of their control?" I asked.

"I don't know. Perhaps if you could have someone who is not under their influence, instructing your movements then you could find an opening," Orion said.

I thought for a second. "You're not under their influence, right? You can tell me what to do!"

"That's I can. Jump back," Orion ordered.

I did as he said and narrowly missed the male Envy's claw.

"Left!" Orio ordered.

I rolled left just in time to avoid the female Envy's swipe. I looked up at the two of them with a panting breath. I was exhausted. I could barely do this. My body was still sore from everything. But I can't just let this go. If I let Envy have the Horn then everyone dies.

"Yes! Keep this up. You're fighting their influence," Orion revealed.

I smiled and avoiding the next attack on my own. I could do this. I had to do this. I could easily do this!

"Don't get too prideful," Luci warned.

"What do you know about pride?" I spat.

"What's that supposed to mean? Or did you forget who I am?" Luci spat right back.

I jumped out of the way of another attack. I looked up and realized that I had no idea where the sister was. I gritted my teeth and looked around as I tried to get out of Envy's reach.

"You heard me. You're my most prideful thing I've ever met," I said.

"Obviously you don't spend much time with yourself," she claimed.

"Luci you are not helping," Orion chimed in.

"Yeah, you're not helping, April-" my legs stopped moving. I fell to a dead stop and my head got quiet. I pushed myself off the ground and felt a numbness in my legs. I rolled over to see that my lower half was burning the ground below me.

The male Envy came over to me and looked down at the ground with the curiosity of a kitten. He looked over the burn marks on the ground and then around my legs. He was clearly very interested in what was happening.

"How do you know that name?" Luci finally asked.

"Does it matter?" I asked.

A burning sensation traveled up my legs and through my spine to my head. The pounding headache made me cry out in pain. "Damn right it matters!"

Smoke filled my view. I looked down to see that there was smoke coming out from my mouth. Envy turned to me and stuck his hand into my mouth with a quick motion. He pulled out a tooth and I screamed, biting down on his hand.

"Dude!" I yelled.

I spit some blood onto the ground and looked at the crane headed Sin. He replied by jumped back and twitching his head as he looked over my tooth. I rolled my eyes and winced as the motion made my head hurt more.

"I'll ask again. How do you know that?!" Luci yelled through my mouth. Smoke filled the air as she spoke.

"The man in the fancy suit told me it," I answered. The headache was killing me.

"Man?" Orion asked.

"Yeah. When I was passed out for several days I was at a job interview with this guy in a fancy suit. He showed me how Luci became the Angel of Hell and told me to ask you who suffered for you to become the Angel of Heaven. I wasn't going to bring it up to be honest but you two have been nothing but controlling. I'm sick of it!" I yelled.

"Awe, he's so cute~"
The female Envy appeared behind me. The horn case was still in her hand. She mewed and circled around me. I still couldn't move my legs.

"I'm going to take him home," she ensured. "But I have first dibs. I found him. And I'm the oldest."

"I'm the oldest! And I had him first."
The female Sin picked me up and held me tightly in her arms, like I was a doll.
"Sister, he's mine."

"Mine."

"Excuse me," I choked out.

"Yes?" they said together.

"We need to think on our feet. We can work out our differences later. For now, let's focus on getting back the Horn and staying alive," Orion said.

"Fine, but this isn't done. In fact I think I have a good idea if you're willing to listen for a change," Luci offered.

"If you give me a chance," I whispered.

I cleared my throat the best that I could and listened. Luci took a moment and looked around the situation before speaking again. "Envy hate each other. Their ability to inflict envy is both a gift and curse. They are envious of each other. Use it," she instructed.

So I needed to get them to turn on each other. They acted like children, I guess I was doing the same. I really owe Luci an apology and Orion too. But, the best thing I can do is listen. I can't do this alone. An idea popped into my head.

"I want to go with her. She's the better Sin, after all. She knocked me out, got the Horn, and captured me. I think you're just slowing her down," I said.

"You're crazy! I'm obviously better!"

"You heard him, dear brother. Haha, looks like I win."

"You're nothing without me. This was my plan and that should be my Horn!"

"Well, you don't have it. Do you?"

"Whore."

"Bastard."

"Pathetic!"

The female Sin dropped me and the case for the Horn before she rushed for her brother's face. The two started to go after each other. They looked like alley cats who had just found enough food for one of them. The male Sin did his best to scratch at the mask of the his sister. The sister avoided each attack with grace. She was literally dancing across the battlefield. While his movements were sharp and accurate, hers were graceful and fluid. They were complete opposites.

I grabbed the case and ran away from the Sins and back towards the car. As I was running I felt something grab my legs and pull me back against the desert ground. I yelled and looked up to see the male Envy holding my ankle.

"Where do you think you're going?"

"Where indeed?"

"You're the prize."

"Can't have you running off."

I swallowed dryly and held the case close to my chest. I can't let them get their hands on this. It's mine! No. No it's not. This belongs in the afterlife. I can't let anyone get their hands on this. We all depend on this.

"Alright. Alright, you win. I'll stay here. But, I think that he's the better Envy now," I revealed.

"You little-"

"Ah, I knew he'd come around."

"That's what you call a psychotic break?"

"He only speaks the truth."

"He's our enemy."

"He wasn't our enemy five minutes ago."

"That's because he was making sense then."

"You're only jealous."

"You're only hopeless."

"Ok, they're distracted. But I still can't focus enough," I told the voices.

Orion hummed as he looked over the situation. He seemed to be in a deep thought as he would mumble from time to time.

"Got a plan, old man?" Luci asked.

"Working on it. Terrance, the best way to get rid of Envy is to clear your mind. Focus on giving. That's the best I can come up with for now," Orion said.

"It's better than nothing," I said.

I took a deep breath and did my best to think about giving. I went to birthdays and holidays. I thought about church on Sunday and when Dad and I would go help out Mrs. Shelly with her yard work once she was too old to work. The thoughts made me much sadder than happy. My brain was fixed on my Dad. If he had just gone down into the cellar none of this would have happened. He would be the Vessel and I wouldn't have to be saving the world in his place. How much easier would that had been? He could have saved everyone. I can't even save myself.

I wiped a tear from my eye. I needed to stop thinking like this. I felt like my heart was going to tear apart my whole body. I mean what was even the point?

They didn't want me. I wasn't the one who was supposed to save the day. All I am is the kid who got in the way.

"Damn it, I'm useless," I confessed.

"No you're not," Orion began. "You have done more than anyone could have imagined. You weren't the chosen Vessel, oh well. You stepped up when it mattered and you've taken every challenge head on."

Luci sighed and let out a small groan. "Alright, fine. Maybe we were being too hard on you. I know we can both be a bit demanding and well, controlling but you have stuck through it and I'm thankful. This isn't easy," she admitted.

I had no idea why these two were apologizing to me. It seemed misplaced and odd to even hear it. This whole time they had just been riding my body along. Then...what I just said. I didn't have an excuse to talk with them like that. This is the end of the world. We didn't need to be arguing and I didn't need to be petty. Sure, they were taking control of me but from the way Frank talked m, it seemed like that's what they were supposed to do. A vessel was, well a vessel. It was just a body. But since I still couldn't have them fully take over me, I guess they're just not use to a third voice in the mix. I can't say I blame them.

"I'm sorry too. I've been acting like a brat. I don't know what came over me. I think it's just the buildup of everything. This is a lot of pressure, okay? Speaking of, what should we do? We can't just leave these two and I can't break from their grip," I said.

"We could trap them, you know?" Luci offered.

"That's not very angelic of you," Orion replied.

"What's the harm? It's not like we're leaving them here forever. Just until one of the Crusaders can get down here and take care of them. Besides we have the Horn, what's the harm?" Luci added.

"Trap them? We can do that?" I asked.

"Yes, we can draw a devil's trap and make it so they can't leave. Honestly they're arguing so much, I don't think they will notice," Luci answered.

"Alright, how do we do that?" I asked.

"Take off your shoes and socks. Then walk were I tell you. We can burn it into the ground," Luci suggested.

I nodded and quietly took off my cowboy boots and socks. The smell from my feet was enough to make me gag. These were old boots and I had been wearing the same socks for two weeks now. I put them to the side and stood up. My feet felt hot, burning actually, as I walked around the Sins. I cut through a few times and made different symbols with my feet. If Envy began to notice me, I would just say that one was better or looked better than the other and they would fight again. When I was done I put my shoes and socks back on and looked over at the now trapped Envy.

"Hun, we should use that more," I said.

"Other Sins won't stand still long enough to try," Orion reminded.

"You have a point," I laughed before I walked back to the car with case in hand.

"Hold on, Terrance. Check to make sure the Horn is still here. We can protect you from any of the Horn's callings," Orion said.

I nodded and put the case on the trunk of the convertible. I unlatched the case and slowly lifted the top. I looked over the horn. It was long and cylinder shaped. It looked like one of those horns you see in medieval movies. I picked up the instrument and looked it over. It felt weird. Almost like-

"Shit!" Luci barked.

I jumped and dropped the horn to the ground. It clang against the dirt. I quickly picked it up and noticed a dent in it. I actually just dented the Horn of Gabriel.

"I'm sorry...I-I," I stuttered.

"It's a fake," Orion revealed.

"What?" I said.

"Look, there on the side," Luci pointed out.

I looked at the side of the horn to see a carved in warning "Property of Excalibur Hotel and Casino".

"It's a prop? Then where is the real Horn?" I asked.

"Well obviously these two don't have it. Gluttony and Lust are out of the picture too. I hope that Lust didn't just hide the real horn," Luci said.

"If Lust did, she wouldn't have advertised it, right?" I asked.

"Unless she was advertising because she knew the Horn was a fake. She wanted whoever has the real Horn to show up," Orion revealed.

"But why would they show up?" I asked.

"I could see several reasons. Pride would want to prove that he had the actual Horn and would want to punish Lust for insulting him. I don't think Wrath or Sloth would take the time. Sloth is, well Sloth, and Wrath would punish her *after* she blew the real Horn," Orion explained.

I pulled out my hand and started to count off the Sins listed. After I remembered that I was now missing a finger, and a molar for that matter, I shook my head. "What about Greed?" I questioned.

"Greed would have come for both. Even if he had the real Horn he would want the fake as well. But what surprises me is that he didn't come for it. He wasn't there and I mean there could be a chance that we just missed him, but he can move much quicker than us. I would imagine that he still would have come after us," Luci replied.

I pulled out my phone and turned it on. I typed in the name of the hotel on the fake horn. News articles and video footage came up in an instant. People from all over the world were talking about this particular hotel. Apparently everyone had been winning big. I clicked on a video from a YouTube blogger. They boasted about how they just won two grand on a slot machine and how that hotel had the best chances at winning. People left and right were winning and cheering. I clicked on a few more videos and the results all seemed the same.

The last video I clicked on seemed to be an interview. A very nice dressed man sat in front of the camera. He had a million dollar smiled. His hair was neat and perfectly sculpted. He looked like a Ken doll, almost not real.

"You've recently made some major changes to the gaming experience here in Las Vegas. Why don't you tell us about it?" A woman asked from off screen.

The man let out a fake laugh and his smile grew. "What can I say? I hated the feeling of losing. I hate to lose, actually. So my partner and I bought our own casino. Now no one has to feel like they need to lose," he said.

"But how do you keep money? You are still running a business, aren't you?"

"If you must know, we know ways to keep all of the money still circling inside. If you want a good time, then why don't you come down and have a taste of the good life for yourself?" He offered. The host laughed and the man followed. "And one more thing, to a dear friend of mine who I'm sure will be watching, I'm all prepared for your arrival. Don't keep me waiting."

The video ended.

"That's Greed, alright," Luci spat.

"And that sounded like an invitation," Orion added.

"Or a warning," I concluded.

"Either way, we know where we need to go next," Luci insisted.

"Vegas here we come!" I called.

20
IT'S THE PERFECT SIZE

It took me three days to drive out to Vegas. Turns out more people recognized me than expected. I was either being asked for the secrets of the afterlife, to put my hands behind my back and come peacefully, or for an autograph. Some people thought that I really was a superhero and others thought that I was the sign of the apocalypse. Some even thought that I was the next coming of Christ. I tried my best to shut that one down real fast. But crazies are persistent.

Things weren't much better in my head, either. Luci and Orion demanded every detail of my dream with the fancy man. I told them everything but still kept demanding more. I did my best to answer their questions but I couldn't explain something that I could barely understand. Everything felt like a dream but I wouldn't have another way of knowing what I knew if it wasn't real.

"Luci, for the last time, I don't know anymore," I sighed.

"You have to. There's no way that some strange blind man came to you in a dream and told you why we became angels," she spat.

"To be fair, he only told me yours. He told me to ask Orion," I clarified.

"And he's keeping his pretty little mouth shut," Luci barked.

"It's not important to our mission," he replied.

"Then why does the kid get to know mine? Not fair," she growled.

"To be honest, I really didn't want to know yours, let alone, witness it first hand," I interjected.

Luci blew out a puff of air. "And I didn't want you seeing it, still doesn't mean metal head here gets the right to keep his shady past, shady."

"It's not shady. It's just not important," he insisted.

"If it's not important then why don't you share with the rest of the mind?" Luci asked.

"Well, I...Terrance," Orion stuttered.

"At this point, I realize she's not going to stop till you tell her," I admitted. I was curious too but I respected Orion's choice not to tell me. If it was anything like Luci's past, I really don't want to know.

Orion let out a long sigh and was silent for a few moments before he let out another puff of air. "Like I said, it's nothing too amazing, nor is it important to what we are doing but...I was gone. I let my family live without me. I didn't come back, but it wasn't because I died. I was just in a position where I couldn't return home. After a while, my wife assumed my death and was remarried. I don't blame her nor do I hold any grudge against her. My countrymen needed me."

There was a long silence with only the sounds of the busy diner. I took another bite of my sandwich.

"That's it?" I asked with a mouth full of food. I had gotten over the stares that I had gotten for talking to myself in public. To be honest so much has happened in the last few weeks that I didn't even care anymore. Plus, I was outside of Vegas, I was not the weirdest person here right now, even if I was talking to myself in the same clothes I had been wearing for two weeks.

God, I reeked.

"And that got you to be the Angel of Heaven?" Luci asked, there was disgust in her voice.

"I put my countrymen above myself, is there something more that needs to be done?" He asked.

"I gave up my place in Heaven to get revenge on the dirty, lying, bastard that sacrificed me to a demonic cult. And you just, what, gave up your free time?" Luci lashed out.

"I abandoned them," Orion added.

"You did nothing," she continued.

"Luci-" I began.

"No, he didn't do anything. He didn't suffer or learn some valuable lesson. This is bull!" She was obviously very worked up around all of this.

"Can I get you anything else?" the waitress asked as I flinched from the angry yelling in my head.

"Can I actually get another apple juice? Boxed please," I asked.

"Not a good time, kid!" Luci barked.

"What? I'm thirsty. Sue me," I replied.

The waitress rose her eyebrow at me but shrugged the comment off and went back behind the counter.

"Luci, why is this bothering you so much?" I questioned.

"Because," she blurted. "Because, I had to give up everything to be the Angel of Hell and he just gets it for that? It's not fair." Her tone was softer, she seemed more like a child than before. Luci was really bothered by this, but her voice wasn't angry, it was regretful.

"Do you regret it?" I asked.

"Of course I do. Tony, I'll spend the rest of eternity in Hell for my choice. I will never get to see Heaven. Why wouldn't I regret that?" Luci revealed.

I wasn't quite sure what to say. It seemed sudden and out of the blue. I really didn't think of these guys as the regretting type. Luci and Orion both seemed so confident in their choices, the idea that they were regretful never really passed my mind.

"I regret my decisions too," Orion chimed in.

"Really?"

Orion sighed and my head grew quiet again. "I gave up the only thing that really mattered to me in order to serve my country. A country, that doesn't even still exist. I gave up the love of my life, my two beautiful daughters, Maria and Mary. And I gave up my son, Peter. I didn't even know he died for a year after his passing."

A haunting chill went over me. I think I understood what the fancy man was saying now. While Luci suffered for her own position, Orion had others suffer for his. He was an Angel of

Heaven before anything, even a father. He served to the day he died and now in the afterlife, he had to serve again. He didn't even get the choice that Luci did. He'd have nothing to go to in Heaven, or rather no one.

They were both alone.

I swallowed the last bite of my sandwich and put out the last of my money on the table. I took the apple juice and left the diner. We were all quiet. I think we were all letting everything set in. This was a lot of information to take, not to mention that none of it really mattered. We didn't know who the fancy man was or what he wanted. We didn't know what Greed had planned for us, and we didn't know where exactly the Horn of Gabriel was. Overall, we were taking a shot in the dark. It was a Hell of a gamble but at least we were in the right place for the risk.

I took a sip of the new juice box.

"You really need to drink like an adult," Luci broke the silence.

"But juice boxes are the perfect size. It's just enough to fill my craving but not too much," I argued.

"You're an odd one," Orion added.

"You're one to talk, disembodied voice," I laughed. This situation was far too serious to just let brew. We needed the laugh. Lately, we've been at each other's throats. It couldn't be helped. So much has happened and now it was all coming to the end. One way or another this would be over. I just hoped that the Sins still believed Luci's lie about Halloween. But from what we've seen about them, I doubt that they did. The Sins were smart, well most of them. They were powerful too. Luci seemed to have a very hard time keeping control of them. Not that I judged her for it. I mean, she was just a girl and then she was given all of this responsibility. It had to be hard. It had to be hard for Orion too. He just has to follow orders. He's alone and orders are all he has, and Luci and I haven't been making it easy on him either.

This hadn't been easy for any of us. But this was the way it needed to be. Unfortunately, we were stuck in this mess but I still hope that we can do right. We had a chance to make this all better. It was what we owed the world. It was what I owed them for saving my life, even if they didn't mean to.

We drove down the Las Vegas strip and I took in the sights around me. The flashing lights and music were like something out of a fever dream.

Movies got it right. This place did look like an adult Disney World, if Disney World involved so many poor decisions.

We drove until we spotted the Excalibur hotel. It was a huge castle that towered high into the neon light-filled sky.

I pulled up to the hotel valet service and handed them the keys when they asked. It wasn't my car to begin with. I wasn't too protective over it.

Before I got out of the car I took the case that used to have the fake horn in it. I had put my shotgun in the case so that it was easier to take into diners and now the casino. It was an easier way to move around without being cornered and arrested.

"I can smell it. Greed is definitely here," Luci said.

"I'm more worried about the Horn. If I can get away without fighting this guy, that would be ideal," I admitted.

I walked into the casino. People were going crazy as they were winning left and right in the casino. People were stuffing the money everywhere they could. Every face had a huge smile on their face. The place was bustling with energy. I looked around and shortly saw the man from the news. He was standing on the second-floor balcony. He was holding a drink and a wide smirk on his face. I met his eyes.

The man smiled and waved to me before walking away. I ran up the stairs to follow him but I didn't see any sign of him.

"He's fast," I huffed.

"This is his playground, Terrance. He would be very dangerous to directly fight. We should try our best to just find the Horn and get out of here," Orion suggested.

"You're right. But there's something about this that feels uncomfortable. I don't know, I guess I feel conflicted now. I want to get some of the money that's floating around, I mean I really want it. But I also want to take a nap. I feel exhausted still. The feels are kind of canceling each other out," I revealed.

"Perhaps your body is still recovering?" Orion reasoned.

"Or Sloth is near," Luci pointed out.

"I can't handle two Sins. I can tell you that right now," I ensured.

"You wouldn't have to. Sloth isn't one to fight. He's a pushover. Greed is probably keeping Sloth here to keep people from wanting to leave. If they are too tired they will get a room here and eat at the restaurants here," Luci explained.

"Greed did say he had a way to keep money at the business. Maybe that's it," I stated.

"It's a thought. It would probably still be best to avoid them both if we can," Orion added.

"And what about all these people?" I questioned.

"At least they are happy. Gluttony and Lust were killing their captives. Greed will not want to lose a single person. For now, they are safe," Orion ensured.

A finger tapped my shoulder. I jumped and turned around quickly and readied the case to hit whatever was behind me. A twenty-something year old man stood behind me with a tired expression. He was pale as a ghost and looked like he only weighed a hundred and twenty pounds, despite his lengthy figure. He had long and tangled black hair. His eyes had dark circles under his eyes that nearly reached to his several day old stubble. He wore a large grey bathrobe with the hotel logo on it and a pair of baggy sweatpants with slippers under. All looked like it came from the hotel and had some sort of logo on it.

"Luci, your smell woke me up," he grumbled.

"Sloth?" I asked.

He slightly held out his hands before letting them fall back to his side. "One and only," he groaned.

I pulled out my shotgun form the horn case and pointed it at the Sin. He didn't move. He yawned and rubbed his eye.

"W-where is the Horn?" I barked.

"He probably doesn't know," Luci commented.

Sloth stuck a finger into his ear and dug a bit. He flung some ear wax onto the carpet before he wiped his finger on the robe. He smelled worse than me, and that was saying something.

"Greed has it. He was going to blow it but he wanted to have some fun first. I like the pool and I have a nice bed. It's so dark in that room, even during the day, it's perfect," Sloth muttered.

He was being surprisingly helpful.

"Should we believe him," Orion asked.

"I've never had trouble with Sloth. He never really questioned my commands. He just didn't really do anything. So I don't see a reason why we can't," Luci answered.

I lowered the gun some but I didn't drop it fully. I could still shoot him in the leg right now if I needed to.

"Why should I listen to you?" I asked.

He shrugged. "You don't have to. I'm not going to try to convince you that you should," he said.

"Fair enough. So where is the Horn being stored?" I asked.

"Greed's office. It's on the top floor of the casino," Sloth answered.

That was too easy. I didn't know if I trusted this guy. But Luci didn't seem to think that he was a threat. I was not a lazy person either. I was sure that if it came down to it, I could kill Sloth.

"Once we have the Horn, return to Hell. You don't belong up here yet," I ordered. I did my best to sound like I had the right to even order a Sin around. But overall, I think I was trying too hard.

Sloth yawned again and nodded. "Fine. I didn't even want to come up to begin with. But the other six don't give much of a choice when they want to do something. But I want something in return," Sloth began. He cleared his throat and rubbed his eyes again before sitting down, then laying down on the floor. He motioned for me to bend down too. I sighed and followed his motion. I laid next to the Sin and looked up at the high ceilings. He pointed to one of the hotel rooms that could be seen from our position. There were thick shades against the window. "If I go back, I want some of those," Sloth said.

Luci sighed. "If that's all it takes then you have yourself a deal," she said through my mouth with her voice.

I covered my mouth and coughed. "I hate it when you do that," I spat.

"Yeah well, I hate it too. You need to start brushing your teeth more," she retorted.

"I'd actually kill to. It's not like there's a ton of hygiene that I can have in a car," I replied.

"Are you done?" Sloth groaned.

I stood up from the ground and patted myself off. "Yeah, yeah. Just make sure you go back when we're all done," I warned. He seemed almost nice, too lazy for his own good, but nice. As long as he did what he said, I didn't see much of an issue letting him stay till we got the Horn.

I looked down at Sloth who was now asleep on the floor of the casino. I had no idea why he didn't just go to one of the hotel rooms but I didn't really have time to question it right now. I had to get the Horn and get out of here. Hopefully, I could do it without Greed interfering.

I followed Sloth's directions and did my best to avoid the slot machines or the card tables. I was being drawn towards them but I was able to bite my tongue enough to avoid them. I was rather disgusted by the people around me. All they did was fight, talk, and laugh over money. It was disappointing. All I could think about were the men who were trying to buy the farm from Dad and me. They were just as greedy as the men and women in here.

I went up the to the office. I stood outside the door and looked at the handle. More likely than not, Greed would be waiting for me on the other side. I wasn't too worried. I had managed to take down three Sins now, well, kind of four. I was growing much more confident in my skills. I felt that Luci and Orion trusted me more too. I think I also trusted them more because of everything. I was still mad at them for everything that happened but there was a sense of duty. I had to see this through to the end. I had to get the Horn and send it back to Hell before I took down the rest of the Sins.

Everything was going to be over soon. Then we three would go back to being alone. But the world could go on turning. I guess that was worth it in the end.

I took a deep breath and opened the door. No turning back now.

21

GREED

Greed smirked at me while he danced a chip across his fingers. "I guess I made it a bit too obvious with hiding in Vegas, huh?" He asked with a laugh. It was true, he kind of went to the most predictable place in America for greed. Which means he did not care about being found. I just needed to figure out why.

I pulled the shotgun out of its sheath and pointed it towards him. He did not even flinch. I couldn't take a shot yet as his influence was clouding my vision of where his kill spot was. I kept feeling a need to have more stuff. It took all my focus to not jump onto a nearby slot machine. It was easy money after all.

I shook my head, I had to stay focused. His smirk grew a bit more as he realized that I was getting influenced.

"You know Toby, if you just beat him until he can't move anymore then we can just take out time clearing your mind," Luci hinted.

I didn't even have time to reply to Luci's suggestion before Greed took a swing at me. I avoided the swing thanks to Orion's quick reflexes.

If that's how he wants it, then fine. Two can play at this game.

Greed dodged my attack and backed up. He looked me up and down before he began to become black and smoky. It looked he was made of semi-solid smoke with it rolling off of him and flowing on the ground. He gave me a salute with his hands, and before I could react, dashed further into the casino.

"Luci, looks it is time for a chase," I said slightly excited. I checked my back blast to make sure it was clear of any people, and then focused on summoning the wings. I felt the familiar burning rods rise out of my back. I ran forward a few steps and heard the wings' flames start flaring up. In a moment I was jetting forward at incredible speeds. I caught up with Greed as he flew through the front doors of the casino in his shadowy form. The glass exploded out as he passed through but his speed did not waver. He had to be the fastest sin I have seen yet.

I followed a few seconds behind and followed his path. I saw people outside visibly confused at what just happened. I turned my attention back to Greed as I saw him fly low to the strip heading further into it. The heat of my wings were intense and I felt like I had a jetpack strapped on but I was managing to keep control. I followed behind him dodging the traffic on the strip. He dodged around cars expertly giving no thought to how closely he was cutting some dodges. I was struggling to control myself as cleanly and had to rise up slightly to avoid being a large bug smeared on someone's windshield.

Every misstep with this chase put more distance between him and I. Plus by weaving through traffic there was no way for me to take a shot with my shotgun. We continued up the strip until he veered right towards the replica of the Eiffel Tower. His shadowy figure flew around the tower heading straight for the top. Luckily, his shadow was easy to pick out in the hot noon sun of the desert. I heard some screams from people as I passed over their heads. Hopefully they realize I am here to help them.

I saw his shadow land on the tip of the tower and peer down at me. I stopped for a moment about halfway up the tower. I felt great. This adrenaline high was one of the best feelings ever. I had to be careful though I know it is because Luci's influence is strong after demanding so much speed.

"I can do this all day Angel Boy," Greed yelled down to me. "This is my home turf outside of Hell." He was right about that. Las Vegas was basically as close as you could get to being under Greed's control without him being around.

That wasn't going to deter me though. Greed may be fast, but I am pretty sure Luci is the faster.

"Luci, let's give it all you got." I whispered to her. Greed looks like he was getting bored so I had to take this moment fast.

"Alright Terrance but this will use a lot of energy on both our parts. Plus I'll need your eyes for steering," She said.

"Let's do it," I replied confident even though I wasn't sure if this would work. I focused on myself and looked at myself from third person. I saw Luci's outline over me and Orion in the background. Even he knew that at this moment we needed all of the speed we could get. I saw Luci cover my body as she took over.

Suddenly, I was yanked back into my body as everything was a tint of red. I knew Luci was in control now. I felt the wings flare even harder and noticed that my chest had even changed over to Luci. My chest was now covered in cracks that flowed with lava and my skin had the texture of charred wood. As she leaned back to take off I felt steam vent off from the sides of my ribs. She must need my chest to help keep me from overheating. I did not like having my chest covered as it felt like I was being constricted.

Greed raised an eyebrow at us but still stayed at the tip of the tower. I guess he assumed that we would never be able to catch up with us. Though I felt a deep feeling that he was about to be very wrong. The wings flared to life as I heard and felt a torrent of flame explode out of them. The exhaust felt hot on my arms as Luci lifted my arms.

I shot at Greed at incredible speeds. I could feel the wind slam into me as I went from zero to sixty in what felt like a second. I quickly approached Greed as he scrambled to jump off and fly away. Before he could get off I slammed into at full speed. The shock of the impact hurt but it hurt Greed a lot more. I heard him cough as I hit him straight in the gut. We flew up in the sky as I held tightly onto Greed. He scratched on my arms cutting in deep. I yelled out in pain and loosened my grip slightly.

He used this to his advantage and pushed off of me breaking my hold. He glanced at me before taking off towards the Luxor Hotel. Looks like he stopped messing around as he sped off incredibly fast. I wasn't worried though Luci showed me that we were more than fast enough for him. I felt heat rising up my throat. I burped and some black smoke came out. *I really hoped that was normal.*

"Just a little extra exhaust there don't worry," I heard Luci say while panting. I took a moment to glance over myself before we took back off after Greed. Luci's ribs were opened up and looked almost like gills but smoke billowed out of them. *I will admit it was a bit odd to look down and see myself with a feminine torso.*

"One moment. I can only really use this for short bursts as it tires me out really quickly. Plus it is really hard to turn," Luci explained. I was forced to take a deep breath before I felt the wings flare up again. I jetted off towards the Luxor seeing Greed in the distance. My face skin blew back and I looked like when astronauts do their G-resistance training. We cleared the distance quickly before seeing Greed blast through the top of the Luxor. The glass rolled down the side of the hotel.

I skidded to a stop near the top of the pyramid where he busted through. I felt the burning in my chest die down as Luci's chest returned to mine.

"Now is time for some finesse," She said. I still had the red haze over my eyes as we flew through the broken hole. As we came through I noticed that people were still milling about gambling and buying things even though part of the roof had broken. It seems that Greed's influence covered a lot of the Las Vegas Strip. I also oddly enough saw Sloth just milling about with the crowd. He was still wearing his robe and seemed to be just flicking a few switches here and there before sitting back down and looking at me.

My head snapped to the side as I saw Greed dash into part of the pyramid towards where the hotel rooms were. I was about to jet in there before Orion piped up, "Stop. He is wanting us to follow him. He wants to create an opening where he can get through and continue the chase. He just wants to tire us out."

"Okay, what do you suggest fly boy?" Luci asked. She was sounding a bit rough, and I felt exhausted. It was like I had run four marathons. Orion was right we could not continue like this.

"He is going to rush around the maze of hallways back there hoping to waste time before coming back out into this area to finish us off. So, we will just make sure we predict where he is coming out. Luci, I need control for this," Orion listed off.

"He's all yours," She said sounding slightly relieved. I felt a bit of invigoration from Orion. My eyes glazed over yellow and suddenly Luci's tired wings billowed out into two pairs of pure white feathery wings. It was odd as it felt like I had refreshed limbs. I still felt exhausted and this was taking a huge toll on me. I coughed slightly and saw some blood in my hands.

"Orion I don't think I have any more switches on me," I said haggardly.

"I agree Terrance, but do not worry this should help end it," He replied with confidence. I can see why he was such a great general as I had full confidence that this plan would work out.

"Go for the hallway opening to the right there," He said thoughtfully. I realized I had control of my wings and flew over to where he directed. The hallway was empty but Orion did not seem surprised by this."

I heard what sounded like quiet counting in my head. "Alright, and now." I heard him firmly say. I felt the wings flow back on their own before flapping strongly towards the hallway. Just as the flap finished I saw Greed blast around the corner. Orion had actually predicted right where he would come out. I shot backwards from the strength of the flap. The wind slammed into Greed and sent him sprawling back down the hall into the wall.

He hit the wall with a satisfying thud before landing on all fours on the ground. He looked up at me confused before jetting back off to the side hallway again. I felt Orion's wings take me over to a hallway on the opposite side of the hotel. Once again I heard the light counting before Orion's pulled back and launched another strong gust down the hallway. There were some trays left out by the people staying in the different rooms that were immediately pulled up by the wind following the gust. Greed once again rounded a corner straight into the gust.

He got slammed into the wall and looked at me with utter hatred in his eyes. The wind dissipated and he slid down to his feet on the ground. I immediately aimed and took a shot. The pellets hit him in his chest pushing him against the wall again.

"Enough of this," He spat out as some black blood leaked out of his mouth. He turned and quickly flew down the hall. I heard a few screams and the shatter of wall and glass. He straight up busted through a wall in frustration.

"Oh crap, where do you think he went?" I asked slightly worried that he would just flee town.

"He is going back to the castle as that is where he has most fortified," Orion said matter-of-factly.

"Alrighty then, I will take your word for it," I replied impressed by Orion. I took over fully as the yellow tint cleared from my vision and I flew down towards the front door. I also noticed that Sloth was no longer hanging around. I wondered where he went off to.

I flew into the street and over next door into Excalibur. I busted through the doors into the hustle and bustle of the casino. Sloth was next to me and made me jump. I saw him flip a switch and then look at me unimpressed. He just grunted and wandered off into the crowd. I raised an eyebrow but put my attention back into finding Greed. A little flying around and I found him in the main room of the casino near all the slot machines. He was leaning against it trying to look cool but I saw that he was breathing pretty hard. The shadowy smoke flowed off of him and around the feet of the people around him. The people within this smoke were frantically pulling the levers of the machines.

I even felt compelled to sit down and start gambling but shook my head to get over the feeling. I flew towards Greed and he dashed through an aisle of slot machines. I could not get in there with my wings so I quickly focused on them and made them dissipate away. I landed on the ground running with shotgun in hand an dashed into the same hallway. Greed was definitely not moving as fast as he once was. He looked back at me and slapped the side of the last slot machine as he left the aisle. Suddenly chimes went off all around. I glanced over as everyone started shouting in excitement.

He had caused every slot machine near me to get a jackpot. People began pushing around grabbing all the coins they could. I reached down to grab some coins as well.

I was a hero after all, I deserved a salary.

No. I pulled my arm back and continued towards Greed.

I finally dragged myself through the crowd and looked around for my target. Sloth was nearby again adjusting something on a table. He looked at me and nonchalantly pointed his finger towards the direction of a hallway leading to what looked like the card tables. Was he really leading me towards Greed?

I shrugged and ran down the hall in the direction he pointed in.

"Go get him champ," I heard Sloth mumble as I passed by. *He was a very strange Sin.*

I cleared the hallway and immediately took a punch from my right. I scrambled on my the ground before getting my footing and jumping up ready to fight. My shotgun had slid out of my hands and was now lying on the ground near one of the card tables. Greed and I both glanced at each other and made a dash for the gun. I jumped and was able to grab it before he did. I spun around to see him about to land on top of me with fists at the ready to pummel my face.

I wasted no time and took a shot at him. The shot once again slammed into his chest and caused him to fall back and not land on me. He let out a horrid screech but got up drooling a good amount of black blood. He wiped it from his chin and stared at me with hate.

I cracked open the shotgun and let the two shells fly out. I attempted to grab some more while Greed stared but he reacted to quickly. He dashed forward at inhuman speeds and tackled me sending me flying with him. The shotgun flew out of my hands again and clattered on the ground unloaded.

"Orion, need protection," I called out. I felt a burning on my back as I felt hot metal cover my back. As the burning subside, Greed and I slammed through the wall. Nothing broke but I felt the wind get knocked out of me.

We both fell over each other on the ground with a huff. It seems both of us were running on fumes. My body felt like Jell-O but I had to keep fighting. I yelled out wanting to make sure no one ever got hurt by this horrible Sin ever again.

I rolled over on top of Greed and slammed down into his face with my fist. He let out a groan as I hit him. I yelled out again and felt my fist burn away into claws. I slashed down towards but he reached up and grabbed my arm. He used his free hand to push me off of him. I fell back onto my back a little away from his feet.

Greed slowly got up and then jumped up into the air before falling towards me with his elbow out ready to strike. With my non-Luci hand I raised it up and felt it covered with armor. My body felt crowded as our souls tried to gain control of certain parts. I felt like I was being ripped in half.

His elbow hit the hand but the hand remained firm in the attack. I then took my claw and stabbed it into his side using his momentum to launch him over me. He crashed into a table ruining some card players' game. They looked upset and then confused as they saw the creature and me. They then quickly got up from their chairs and ran down the hall.

He groaned but got up again slowly. My arms returned to normal as I reached my limit. I pushed off the ground almost falling back over. I stayed standing though and raised my fists. I knew though that I could not fight this anymore, but I could still bluff.

He raised up as well but did not immediately attacked. We stood there panting at each other.

He smirked and said, "You-" Before he could finish his sentence a blade appeared cleaved into the top of his head. His eyes rolled back into his head and he fell to his knees.

Sloth stood behind him with the blade in his hands looking tired as always. He calmly raised his foot and kicked Greed off of the blade. Greed fell with a thump unmoving.

Sloth looked at the blade and yawned. Looking back at me he said, "Now it is your turn."

22

SLOTH

Sloth's blade pointed up to me as I panted. This was great, I was already ragged from Greed and now I had to immediately deal with another Sin. I did not think I had enough power to even put up a fight at the moment. Sloth did not approach yet though. He just stared at me with tired eyes as his blade dripped with the black goo of Greed.

"Why did you kill him?" I asked. I was genuinely curious, but also if I kept him talking maybe I could get enough energy to get away.

"Oh I planned this from the beginning. He was very annoying, but useful to help me keep the horn." He answered. "Though like the competition says there can only be one new horseman. So, by letting him do the hard work of fighting I could reap the rewards," He gestured at me. I glanced behind him and saw my shotgun laying by the hole in the wall Greed and I created. If I could dodge well enough when Sloth attacked I could possibly make it back to my shotgun and buy more time. This whole fight would be me just buying time to escape.

"Terrance this fight will be nigh impossible. I think you might have enough for just a couple more transformations," Orion warned in my head. That was great info to have but I did not want to respond as I wanted Sloth to be guessing on how well I was doing.

"Come on then let's end this," I ordered, hoping to prod Sloth into attacking. He looked at me once over, shrugged, and then turned around walking away from me towards the hole. I was absolutely confused why he did not attack. As he got close to the hole he nonchalantly flipped a switch.

"Alright hero, we will finish this," he replied with a smirk. I was visibly confused until I heard a latch open on the ceiling to my right. Two panels slid to the side as a giant hammer came swinging down towards a poker table filled with people. The people were not gambling anymore but instead sat slumped in their chairs almost looking asleep.

I immediately took off towards the table. This was going to take a lot but I had to save those people. "Orion!" I shouted. His wings shot out of my back and launched me towards the table. I landed and raised my hands towards the hammer. I hoped it was not too heavy. My arms screamed but I flexed every muscle in them and forced Orion's armor to cover my whole arms. I felt the armor cover over my shoes as well to support my legs.

The giant hammer slammed into my arms. I yelled as it felt like a truck just slammed into my hand hands. My arms got pushed back some and I skidded slightly but I held my ground. My arms were falling asleep and I could see the armor on my arms receding a bit.

"Let's take out the rod holding it," Orion called. It was a good idea. I took a deep breath and flapped the wings launching into the air. I pulled back my arm and slammed my fist into the side of the metal pole holding the hammer. The metal bent as Orion's gauntlet collided with it. I then grabbed and pushed with the bend. With all the weight of the hammer this caused the metal to easily fold in on itself. The hammer creaked before snapping and falling on its side and stopping just in front of the people. Their eyes looked terrified but still they did not move.

I landed on the ground and the armor on my arms and legs dissipated. The TV static feeling immediately returned and I noticed bruising along my arms. Dark blue and purple splotches covered parts of my arms. I was truly pushing my body to its limit. I did not have time to worry about it too much as Sloth had the horn and was getting away. I focused on my back returning the wings inside me. I needed to conserve as much energy as I could.

I jogged back towards the hole in the wall. I stepped carefully through and saw my shotgun still sitting a couple feet away from the entrance of the hole. A sigh of relief escaped my lips. It would give me a bit of confidence to have something ranged against this wild card, Sloth.

I reached down and grabbed the shotgun. I lifted it up and noticed a string attached to it. I stared at it curiously for a moment.

Suddenly Luci shouted, "Behind you!" I whipped around to see another hammer swinging down towards me. I immediately dropped to the ground narrowly escaping getting slammed by the hammer. I felt the hammer graze my nose as it passed overhead. I rolled over before it could make another pass, shotgun still in hand. I stood up slowly and wiped the sweat off my forehead.

"How'd he get the whole place booby trapped like this?" I asked.

"Remember him hitting those switches, he probably was wiring everything," Orion answered.

"I will be honest. I knew Sloth was smart but did not realize he could get so much done," Luci said sounding slightly impressed. I saw Sloth watching from the end of the room. He waved at me with a smirk on his face before heading further down the hall. He made me mad but I was hesitant to charge after him. Who knew what was waiting for me?

"Terrance we need to head both carefully but quickly. The quicker we catch up with Sloth the less traps we can expect," Orion explained. Orion was right if I went too slowly then Sloth could just hit me with trap after trap. If I went too quickly I could have my head taken off by a hammer or whatever else he had in store for me. So, I just needed to be quick but vigilant.

"Alright guys, we got this," I said trying to instill some confidence into myself. I could barely feel my arms, my back had splitting pain, and my feet felt like cinder blocks.

I took off jogging down the hall watching my feet for anymore wires. About halfway through the hallway everything was going good so far. It was possible that Sloth did not have too many traps set up and expected the first couple to finish me off. My foot then stepped on a tile that clicked.

I heard panels shifting to the left and right of me. I saw small holes open up along the room leading to the hallway.

"Luci I need speed," I said very quickly. I focused hard on my back and felt the flaming wings bloom out of my back. I almost blacked out from the exhaustion of this though. I immediately took off as fast as possible to the hallway Sloth headed down. I heard bangs behind me as I realized what looked like holes were actually barrels. I put everything I had into the wings to get me out of there. I got just to the end of the room when the last set of barrels by the door went off out of order. My eyes went wide as the world seemed to go in slow motion.

I could see the bullet heading towards me as I was racing by slowly out of the line of fire. I took a deep breath and made it to the hallway crashing and rolling along the ground sweating profusely. The wings were completely gone and I did not think I had another one in me. In spite of myself I laughed, I had made it.

"Wow, nice job Luci. We actually made it," I complimented Luci as I stood up. When I put weight on my left leg though I immediately let out a yelp of pain and fell to my left knee. I looked at my calf and saw blood streaming out of a bullet hole.

"Well, we didn't quite make it," Luci replied with worry in her voice. I could see the faint glow as Orion was attempting to mend the wound. The bleeding slowed but the hole was not going to close anytime soon. I could feel that it tore into the muscle. I was exhausted but I had to keep going. The longer I sat here the more time Sloth had time to get ready with traps.

I finally took the time and loaded two shells into the shotgun. I had four left as a few got knocked out with Greed. I closed the breach and put the end of the barrel on the ground. I had tears in my eyes and bit my lip as I used the shotgun to push myself off the ground so I did not have to put too much weight on my left leg. The shotgun sadly was a little short for a crutch but it worked okay. I leaned on it and hobbled down the hall. I came out into the main hall which was oddly empty. Sloth stood at the top of these large ornate stairs staring down at me. He had a woman in his left arm and a gun against her head with his free hand. I felt rage burn in me.

"Let her go Sloth this is between you and me" I said up to him with rage in my voice. I began to hobble to him quickly almost losing my balance. He pressed the gun harder against her head and I stopped. It was clear he wanted me to wait.

"Just one moment, boy," Sloth sneered, "I want you to stand there a moment so something can get set up for you." The lady he was holding was crying but she did not resist much. His influence was keeping her too tired to push against his arm. I grimaced but stayed still. I could not risk him pulling the trigger.

I raised up my hands in compliance. He smiled as he knew he had me. I could not risk her life to charge in there and I could not risk a shotgun shot.

"Terrance we have to do something," Orion mentioned in my head.

"If we do something she is dead," I whispered.

"I know you want to save as many people as possible but sometimes you have to sacrifice someone for the greater good," Orion pleaded.

"Not if I can help it," I stubbornly replied. I stood there patiently listening to the lady gently sob. Sloth was loving this and just stared at me smiling. The quiet was maddening as we just stared at each other. It seemed like Sloth caused everything to just slow down. The games were not making their usual ringing and there were not crowds of people loudly talking. Just Sloth, the lady, and I.

Sloth tilted his head for a moment and then nodded. "That should be long enough," He said thoughtfully.

"Alright then, so can you gently put her down please?" I asked. I was hopeful that he was just using her as a pawn and would have no reason to kill her.

He looked over at the lady absentmindedly, like he almost forgot she was there. "Sure," he answered. With that he pushed her down to his right and without hesitation shot her.

"No!" I screamed. I felt white hot rage in my gut. I exploded with fury towards him as Luci's wings carried me at a new incredible speed. Just as I was about to hit him I saw, myself. I was almost complete transformed into Luci. My body and face turned into her Hellish angel form.

I then slammed through glass rolling along the ground. I quickly got to my feet and saw Sloth opposite to me. I launched myself again at him. Just as I approached him once again I saw myself and slammed through glass. He was using a bunch of mirrors to hide his location. I coughed as flame and smoke spilled out of my mouth.

"Terrance," Luci called out, "you can't keep going this hard. Your body is about to exhaust itself." She sounded exhausted as well. I couldn't stop though. I wanted Sloth dead.

I saw him one last time down a little ways away from me to my right. I put everything into flying towards him. I screamed out as the pain was enormous. I flew and once again broke through nothing but glass. Luci's form melted off of me and I laid there for a moment coughing. The smoke from my mouth was replaced with blood.

I stood shakily to my feet and wiped the blood from my mouth. Sloth slowly walked up to me sword at the ready. I raised up my arms in defense. He slashed down at me with the blade with a grunt. I barely got my arm in the right place as the blade connected with it. It got deflected off as a small piece of Orion's armor appeared.

Sloth kept slicing and I kept blocking. The armor getting smaller and smaller with each slice.

"Terrance, we have to do something," Orion called out with worry. There was one last thing I could do. Sloth came down with one last slice, I barely blocked it with a small speck of armor. Part of the blade slid past and caught a piece of my arm.

As the blade passed on its downward swing I raised my free arm and put all my focus on it. Orion's holy light formed in the palm of my hand and hit Sloth in the face. He put his hands up in defense as the holy light burned and blinded him. He started backing up and I followed him limping. I was actually doing this. I focused on his form and saw the weak point in his shoulder for a split second. I took one last step forward as the light faded and raised my shotgun.

As I put my weight on the ground though I heard another click. A pole shot from the ground hitting my hand as I shot. I missed the mark completely and fired into the air. Sloth lowered his hand grabbing quickly onto my shotgun with his left hand.

His right hand then raised with his sword and thrusted forward. I sucked in a breath as I looked down and saw the blade pierce my chest. In reflex I fired off the second shell into the air.

"Terrance no!" My two angels yelled in unison. I gasped for breath finding it hard to breath. My head got really light as I stared at Sloth smilingly widely at me. I actually lost. I looked over to where the woman would be to see if she was really dead. I saw her lying on the ground unmoving but suddenly shadow seemed to melt off of her. Once all the shadow was gone it was revealed that it was a mannequin the whole time. I did all of this for nothing.

I looked up one last time at Sloth, and spat on his face. Then everything faded to white.

My eyes opened and I saw myself from third person. I was slumped over the blade as Sloth reached up to wipe my blood off his face. Suddenly he stopped, frozen. Everything seemed to stop in the world, and I heard a distant ticking. I looked around and noticed I was floating in the casino. I could see myself but it was like I was slightly see through. I marveled at my hands for a moment I couldn't believe that I had died. I felt tears well into my eyes as I realized the world was now doomed. I had just died and now there was nothing that was stopping the Sins from summoning the Four Horsemen.

The light ticking began to grow louder and louder. I was so confused, I looked around for the source of the ticking. Out of thin air I saw a door appear, and the ticking stopped. With a creak the door slid open, and suited man walked out. It took a moment before I realized it was the fancy man from my interview. He glanced up at after closing the door with a warm smile.

"What's going on?" I asked feeling like I was a kid again. I was so scared of what was happening and just needed to hear someone else's voice.

"You died Terrance, I'm sorry," he replied. His voice was warm and had a comforting feel to it.

"Why are you here?" I asked.

"Well, I came to announce that you got the job," he replied cheerily. I gave him a very confused face. How did that have to do with my current death?

"I see that you are confused. Check your pocket." He said gesturing to my pants pocket while walking up to me. I stuck my hand in my pocket and felt a card. I pulled it out and saw one of the black tarot cards he had me draw. I turned it over to see its face.

"Judgement," I read aloud, "What does that mean?"

"It means rebirth Terrance. I will take it from here," He replied putting a hand on my shoulder, "Also, my name is Pitch." He looked down at Sloth and my body. His normally warm expression turned hard. His hand left my shoulder and he started towards Sloth and my body. His eyes in that moment were not clouded over. As he walked by me his form began to change.

Pitch's suit flowed out into a cloak that surrounded his body. On this cloak were clocks everywhere all ticking at different speeds and different times. His hands transformed from the dark brown color to bleached bone.

His face also began to decay but did not turn to bone completely. He looked more mummified. From his nose up passed his head it was all bone, but his mouth still had some skin. There were holes in his cheeks revealing his teeth beneath. His lips were also gone giving him a skeletal smile. Where the eye sockets should have been there was nothing but bone. Beneath the bone there was a slight glow of green. It finally hit me who this was. This was the Reaper, the Angel of Death. Two wings of bone furled out from him and wrapped over his shoulders.

Pitch's form passed over to my body. I saw his hand touch my corpse as it still hung on the blade. Suddenly his form seemed to get swirled into my body, and I saw my finger twitch. Suddenly, time seemed to start again as Sloth wiped the blood from his face, and my shotgun dropped to the ground. I was still up here though. I spirited my way over to look at myself from over the shoulder of Sloth's perspective.

Suddenly, my body's hand grabbed onto the blade of Sloth's sword. Sloth looked at me with confusion. He knew that by all accounts I should be dead. He was right I was dead but I think he had bigger problems. I saw my head snap up and stare at Sloth with a huge grin on my body's face. Blood still dripped from my mouth but now I certainly looked alive.

My body pulled itself further onto the blade closer to Sloth. My body's eyes turned green and the skin began to flake off from my face. Sloth went from interest to fear in a millisecond. He dropped the sword like it was red hot and jumped back. He looked at the corpse on the blade with horror.

"You summoned him? Are you crazy?" He shouted to what I assumed was me. My form shifted and became more and more skeletal. It seemed Pitch was using me as a vessel but without my soul in the way. Pitch grabbed the blade and pulled it out. It slid out with little trouble and glistened with blood. He dropped the blade on the ground and stared at Sloth with intensity.

Sloth immediately took off running down and jumped off the balcony to the lower floor. He didn't miss a beat and kept sprinting back into the card room. Pitch seemed unfazed and just stared at him as he fled.

Then Pitch leaned over and picked up my shotgun with his skeletal hands. My body was now mostly skeletal. Beneath the hole in my shirt I could see my ribs. My face now was the same as Pitch's, with the smoothed over bone eyes. It was terrifying to see myself this way. Pitch rustled in my shotgun pouch and pulled out a shell. It turned pitch black in his hands. He cracked open the shotgun and loaded only that one shell into the gun.

He then walked, not ran, to where Sloth went. He jumped down railing and went into the room where Sloth ran. I floated along following Pitch. As we entered the room there was people everywhere. It seemed they were trapped in here while Sloth and I were fighting in the main room. I saw Sloth near the back of the room struggling with a locked door.

The people all looked at Pitch and turned as white as his bones. They all looked like they knew exactly who this was and what it meant. Maybe it is ingrained into every human who Death is. Pitch waved his hand for them to get to the side and they obliged. Sloth noticed the movement behind him and turned around quickly.

Sloth pulled the gun out of his belt and shot Pitch/my corpse twice. The bullets seemed to pass harmlessly through.

"My turn," Pitch replied in a raspy voice as he raised up the shotgun. Without hesitation he pulled the trigger. Instead of pellets chains shot out of the barrel, more than what could have possibly fit in there. They furled out seeking their target while avoiding all the other people in the room. Sloth jumped out of the way of one of them and tried to use his demon form to fly out of the room. Before he could get to a wall though one of the hundred chains grabbed onto his leg and pulled him to the ground. The others then followed suit wrapping his legs up.

Sloth screamed and attempted to pry the chains off but they were holding tight. Pitch then placed the shotgun on the ground and approached at walking pace. As he got closer my body's clothes turned into his cloak. The long sleeves covering his arms. From these sleeves two nasty looking weapons fell into his boney hands.

They were scythes pure silver in color with white spines. Chains lead from the scythes and up into the sleeves. He spun the scythe blades on their chains absent-mindedly. Once he got to Sloth, he stopped still spinning the scythes. Sloth looked up with defeat in his face. He knew there was nothing he could do.

"Sloth, I find you guilty on multiple counts of interrupting people's natural times," Pitch announced, "With that it seems your time is up." Pitch spun his scythes quicker preparing to I presume strike Sloth. Suddenly, ticking began in the hole room. Everyone was looking around as it seemed to come from everywhere. The ticking slowed before an old time ringing alarm went off.

Pitch took that as his cue and let both scythes slam down onto Sloth's shoulder. Sloth let out a gasp as all the color from his face drained. His eyes rolled back into his head and Pitch removed the scythes in one swift movement. With a flick of his wrists all the chains in the room shot back up into the sleeves of his cloak. I saw him pull out a pocket watch from the front of his black cloak and look at it with mild surprise.

"Looks like I am running a little late," he mumbled. He looked up directly at me and said, "Time for you to take back over. I hope you realize this is the one time this will ever happen. Though I am glad you got the job." He smiled at me with that skeletal grin. Suddenly I felt myself being vacuumed towards my body. I was forcefully pulled down until my foot touched my body.

The world spun as it felt like I was being flushed and then everything faded to black.

23

TWO IS COMPANY, THREE IS A CROWD

The world around me was dark. My breath was low and nearly nonexistent. I was cold but I didn't shiver. I just laid still against the flat surface. In an instant, all of my senses came rushing back to me. I gasped and opened my eyes to see the same blackness as before. I coughed and tried to kick and swing my arms but they were constricted. I groaned and whined as I tried to get out of, what sounded like a plastic bag.

I yelled and soon I heard yelling around me. People. There were people here! I twisted and tried my best to get out of the black bag but I didn't get any more grasp on my situation.
The conversation outside of my prison was growing louder. I heard the sound of a slow zipper and suddenly I could see light. I took my opportunity and stuffed my fingers through the hole. I pulled open the bag and gasped as the fresh air entered my lungs. I didn't realize how stuffy it was in there.

I looked around at the scared officers who were standing in the same room where Sloth and I had fought. There were several black body bags around the room and plenty of white outlines, yellow markers, and plenty of blood. It looked like something had been splattered across the room. It was on every wall and everything in here. In the center was a mummified person. It looked like something from a museum; like something that would be thousands of years old. It was completely out of place here.

I looked down at my shirt and saw the cut and blood stain. This wasn't a dream. It was obvious. I pulled off the shirt and threw it to the side. There was nothing there, not even a scar.

I touched my skin and sighed. I looked up and saw the fear in the eyes of everyone still alive.

"Howdy," I said. This was crazy. This was absolutely crazy. I knew that it was absolutely crazy. But for some reason, I laughed. I couldn't help myself. This was funny. I just cheated death! I really did this!

I stood up and looked down at the body bag that I was in. I kicked it off my feet and took a step forward. One of the officers pointed his gun at me. I rose my hands.

"Easy," I said.

"What are you?" A cop yelled at me.

I stopped for a moment and looked around the room again. I couldn't believe this actually happened. I felt like I was on top of the world right then, nothing could take me down.

"I'm a superhero," I said, confidently.

I took a few more steps around the room as I got my bearings. I felt like I just woke up from a long nap. I was very refreshed and honestly felt really good. I didn't have any pain. I hadn't felt this good in a long time. I cracked my back and jumped. I felt really damn good right now!

The cops still didn't seem sure of me. I didn't blame them. They apparently just thought I was dead, so did I for a while. I still couldn't even say exactly what happened. I put my hands in my pocket and felt something. I pulled out a folded up card. I unfolded it to see the tarot card that I had been given by the fancy man, or rather by Pitch.

I felt a pain in my head. I winced and grabbed my skull as the pain intensified. It was like a migraine on steroids. I closed my left eye and put my hands up to my temples. I felt some tears escape from the corner of my eyes. I honestly felt like I was going to pop like a pimple.

The cop who had his gun pointed at me was shaking. I heard the sound of the gun go off, but I didn't feel any pain. I opened my eye and saw a large white wing in between me and the officer. I looked up with as much surprise as the officer. The pain was going away.

"I am your shield," Orion's voice boomed in my head.

"You gave us quite the scare, cowboy," Luci added.

"Guys." I smiled. "You're still here."

"We can't leave till your cold and dead, and apparently until there's no chance of you coming back either," Luci laughed.

"Speaking of, do you care to explain?" Orion asked.

"Will do, but let's get out of here," I answered.

"But first the Horn," Luci corrected.

Orion's four wings bellowed out and flapped several strong gusts of wind, knocking over the officers. He lifted me off the ground and we flew out of the casino and back towards Greed's office. I landed in the office and looked around. The office was trashed from our previous fight. There was money, poker chips, paper, and furniture scattered across the room.

"Got any idea where it is Luci?" I asked.

"No, the reek of those two is still too strong. I couldn't tell that our previous horn was a fake because of Envy and Lust. Honestly, I don't trust my sense of smell too much right now," Luci admitted.

"Really? I think you smell fine," a new voice called.

The three of us jumped from the voice. It was clearly coming from inside of my head. It was rough but had a warming feel and a heavy African accent.

"Who's there?" I asked.

"Hi," the voice called again.

I rose an eyebrow. "Guys?"

"Yes?" All three voices said.

"No, Luci and Orion," I clarified.

"Oh, so just me then?" The voice asked.

"No. Just Luci and Orion," I repeated.

"You heard him. You two stay quiet," the voice said again.

"No! I said-...fancy man?"

"I already told you my name. It's-" he made the same gasping sound as before. "But you can call me Pitch, if that's easy to say."

"Pitch?!" Luci and Orion cried out.

"You know this guy?" I asked.

Orion let out a long sigh and seemed just done with everything. "That explains so much."

"Really? How?" Pitch asked.

"Pitch is the Angel of Death. As you can probably guess, he's not one for following protocol or anything for that matter," Orion filled in.

"He's a nut," Luci clarified.

"I figured that much out. But why is the Angel of Death now in my head?" I questioned.

"I'd like to know why too," Orion said.

We waited for Pitch to answer but he didn't make a sound.

"Pitch?" I asked.

"What? Sorry, I was doing something. Terrance you really have a juice problem," Pitch said.

"They are the perfect size! Wait, why even bring that up? How do you even know about that?" I asked. This man was the living embodiment of nonsense.

"Because your life flashed before your eyes. It was quite funny," Pitch exclaimed.

"It's not funny," I spat.

"Terrance! This is very important. A matter of life and death. Go to the computer on the desk," Pitch ordered. His tone was suddenly serious.

I didn't waste time. I went to the desk and looked at the computer, the screen was cracked but I could see my reflection in the black. My face moved on its own. My eye half closed and my tongue stuck out. A "Blah," sound came from my lips. I shook my head as I regained control.

"That's what you looked like," Pitch ensured.

"I did not go blah," I argued.

"Yes, you did. I was there," he assured.

I rolled my eyes and sat down in Greed's chair. A click sounded from the chair and it turned me around. I watched as the Tv screen on the wall rose up and behind it was a safe. I rose an eyebrow and got up. I walked over to the safe and tried to pull it open. I felt my hand burn as one of my fingers turned to Luci's.

"Try melting it," she offered.

I nodded and used her heat to melt the lock of the safe. I opened the safe and inside was an instrument case. I reached in and took it from the hidden room. I looked over the case, it was solid black with two locks on the side of it. I rose an eyebrow and ran my hand against the casing. It was velvet.

"Is this it?" I asked.

"It is," Pitch assured.

The Horn of Gabriel was now in my hands. The end of the world could be stopped, at least for now. Five of the

Seven Deadly Sins were gone and I held the end of the world in my hands. This was all over. It really was over.

"It's really over," I said. There was total disbelief in my voice. I felt my body relax in an instant. "It's really over! We won!" I cheered.

"We did it!" Luci exclaimed.

"Your hard work and dedication made this possible. You should be proud of yourself Terrance," Orion said.

Pitch clicked his tongue and sighed. "Don't you wish this was the end?" he asked.

"What are you talking about? We have the Horn," I said.

"Is the Horn back where it belongs? Are the Sins back where they belong?" Pitched asked with a serious tone. "Your work is not done until the time where you can proudly say that no one on Earth can get their hands on the Horn of Gabriel. Until that time, you are not done."

I bowed my head. I felt like a child who had just been scolded by a parent.

"But we just have to do Luci's ritual, right? Then we will be done?" I asked.

There was no reply. I waited for several minutes but there still was only silence.

"I think he's gone," Luci chimed in.

"Great," I sighed. "Well, let's get this over with. What do I need for the ritual?"

"Nothing we can't get easily. But, we could use a bit of help with the Latin. I'm assuming you don't know any? Well, it has to be a mortal who says the spell. Maybe we could find a priest," Luci reasoned.

"I could call Frank," I offered.

I began to dig through my pockets but I couldn't find the number. I rose an eyebrow and emptied my jeans but it was nowhere to be seen.

"I lost it," I admitted.

"You didn't memorize it?" Luci barked.

"No one remembers numbers anymore!" I argued.

"This could have been a life and death situation," Orion replied.

"But it wasn't."

"That's not the point," Orion said.

"Look, I'll see if he called me. I mean, maybe he put the number in while I was out? You never know," I reasoned.

I turned on my phone and saw that I had nearly thirty missed calls, most from the same number. I figured that was a good place to start and called the number. It rang three times before someone picked up.

"Hello?" I said.

"Terrance?" Frank's voice said on the other end.

"Frank! Thank God. I lost your number. Sorry I didn't call sooner. But, I got the Horn," I said.

"I realized. You left the paper I gave you in the parking lot in Dallas. I've been calling just about every Terrance Homwell in Ohio looking for yah," Frank said.

"Sorry about that. Look, the reason I'm calling is that we need some help with the ritual to return the Horn to where it belongs. Where are you right now?" I asked.

"I could ask you the same thing. After you didn't show up in El Paso, I moved on to the next info I get. I'm in Hollywood now. Looking like there may be a Sin out here. There's lot of videos about you out here. Sounds like some big shot is making a movie about you already. Trailer just came out yesterday. I've got no doubt that a Sin's behind all this. Or one dedicated director," Frank explained.

"Really?" I asked. I couldn't help but smile at the idea. I really was a superhero, why shouldn't I have my own movie?

"If you meet me out here I can help you with whatever you need. Where are you anyway?" Frank questioned.

"I'm in Vegas. I just took out Sloth and Greed. Turns out the Horn Lust had was a fake. I got the real one now," I explained.

"Not a far drive. I'll text you the address. I've got myself on one of them movie sites. When you get here give me a call and I'll get you past the gates. Be careful. I'm sure a Sin is near but I haven't gotten them to show themselves yet," he warned.

"Alright, I got it. I'll see you soon," I said and hung up.

"Are you sure you want to take the Horn there?" Luci asked.

"If you come anywhere near a Sin with the Horn, I have no doubt they will reveal themselves," Orion warned. "Perhaps we should find someone else."

"But what if that other person is a Leech or a Sin in disguise? Look, we know Frank and he's not that far from here. Besides, if the Sin is there Frank and I can take them down," I argued.

"Be careful Thomas. You're getting a full head," Luci warned.

I shrugged. I felt on top of the world right now. I felt like I could do anything. I wasn't worried. Even if we did find another Sin, I could take them down just like how I took down the other Sins. With Frank, it would be even easier.

"We can do this. I promise to keep on my guard. But I know us, we can do this. We're so close," I said.

"Fine, let's go. But Terrance, be careful. You're still human. Pitch may have saved you this time but he's an odd man. He is very particular about his cards. If you lived this time it means you just drew luckily. You may not be as lucky the next time around," Orion warned.

I looked at the Tarot card from my pocket. It already looked older and more worn. This card saved my life? If I was running on luck then so be it. Sometimes that's all it took. A little luck and a whole lot of guts. We were close, we didn't need to let this opportunity slip away. If we could get Frank then we could end this all before it can even begin.

We can do this.

I can do this.

24

IT'S A REFERENCE!

It was only a few hour drive from Vegas to Hollywood. I think I understood what Frank meant by signs. This place seemed to be crawling with mindless zombies and sinful freaks. Then again, it is Hollywood. That could be normal for all I knew.

Despite Luci's will, I did not take the stolen car out of the valet parking. I instead took a few stacks of Greed's winnings and bought myself a used truck. On my way I also bought myself new jeans, short sleeve shirt that said "What Happens in Vegas, Stays in Vegas", and sneakers. My feet were so blistered from the boots that it felt like heaven to put them in something actually made to run in. But I still kept them. I mean they were still my clothes and my boots. I took a very long time to break those in. They just needed a good wash down and they'd be fine. But that wasn't anything that I was concerned with now.

I drove down Hollywood plaza and found myself near a large film studio. I looked through the gate to see people rushing around. They were obviously very busy. I pulled up to the gate and text Frank that I was here.

The officer at the gate asked for ID, which I had none, and then he asked for my badge, which I also didn't have. I was starting to get a bit nervous but Frank sent me a picture of a badge and said to tell them that I was auditioning with Mr. Superbia.

I showed them the badge and the man gave me a once over.

"You don't look the evil type. They don't want a kid for the villain," the man said.

I smiled and rubbed the back of my hair. *Now I don't like to lie but I understand there are times in one's life when they need to, like when I broke the tractor joyriding and I said that it just stopped working randomly.*

"Oh? Really? The description said they were looking for someone younger. It can't hurt to at least try," I said.

The man looked me over again and shrugged. "Fine. The trailer was pretty vague anyway. Who knows what direction they are going for," the man said and opened the gate.

I shrugged with him and pulled into the lot. Frank said I was looking for stage 19. That's just what I needed to go on right now, and hopefully, I wouldn't get jumped in the process.

"Tony," Luci said once we were clear of people

"Superbia means pride," she revealed.

"So Frank found Pride?" I whispered. There were a lot of people here and if there was a Sin, I didn't want them hearing me through a Leech.

"Maybe, it would be best to stay guarded. We don't know what may be lurking in the shadows," Orion warned.

"We've been through this a few times. I'm pretty sure I know what's lurking in the shadows. Still, it would be nice to not get thrown around like an actual doll," I replied.

"Don't be a smart ass. Let's find Frank and get this horn back to where it belongs. Then you can be as confident as you want," Luci insisted.

"Fair enough," I added.

We parked and I grabbed the case and my shotgun. At least it being Hollywood, I didn't have to worry about sticking out too much. Hell, I'm pretty sure that I could have Orion's wings out and I'd be fine. I walked through the various sets and watched the people around me with a careful eye. Everyone seemed to be working hard and didn't seem to have much time to notice us. I tried asking for directions a few times but I was normally asked to get a coffee or to buzz off.

I rolled my eyes and eventually found where I was going. I saw Studio 19 with a large sign out front of the building. It was a billboard with a city landscape with a sun set in the background. There were words printed across the front of the billboard in the center. They read "Pride and the Angel: The Final Battle" in large golden letters. I rose an eyebrow and looked around the set. People were not coming in and out of the set like they were at the other studios.

The more I looked around the weirder the sights around me became. Before I just thought that people were working but they seemed beyond that. They were driven but to a frightening level. The people, they were foaming, drooling, and twitching. Many were mumbling as others were screaming.

"This is my shot! You will not ruin this!" One yelled.

"I can do better that that trash! What were they even thinking? They should have just asked me. I'd get it perfect the first time," another called.

"Horrible! All of it!" A third cried.

I looked up at the billboard again and felt a chilling horror come over me. It couldn't be that good. I pulled out my phone again and looked up the trailer for the film. There were millions of results. People claiming that they could do better or that they would be perfect to star in the film. Eventually I pulled up the video, it was only sixty seconds long.

I played the video. It faded in from black and went to a stock video of a desert as several days and nights quickly passed. Words faded onto the screen. "In a world where demons walk among us..." The footage changed to what looked like cellphone footage of four teens being chased down by humans with black eyes and foaming mouths. They screamed as the possessed people darted towards them. "There is a so called hero who has risen..." The footage changed to a video of me fighting Gluttony at the fairgrounds. "But demons can take many forms..." The footage switched again to me screaming as I forced out Luci's wings in Dallas. The video was from one of the people I burned and the video did not cut that part out. "Who will step up and destroy this threat before he brings the end of the world? Coming this Summer...Pride and the Angel: the Final Battle".

I rose both of my eyebrows and looked around. "Guys I think this may be a trap," I said.

"Oh you think?" Luci spat. "What was your first clue?"

"I am not a bright boy, and I can admit that. Look, that was definitely Frank on the phone. I don't know, maybe Pride has him now? The last message was a text. But, if it's Pride that means they have Frank. We can't just leave, even if it is a trap," I retorted.

My phone vibrated. I looked at it with the realization that I forgot to turn it off after Frank text me. I looked at the new message. Speak of the devil.

"Did you figure it out, cowboy?" the message read.

"Where is Frank?" I quickly replied.

"Terrance. Get out of sight," Orion said.

I nodded and ran into a nearby trailer. I peeked inside before I went in fully. I closed the door behind me and looked at my phone to see a new message. It was a photo. I opened the message and looked at the picture. There were at least fifty people who were tied up on this outdoor movie set. It looked like something right out of one of those old western movies I watched with my Grandma but the people were all dressed in modern clothing.

"If you want to prove that you're a hero, why don't you come and save all these people first?" the message asked.

I flurried my brows and stared at the screen. I was lead right in this trap and I didn't have anywhere to go. If I didn't save these people then what the video said would be right, but if I did save them there was a good chance that Pride would get his hands on the Horn of Gabriel. I had to save them, it wasn't an option.

"Terrance think of the big picture here," Orion warned.

I bit my lip and stared down at the screen, my thumbs unmoving. I didn't know how to reply. I wasn't sure what to do. My gut was telling me to track Pride down and cut off his head, but the voices had another plan.

"We can find someone else to say the spell," Luci said.

"But that's not fair. It's not fair that I leave all those people to die, that I leave Frank to die," I argued.

"We can't let the Horn fall into the wrong hands," Orion yelled.

"Hey!" I yelled over him. "Why don't I just leave it here? I mean Pride is expecting me to have it on me, right? I can beat him and rush back here with Frank."

They were silent.

"No one would be that idiotic," Orion began.

"Which means no one would be expecting it," Luci finished.

"Put a devil's trap on it. That way if he steps foot in here, he'll get stuck. We can just hide it somewhere," I explained.

"That's dumb enough to work," Luci agreed. "Although, I'm not sure how well that's going to work for you. Tony, if you haven't noticed, you're not the most humble person. How are you going to get out of his grasp? You're already getting full of yourself."

"Ok, one, I have noticed. Two, he's a Sin. He will die just like any other Sin. I just need to find his weak point," I said.

"Orion, help me out here," Luci sighed.

"What she means is, the more sinful you are, the more control a Sin can have over you. I'm sure the only reason you haven't been taken over by one of those Leeches out there is because of us. We're keeping your mind just clear enough. Though, we can't protect you forever and what happened with Envy-"

I cut Orion off. "Ah, can we not talk about that, please? I'd like to avoid that pain in my head for the rest of my life, thank you."

"Shouldn't have called me April," Luci barked.

"Should have been such a royal...mean woman," I corrected. I cleared my throat and shifted some on my feet.

"Tonoki, I'm not some saint. I don't care what you call me," Luci ensured.

"Well, that don't matter much. You're still a lady...barely but still. And you don't swear at a lady," I revealed.

Luci started to laugh and I felt a blush go across my cheeks. This was bull. She can wrap anything to make me sound stupid. "Not funny."

"I mean to believe she's anything similar to a lady is humorous," Orion chuckled.

"Not funny bird brain," Luci growled. Her laugh suddenly stopped.

"Then why are you laughing?" I asked.

"It's funny to me, doesn't need to be funny to him," she corrected.

Orion and I were in quiet confusion for several moments before he broke the silence.

"Anyway, did Pride say anything else?" Orion asked.

I looked back at my messages and saw a new one. It was video this time. I opened my messages and clicked on the video. Frank stood in front of the tied up people. He wore a large smile and his eyes were black. "Better hurry cowboy, for every ten minutes that you're not here, I'll kill someone. Look, I already killed two," Frank laughed and pointed the camera over to two dead people who were slumped over each other near a table with food on it. Frank re-centered the camera on his face. "Oh, and why don't you come dressed for the part? If you come without costume, I'll kill everyone here," his voice got dark and sounded like two people were speaking at the same time. Frank smiled and seemed to pose in the camera view. "I'll be waiting."

The video ended and I felt my heart swell. Pride has taken Frank. Whether he was Frank all along or just recently took him, I didn't know. But what I did know was that I was mad. I was beyond mad, actually I was pissed!

I slammed my fist into the wall of the trailer and gritted my teeth. This was too much and too far. Frank was the last connection I had to my Dad right now and Pride just too that way.

"What are you going to do?" Luci asked. I had no doubt that she could feel the rage burning inside of me.

"Something that will not be allowed on television."

25

PRIDE

I stood in my cowboy outfit uncomfortably staring at Frank. I had new cowboy boots on that weren't broken in, which is a horrible feeling. I had my shotgun in my hand but not aimed at him. I was still having problems believing that this man who helped train me and saved me would just be another Sin. Though after the fight with Sloth and Greed I could believe that two Sins would kill each other.

Frank smiled at me. He knew that I would not be able to resist coming here to protect people. I was too proud to let people die in my stead. Actually, I was feeling pretty good about myself against him. I may have struggled with Greed and Sloth at the same time, but it was only him here now.

I took a step towards Frank and my spurs clicked. Well if I am going to look like this with all these cameras on me I might as well own it.

"Well, howdy Frank. Or should I say, Pride," I called with a tip of my hat. I took the moment to sneakily check my ammo pouch. Looks like I had six shells. More than enough to take him down. I knew I could easily shrug off Pride's influence. It did not have any hold on me. *And yes I realize now how prideful I was being.*

Pride/Frank jumped off the stage and walked a few steps towards me on the street. He pulled out that hunting rifle of his and I rose my shotgun. We both stood there frozen. I swear I heard the classic Western standoff music. Out of my right peripheral, I saw a speaker. Frank actually had the music playing. He wanted this to be as showy as possible. Oh well, at least it would make me look better when I beat him.

"Careful Terrance, Pride has a greater influence on you than you think," Orion warned.

"No he doesn't I am shrugging it off easily," I confidently replied. Pride already knew about the angels so there was no use hiding them. In the back of my mind though I knew Orion was right. I felt I was better than everyone. I knew I could take down anything I needed. I mean I had been through so much already. I had literally died but even that couldn't keep me down.

I shook my head. No, I was not better than everyone. It was only because of Pitch intervening did I actually win against Sloth but I could not admit it. I had to be confident after all.

"So, the angels and the boy came to crash my amazing movie. Too bad you didn't realize you are the climatic fight," Pride announced spreading his arms. It was obvious he was more talking to the cameras than to me. I decided to play along with it some. It might give me more time to focus on finding his weak point.

"Yes we have arrived," I announced in a cheesy hero voice, "and we will defeat you, villain." Pride rose his eyebrows. I guess he wasn't expecting me to act along but seemed pleased nonetheless.

"No, Terrance it is you who will be the villain in this movie and the villain always loses," he replied. It was so odd to hear this complete change of disposition from how I first met Frank. Frank was a cool collected demon killer and now we have this movie making loud mouth Pride. Pride was one good actor. *At least when acting like Frank, right now this was pretty painful.*

"This is getting tiresome let's just cut to the action," Pride sighed. I noticed the classic western music cut off. Pride raised his rifle and immediately took a shot at me. I had no time to react, but Orion did. In a blink of an eye, my arm rose and formed into Orion's gauntlet. I felt a slight impact against my hand and saw the flattened bullet clatter to the ground.

My mouth was wide open as I stared at the bullet. I looked up at Pride without closing my mouth. He even looked slightly impressed.

"That was so freaking coo-," I started, "I mean, I was ready for that." I tried to appear confident but I was sure it did not come out the greatest.

"Ha, this is just the beginning," Pride replied lamely. This fight was becoming a bad acting contest. Pride tossed his gun aside and began to shred the form of Frank. The skin bubbled and churned as he grew at least eight feet tall. Bubbling black ooze began to form large muscles along his body, and I had seen enough. I immediately shot both shells out of the shotgun into the form. I heard a grunt as both shells hit their rather large mark, but otherwise Pride seemed unfazed. I cracked open the breach and loaded two more shells.

I noticed a more defined head began to grow out of the bubbling muscly body. I took that as my next target and fired twice more. The first spread hit his neck while the other hit him straight in the face. His head got knocked back and he raised his new large hand to cover it but still did not go down. I figured it did not matter if I saw the weak point. If I got lucky enough to hit it then it would end the fight quickly.

I heard something that sounded like growling from Pride, maybe I had gotten close to his weak point. He lowered his hand and I saw absolute rage in his face. His face still relatively looked like Frank's but now it was a pure black color that shined like oil.

"You could have ruined my face. I am proud of my face," He seethed. So instead of killing him outright I just managed to make him very angry, great. Maybe if I could stall him Orion, Luci, and I could figure out a better plan than to just keep shooting him.

"What happened to the actual Frank?" I called up to Pride. I hoped he would not miss the chance to monologue slightly.

"Well I killed him of course," He proudly answered. "He was easy to take down for someone like me."

"Really? I thought that someone who was a mighty demon hunter like Frank would be pretty challenging," I prodded. I took this time to load two more shells in my shotgun. I was getting low but I could still do this. His weak point was not in his face or chest, though I was not certain how deeply the pellets had actually dug into his flesh.

"Ha! Yes, he certainly was a mighty hunter, but even someone like him was no match for me," Pride scoffed taking the bait.

"Nicely done, Terrance. He is eating out of your palm for right now. I expect he will grow bored soon though," Orion complimented.

"Tori, Pride will be one of the most difficult Sin for you to brush off. I expect you realized that since you took four shots randomly at him," Luci remarked. She was right, I was a very prideful man. I was proud of a lot of things in my life and so Pride had a good amount of effect on me.

"You know, you can always just keep stabbing him until you get lucky, sometimes I have to do that," Pitch randomly popped in.

"Wait, Pitch? What do you mean by that?" I asked confused by his sudden appearance and worrying addition to the conversation.

Orion let out a long sigh, "He's gone already Terrance." *As a note, Pride was monologuing this whole time.* "He does raise a good point though. Though it may not be precise, repeated strikes could prove fruitful," Orion continued thoughtfully. *So the plan was just to get the large muscular Sin to sit still long enough for me to repeatedly stab him until I got lucky, always simple stuff.*

I turned my attention back to Pride. He looked like he was giving me a play by play of how exactly he killed the real Frank. His monstrous form was completed. With black shiny skin that was stretched tight by the huge muscles underneath. I could see the veins underneath the skin pulse with each beat. His face was completely smooth, except for the holes I put in it, with small eyes and a large toothy mouth. He did not have fangs but rather enlarged regular human teeth which somehow made him creepier.

"Hey!" I yelled at him to grab his attention. He seemed offended to interrupt his story that I had not listened to a word of. "I know that I am better than you. I have got two angels in my brain and you don't even have a brain," I insulted.

He looked taken aback that I would dare to insult him like that. He frowned deeply then smiled. "Oh really, then why don't you prove it to me," He replied with barely hidden anger. He immediately took off sprinting towards me. Each step caused the ground to vibrate slightly. I took off down an alleyway between two sets next to me. I turned to look back as I saw him skid past the entrance then start pushing his way into the alleyway, cracking the walls as he came. *Okay, so easily angered and does not turn well.* I continued to run down the alleyway before it opened it back up.

I noticed what looked like an open storage house across the street and quickly made my way over to it. If he does not turn well I would use that to my advantage.

"Terri, I can get you out of here quicker than just running," Luci mentioned sounding slightly confused.

"No, if I get too far away from Pride he will probably take more hostages to just force me back. If I keep running like this I can tire him out until I will be able to more easily find his weak point," I explained.

"That... is actually a pretty good idea," Luci replied sounding impressed.

"I am happy that you are using your head more in an actual tactical way instead of using it as a battering ram," Orion remarked with a small laugh.

"I am going to need you guys to help out some of course," I continued. "Luci keep pumping me with adrenaline and heat to help me stay ahead of Pride. Orion, I need you to keep my muscles from tearing and to help me punch my way through some things."

"Sounds like a plan," Orion answered.

"Aye, Captain Tracy," Luci said playfully.

I rolled my eyes a bit but smiled. She could get on your nerves but I enjoyed her jabs from time to time. Alright, it was time to put this shaky plan into action.

I ran into the storage shed and it was filled with boxes upon boxes all of various sizes. This will be perfect I knew this plan would work. *I had no idea if it would work.* I heard a crash as Pride barreled out of the alleyway. He had literally brought part of the wall down making his way through the tight passageway. He looked up and down the street looking for me. Looks like I will need to lead him over here.

I stuck my head out and yelled, "Hey!" again. His head snapped towards me and he ran towards me.

"Come Terrance, the movie is not yet finished," he called. I ducked back into the storage shed and ran into the maze of pallets and boxes. I heard him come in and heard his stomping stop. He was listening for me. It was time to see if I was nimble enough to avoid him for a long time. My heart was pumping like crazy but I did not feel out of breath. Looks like Luci and Orion were keeping to the plan.

I ran out pushing a box over as I dodged over into a separate aisle. The box made a large crash and I heard a large crash as Pride barreled through the boxes. Props flew everywhere as he punched down to where he last heard me. I was glad I had moved over because where he punched the concrete cracked and cratered slightly.

I slowly took a step to gain better vision of Pride but as I put weight on my foot I heard an odd squawk as I felt a chill roll up my spine. I looked down and saw a rubber chicken on the ground. It must have fell out of one of the crates that Pride crushed. I knew Pride had heard that. I looked over in time to see his fist sailing towards me. I jumped forward towards a crate putting my arms up to cover my face. I felt Orion's armor cove my arms as I crashed through the box. I rolled out and kept sprinting down the aisle. Now that Pride was keeping track of me it would be a real chase.

He swung his arm across the stacks of boxes next to me causing an avalanche of cheap props. I focused on my back and had Luci quickly jet me out of the way with her wings. I landed on my back at the rear exit of the building and slammed up against a box. I made the wings go back in so that I could keep being nimble. Even though I had Orion and Luci working together to keep my body I could feel it sapping my energy. So while it boosted my endurance I could not keep it going forever.

I got up to and saw Pride making his way towards me. He was not dumb that was for sure and could predict where I would go pretty easily. I had to stay on my toes otherwise this guy would catch me quick. Pride had pieces of boxes stuck into his skin but did not seem to notice too much. He was also starting to breath a bit heavy. The chase was taking it out of him. He must not be made for endurance.

I got an invigorated feeling as Luci pumped me with me more adrenaline though my heart was beating like it would burst out of my chest. I could not go much longer either.

Pride punched down at me and I jumped to the right. The fist crashed right next to me breaking boxes and concrete. A chunk of wood flew and scratched across my arm. The cut was pretty deep but I could still keep going. It was time to fight back though. While Pride rose his fist from the ground I launched myself into the air with Luci's wings. This was going to take a lot out of me but I needed to have both power and speed.

As I finished the arc of the jump I allowed myself to fall towards Pride's face. Orion's gauntlet covered my right arm and I put a lot of power into the punch as it collided with Pride's face. It made a satisfying crunch and made grunt and tilt his head.

I landed on the ground heavy but immediately spun around with my left arm engulfed in flames as the claws came out. I raked them up across Pride's left calf. It cut through. Though as fast as it cut the wounds healed. I felt the crowded feeling but the pain was not as intense. I felt more attuned with Orion and Luci.

"We can cross out that leg as the weak point," Luci mentioned. So far, we can cross out his chest, face, and left leg. This was taking a while.

"Behind you!" I heard the familiar shout from Orion. I spun around in time to raise my armored right hand as Pride's fist collided with it. The armored hand blocked a large amount of the force but it still sent me flying back further into the storage building. I crashed through several boxes before rolling to a stop in an alleyway. Spots danced in my eyes and I sucked in air after all of it got knocked out. I was still able to move.

Pride walked towards me covering his face. He covered his face but not his leg that I just clawed. Maybe something in his face was the weak point rather than what was on his face. He picked up a few baseball bats out of a box while walking. He immediately chucked one at me. I rolled to the side as it stuck drilled into the concrete.

"Strike one!" I called out in an umpire voice. This caused Pride to stop for a moment in confusion.

"What are you talking about?" He angrily asked. He threw another bat at me I jumped to the side and rolled a bit closer to him.

"Ste-rike two! Careful one more strike and you are out," I shouted out again. Even though he had no idea why I was doing this he seemed to be taking more careful aim with this bat. He threw the bat extra hard putting his full weight with it. Causing him to stagger a bit. I jumped up summoning Luci's wings and flew forward fast over the bat.

"Strike three! You are out of here!" I yelled in triumph as I landed in front of him. I jumped up once more but this time I willed Orion to come out as much as possible. The armor ripped from me and covered everything but my legs. Even my face had an ornate helmet covering though it did not disrupt my vision at all. I slammed both fists into his gut as hard as possible. He got knocked off his feet and sent out of the storage area into the street and landed with a hard thud.

I ran towards him grabbing my shotgun. I cracked it open and fumbled with the few shells I had left. I loaded two into the breach and snapped it shut. I had to make these two shots count I didn't think that I would have time to reload. The plan was that Pride would be a bit tired from healing from the wounds I had been giving him so it would give me time to get on him and start wailing on his face.

I used Luci's wings to boost me over to him and I stood next to his head. Luckily his arms were so muscular that they could not lift up above his head easily to reach me. I aimed for his left eye and took a shot point blank. It obliterated the eye and Pride yelled out in pain but he was definitely still kicking. I flew up into the air to find my next target. Once I got into the air Pride covered up his face to protect himself. I needed those hands down.

"Orion, your turn with wings," I called out. I felt the flames die and be replaced in a plume of feathers as the two pairs billowed out. I put a lot of energy into the wings and flapped them down as hard as I could. The wings created a huge gust slamming Pride's arms against the ground and opening his mouth. It looked like he was riding on a way too fast rollercoaster.

Pride sure liked to talk so I think I knew where to place my final shot. I aimed for his mouth and fired. The shell exploded out and the pellets hit their mark filling his mouth with lead. I heard a choking sound as Pride reached up for me but slowly his arm fell to the ground and his eyes rolled back into his head as black blood poured from his mouth.

I hope this gives the real Frank some peace. I stood there flying for a moment before landing. I stared at the dead Pride and felt a rush of relief.

"We did it!" I shouted. The wings on my back dissipated and all the armor faded away. I fell to my knees panting but I was still able to keep consciousness. I started to laugh. "We actually did it," I repeated.

"Orion, Luci, you guys were fantastic. We really worked well together," I boasted. "Oh Orion all the armor was so cool I felt like a real knight. Luci, the claw up his calf was so awesome."

I took a deep breath and realized how quiet my head was.

"Guys, you there?"

26

I'M GONNA DIE

Crap. Crap. Crap!

"Please answer me!" I begged.

The screech of my tires as I made a turn off the exit, cause my heart to skip. I gritted my teeth and did my best to not lose my focus.

"This isn't funny!" I barked.

There still was no answer. I felt tears trying to force their way from the corner of my eyes. I panted and felt my body shaking. I pressed harder on the gas as I weaved through the interstate traffic. I honked my car horn as I sped down the highway.

"Move!" I yelled as I swerved. I was only nearly missing cars, but I couldn't stop.

There was a parade full of police cars riding close behind me, sirens blaring and lights filling the night. The overhead light of the helicopter that was chasing me down spotlight me. I felt like at any moment I would drop dead from the fear of everything.

"Guys!" I scream. It wasn't helping anything. I hadn't heard from them since I finished off Pride. My head was perfectly empty. The only thing I had was my own thoughts. I never knew that silence could be so frightening.

I am so screwed!

***

This is a bit confusing, isn't it? Let me go back a bit. Let's go back to right when Luci and Orion disappeared.

"Orion, Luci, you guys were fantastic. We really worked well together," I boasted. "Oh Orion all the armor was so cool I felt like a real knight. Luci, the claw up his calf was so awesome."

I took a deep breath and realized how quiet my head was.

"Guys, you there?"

There was no reply. I laughed it off at first but then more and more time started to past.

"Guys?" I called again., "Come on, this isn't funny."

Again, nothing. I was starting to feel uneasy. I bit my lip and shifted my weight on my feet. I didn't really know what to do. I felt like...like a kid. I was alone, for the first time in weeks I was alone in my own head and I couldn't be more terrified.

"Luci? Orion?...Pitch?"

I was alone.

I looked around and tried to think of what to do. I know I gave them a lot of talk about controlling me, but a lot of what they said was super helpful. Right now I was completely lost. I ended up debating what to do for several minutes before I walked back to Studio 19. I went to the people who were tied up, and I cut them free with a knife from the snack table. It took a while with a butter knife. I bet Orion could have just pulled it apart, or Luci could have just melted it.

When everyone was free, they looked at me with fear in their eyes. But one woman hugged me. She actually hugged me! With tears rolling down her face and her makeup smeared she hugged me. When she pulled away, the woman let out a short and nervous laugh.

"I'm sorry. Just, thank you. You saved us," she said.

I wasn't sure how to respond. I ended up standing there with my mouth open for a few seconds as I thought of what to say. I wanted to say something heroic, but in the end, all I could get out was "thank you, kindly."

I helped the people clear out and made my way back to the trailer. I was relieved to see that the Horn was still where I left it. I picked up the case and let out a sigh of relief. At least I still had this, even if Luci and Orion were silent, I at least had this.

"Luci, I need the ritual. We can just try me saying the Latin. We can't keep dragging this around," I said.

There still was no answer.

"Guys, I'm serious," I repeated. I felt like a broken record.

Nothing.

"I'm really alone," I said aloud.

"Freeze!" A voice yelled from behind me. I looked back to see a man dressed in an all-black. He pointed a gun at my head and seemed to be aimed to kill. I looked out of the trailer to see that there were at least four other men in same attire and each had their weapons drawn.

I rose my hands and looked over the men. I couldn't see their eyes. They were all wearing dark shades which blocked my view. I had no idea if they were human or Leeches. Then again, Pride was dead.

"Terrance Homwell? Keep your hands where I can see them," the man ordered.

"Who are you?" I asked. I kept my hands where they could see them, but I was still wearing my shotgun in its sheaf. The Horn case was in my left hand, above my head.

"We are agents of homeland security. You are under arrest for resisting arrest, theft, inducing public terror, assault, murder, and acts of terrorism. Get on your knees and toss away your weapons," the agent demanded.

"What?" I shuttered. "You guys got the wrong idea."

He cut me off. "Get on your knees now!"

What do I do? What do I do? I have to get out of here. Orion! He can use his wings- crap. I need to think here. I need to think on my feet. I can't go against all of these guys without Luci and Orion. I'd end up shot before I could do anything. Plus they might just be normal people too. Why did I have to leave my phone on?

Out of the blue, an idea came to my mind. It was a long shot, but it might work. It doesn't need to work for long. It just needed to work for a few minutes. Just until I could get to my truck, then I could be out of here.

I laughed and shook my head. "This is a joke, right? Very funny. I get it, hazing the new guy," I laughed.

The man did not return my laugh. He tightened his hand on his weapon, and I let the look of shock and fear return to my eyes.

"Wait, you're serious? I just thought you guys were extras for the scene," I gulped. The men seemed to be a bit more confused. "You do know, I'm not the real Terrance Homwell, right? I'm just the actor who's playing him...you know...in the movie?" I said and pointed to the billboard.

"Look, guys, my name is Frank Superbia, Check with the gate. I checked in!" I said with panic in my voice. It wasn't hard to fake.

Remember when I said that I didn't lie to lie? That didn't mean I wasn't good at it.

The agents looked confused. The moment that their weapons drop even slightly I jumped out of the door and started to run. I ran in a zigzag, pattern-less motion. I took a sharp turn and ran through several of the movie scenes, even a few that were recording. I did my best to disappear, but the agents were close behind.

I did my best to focus on getting away and trying to force Luci's wings out, but nothing was working. It was like they weren't in my head at all. I was starting to get scared.

I eventually made it to the truck. I jumped in and wasted no time as I peeled out of the lot.

I think that caught us up. So basically I went on a high-speed chase with the local police and FBI. I have to say, not my most heroic moment but I didn't know what else to do. I really thought that I was going to be killed if I was caught. I guess that's just a side effect from being surrounded by demons so often, anyway...back to the story.

***

Crap!

I took a hard turn and had to slow down. People. There were people everywhere the road was filled with them. They were fighting across the highway. They didn't even notice the fact that I almost hit them. I slid to a stop and looked around as people were basically beating each other to death. There was a huge pile-up of cars that blocked the roads. I looked around with wide eyes and terror swelling in my throat. It was tight and taste bitter. Something was wrong, it felt like everything was happening too fast and at the same time, it felt like I was moving in slow motion.

I yelled and began to beat the stirring wheel. I was so angry. Everything was boiling up at once. I looked in the passenger side. I saw the case and thought for a moment of the worse.

"I can't," I screamed and stopped my reaching hand. To even threaten such a thing would be idiotic. This was the end of the world that I was messing with.

I took a breath and looked around. This wasn't normal, even for LA traffic. Something was very wrong.

Several armed guards surrounded my truck. They pointed their guns towards me. The door flung open, and I was pulled from the car and thrown against the ground. I was pinned down as the people were yelling at me. I really wasn't sure what they were saying. There was a full riot going on around me. The guards created a barrier between the mob and me. After a few moments, the man from before walked over to me.

He was tall, taller than me. He appeared to be in his forties with slick back black hair and tan skin. He had very unique features that made him look sharp. The man removed his sunglasses, and I quickly noticed the tattoo under his right eye. It was the symbol of the Crusaders.

"Good evening Homwell," he said.

"Who are you? What's going on?" I asked. I was struggling against the ground as I tried my hardest to get free from their grasp.

The man looked over at my truck as one of his underlings pulled out my shotgun and the black case.

"Don't touch that!" I warned.

The man rose an eyebrow and motioned for the case to be brought over. He looked over the case before he opened it. He peaked before quickly closing and locking the box back up.

"So the stories I heard were true. You've been very busy. We should be thanking you," he said.

"Don't touch it! You don't understand!" I yelled.

The man smiled and motioned for his lackeys to lift me up. I looked up at the man with a sour expression as I was lifted from the ground.

"I think you may have the wrong idea here. We're the good guys here Terrance," he claimed.

"Oh yeah? Then why are you trying to arrest me? Why is any of this happening?" I spat.

The man snapped, and I was released from the grip of those around me. I pulled away and rolled my shoulder, it cracked, and I turned my focus back to the horn.

"Let me explain. My name is Agent Hopper. I am the current head of the Crusaders, United States branch. We chased you down because of this. We had to make sure that you were the real deal, can't be too careful, now can we?" He said, almost in a teasing manner.

"So the Crusaders are real?" I asked. After Frank turned out to be Pride, I wasn't sure what was real and what wasn't anymore.

"As real as this Horn. Look, we both want the same thing here, and maybe we didn't get off to the right start, but you have been managing to slip through our fingers over and over. I was beginning to think we would never catch you," Agent Hopper revealed.

"Well, you got me. Now give me back the Horn," I demanded. I couldn't help but be a bit aggressive, this guy and everything about him was pissing me off.

"Ah, hold your horses. We need to talk," he revealed.

"About?"

"You. Angels, demons, the end of the world...all of that good stuff," he answered. "We already know you weren't originally supposed to be our Vessel. I do apologize for the loss of your father, but we can't help that now. What we can do is clean up the mess you've made. Apparently, Wrath has a vendetta against you. She has taken the whole city of Los Angeles hostage. She is demanding that you and that horn arrive or she will kill every man, woman, and child within a hundred mile radius of the city center."

I frowned and bit my lip. "Can she do that?"

"We have no idea. But what we do know is that we can't let that happen, but we also cannot allow this Horn to fall into Wrath's claws. You have defeated six of the Seven Deadly Sins, correct? Do you believe that you can defeat one more?" Hopper asked.

I shrugged as a worried expression showed on my face.

"You don't seem too confident," he said.

"Luci and Orion, the angels...they're gone. I haven't heard anything from them," I admitted.

Agent Hopper frowned and pulled his phone from his pocket. He began to type quickly and muttered to himself. I wish I could have been more helpful. To be honest, I felt like an idiot right now. I know it wasn't my fault, but still, I felt responsible. I was supposed to be the hero.

Hopper put his phone back into his pocket and turned to me. "Unfortunate as that is, we do not have the time to spend on it. We will have to go with plan B."

"Plan B?" I asked.

"You will go in, and we will come behind. Here," he began. Hopper pulled out his phone and pulled up a map of the city. "Wrath is here. She is using this office as her headquarters. It has the least amount of people in this concentrated area. I predict that it is because she is using the people of the city as shields. They are gathered around the outline of the city by the boatload while the center is relatively empty, that's not to say that there aren't a few thousand people located in patches through the city. We can get you through the crowds and to the center. Wrath will be expecting you. If you can keep her distracted, we can come in and take her down. You will have an army backing you up, but we are asking you to be bait," Agent Hopper explained.

I blinked several times and felt like my head was going to pop like a balloon that was too full of air.

"What?" I questioned.

"We need you to distract Wrath and prevent her from taking the Horn of Gabriel, or a lot of people are going to die today," he clarified.

I had no idea what to say. I had absolutely no idea how to reply to any of this. I felt like everything was just imploding on itself. I was suddenly alone, and then I was chased down by the police and told that I have to go one on one with a Sin or else millions of people were going to die. What was I even supposed to say to any of that?

I nodded my head mindlessly, and Hopper put his arm around my shoulder. "Thank you for your service Homwell. Now let's get you geared up and ready to go," Hopper said. He lead me to a van. I was lead into the back where several people were waiting. I was motioned in and told to sit. I sat down and the van doors closed. The van started to move, and everyone started to talk to me and offer things. They were going over plans and telling me what I needed. I was given an assault rifle, ammo, shells for my shotgun, and a flash of Holy water. Overall, I didn't hear what they said. I was in such shock that nothing was getting through my head. All I heard was a ringing in my ears and the sound of my heartbeat.

I felt something touch my pants pocket. I reached into my pocket and pulled out a folded tarot card. I opened it up with the expectation of it being Judgement, but to my surprise, the card had changed. There was only one word written on the tarot card, but it was enough to make my heart skip a beat.

"Death."

27

WRATH

Wrath stared at me as I approached her with my new assault rifle and the Horn in each hand. My trusty shotgun was strapped to my back for easy access. I felt armed to the teeth. She stood in the middle of the street. What looked like a usually busy major road was silent with derelict cars everywhere. I heard gunshots and yelling in the distance from where the Crusaders were keeping the Leeches busy. Wrath here was the last Sin on Earth and now I had to take her down completely alone. To say I was nervous was an understatement.

"Stop right there," She called out in a gruff feminine voice. I stopped just as she requested. Wrath was the most intimidating looking Sin yet. Her brow and face were set in a permanent angry scowl. She was completely bald and her skin was pure red. Her arms were covered in a dark red crystal that formed into stony hands. Her legs were also made of the same stony material. I could see what looked like heat waves radiating off of her, and she stood at about seven and a half feet tall. Her aura was still affecting me and I felt nothing but hate towards this Sin. She needed to die but I also needed to remain focused.

"Open the case," She ordered again. I set the case down and undid the two latches. I threw open the lid and stood back so that Wrath could see it easily. She took a step forward towards the case and I raised my rifle. She stopped and stared at me with intensity.

"You said to bring the Horn. There was nothing about giving it willingly," I said. She stared at me for a couple more long seconds before nodding.

"That is fair whelp, I would not mind crushing you before taking it," She answered with steam coming out of his mouth. She raised her hands and cracked her knuckles. This was crazy and I had no idea if I could beat her easily. I felt the back of my belt to touch the vial of holy water for some comfort. I hope this would be enough to actually hurt her.

After a few seconds of more intense staring, she charged me with a roar. My eyes widened at her speed and I jumped to the right over a car. She careened past me flipping any cars in his path. I raised up and rested the gun on the hood of the car. I took aim at her face and as she turned around I fired two three round bursts. Most of each burst hit their mark. She jolted back for a moment and let out a grunt. She brought her head forward and spit out the bullets that hit her. The holes in her face disappeared as well. She let out another growl and pointed her hand at me. It began to glow.

I saw steam rising from the tips and heard what sounded like a loud spark pop off. Suddenly a beam of flame fired straight from her fingers and towards my car. I barely had enough time to run into the street away from the car before the flames hit it. The flames melted straight through the bumper and into the engine. The gasoline exploded causing shrapnel from the car to fly everywhere. I jumped to the ground covering my head and the back of my neck. I felt some glass cut into my arms and back. I winced from the pain but after a second the shrapnel stopped flying.

I heard pounding as I assumed Wrath was running up on me. I spun around to see her nearly on top of me. I raised the rifle again firing three bursts into her. The bullets seemed to more annoy her than hurt her but it caused her to slow down slightly, giving me enough time to roll away from her. I slid myself under a truck to give myself a moment to breath. Wrath had other plans for me though. I heard a crack as she sideswiped the vehicle off of me like it was a toy.

I fired two more bursts into her and scooted backwards. This time though she ignored the sting of the bullets and reached down for me. I kept firing until I heard the click of the empty gun. She grabbed on my leg throwing me behind her. I flew through the air before sliding on the street and hitting my side against a car. The car tilted a bit but stayed on its wheels. Its alarm started to go off with an insistent beep. I coughed and felt my side. It was very tender to the touch. I stood up again and stared down Wrath who looked back at me. I coughed and spit to the side. *What was a few more broken ribs? I feel like my ribs were broken more than not during this adventure.*

I was swung around but was still feeling okay. I was not exhausted yet. I grabbed the rifle and loaded a fresh clip in. I racked the round in and prepared myself to fight.

"Looks like you can take a few more hits than expected," Wrath called sounding like she was having a great time. Before I could reply she raised her hand up and I saw the crystal start to glow as the familiar sparking sound began. I ran away from the car into a nearby building. The car exploded as the fire hit it. I peeked out from what seemed to be an ice cream store to see the flaming car but no Wrath. I hid there for a moment wondering where she could be. Oh wait, the Horn!

I sprinted out of the store and saw her picking up the horn. I put everything into my legs and ran faster than I ever had without the assistance of the angels. She raised the Horn up preparing to blow. I jumped into the air incredibly high as I got close to her. She turned to look at me as I came down with a punch across her face. I was angry that she would have thought that she could blow the Horn while I still was breathing. The punch hit her with a satisfying amount of force causing her head to turn quickly and to drop the horn. I landed to the ground with a roll and sprang up to my feet. I dashed and grabbed the horn out from under Wrath and just kept running down the street.

I had no idea how I jumped that high or ran that fast but I did not have time to question. "Guys, did you come back?" I asked my head. I heard no voices so it looked like my head was still empty. I heard a scream of annoyance as Wrath charged after me. I was running fast but I had no chance of out running her. That means I just had to out maneuver her. I held the now caseless horn in my arms as I jumped through a large glass window display of a storefront. The glass cut my skin some but I was able to keep my footing as I ran through what looked like a clothes shop.

I sprinted and hid behind the counter. I heard Wrath stomp outside.

"Come on out little angel," She called. She must not realize that I did not have the angels anymore. I had a few seconds to think here because I could hear her struggling to fit into the store. God, I was mad. She made me want to just throw a tantrum and rip everything apart. I took a few deep breaths and took inventory. I dropped the rifle outside but still had my shotgun. I had twelve shells, and the flask of holy water on my back was still not broken somehow.

My injuries were not too severe though my ribs hurt like crazy and I was bleeding from a few places. I pulled the shotgun out of its sleeve and put the Horn there instead. The Horn fits pretty well, though it was a little longer than the shotgun. It had been quiet for a little so I peeked over to see what Wrath was up to. I saw her outside the shop pointing her finger at it as her hand glowed.

"Oh crap," I said to myself as I took cover behind the counter again. I heard the familiar spark and saw the flame shoot through a row of clothes. It caught anything it touched on fire. The store was quickly becoming an inferno. I had to get out as fast as I could before my exits were blocked. I dashed for the front of the store again shotgun in hand. She was definitely going to be waiting for me.

I pulled my hand back and unlatched the holy water flask. I jumped out of the window I broke and Wrath immediately grabbed me by the waist with both her hands. She lifted me to her eye level effortlessly. I then got a close look to see that even her eyes were a bright red. She was squeezing me really hard and I heard a few more pops in my ribs. I gasped out but that just let her squeeze harder.

Then I remembered the flask still in my hand. I lifted it up and smashed the glass vial onto her arm. It started smoking and she yelled out in pain. She dropped me immediately while wiping off her arms. They still smoked and I saw her red skin turn dark where I splashed her, but it was still healing. The only way I could take her down was by finding the weak point. She was healing way too fast for me to be able to just beat her until I could get lucky finding the spot. Plus I didn't have the angels to help me anyway.

I started to take off down a random alleyway to put some distance between Wrath and I. I turned my head just in time to see Wrath finish wiping off the holy water and stare at me with glowing red eyes. Looks like I managed to piss her off.

"Come back sissy angel," She bellowed. Why did she keep calling me an angel?

"I'm not an angel," I called back to confuse her. Even though I was confused myself. The alleyway cut around a corner and I ran around it as fast as I could. I knew Wrath would be hot on my tail. As I rounded the corner I noticed that this alleyway was a dead end. There were some doors which I quickly tried to open but all of them were locked. I did not have the power to punch through them anymore. I swore under my breath.

Wrath rounded the corner breathing a little heavy from all the running and began to laugh. The laugh was loud and rough. I pushed myself up against the wall in hopes that it would give way to get out. I wanted to charge her and just beat her but I knew that was her influence talking. I took a deep breath to try and calm down. I only saw one way out which was between her legs. I was starting to sweat and get tired but still felt pretty good. I think I may still be able to pull off a few sneaky moves.

"Angel give up and just give me the horn. I can promise I will control myself and make your death quick," She offered. As tempting as it was I didn't think I would take her up on that.

"Why do you keep calling me angel," I asked. At this point I wanted to keep her talking to catch my breath. She raised an eyebrow at me.

"You're really not smart are you," She asked. I frowned angered by her insult. What was she talking about of course I wasn't an angel I was just the vessel. Before she could make a move I sprinted at her. She laughed and reached down to grab me. I immediately shot her hand with the shotgun causing her to recoil her hand back. As I slid under her I shot her right between the legs as well. She howled in pain but grabbed my head just from under her legs.

I shouted out in surprise as I suddenly could see nothing but her stony hand. It also hurt like crazy as the stone slightly cut into my face. She pulled me up and immediately slammed me back into the ground. I gasped as all the air left my body. She lifted me again and slammed me down. She did this three times before holding me up for a bit longer. My back was bloodied and cut up by the broken cement, and yet I didn't think anything was really broken. What was going on?

Wrath glanced me over and saw that I was still breathing. She made a noise in disgust. She took the horn from my back and threw me back towards the street. This time she was going for distance. I launched through the air and slammed through the brick of the building. I broke through and spun into the back of a coffee shop.

I took a moment to take a self-scan to see if anything was broken. I took a breath and felt some ribs stab into me. That was to be expected. I slowly lifted my arms and wiggled my legs. Those were not broken. It also felt like I was lying on something really soft which was nice. I glanced behind me to see feathers and what looked like wings. Wait, wings?

I sprang up which was a bad idea as everything in my body cracked and I almost blacked out from the pain. "Guys, are you back?" I shouted out in excitement. This would be the perfect time since now Wrath had the horn again.

"Orion, these must be your wings?" I asked again. No answer, my head was still so empty. *Once again I mean there was no extra voices not that I was dumb.* I took a closer look at the wings and noticed that they were not the pearly white of Orion or the leathery wings of Luci. They were a reddish brown and an off-white. They looked like hawk wings. I spun around looking at them for a second. Whose were these?

Wait since Wrath kept calling me an angel does that mean that I somehow have some residual angelness on me. Since Luci and Orion were in my head so long did they have an effect on me. I shrugged I would figure it out later, for now, I was just glad to have something to even the fight a little more. I flapped them once to make sure I actually had control. They were shorter than Orion's but still quite long.

Back to the more pressing matter though I took off outside of the coffee shop and up into the air. These wings felt more natural than both Luci and Orion's wings. I spun around and saw Wrath walking back to the center of town. She must be preparing to blow the horn and assumed I had died. I noticed I was not as wrathful as I had been. I felt like a wave of clarity had passed over me. It must be from having my head knocked into the ground so many times.

I followed her from up high for a bit. It looked like she wanted to go back to the more open area that she was in to summon the horsemen. I felt refreshed like when Orion took over. The residual energy from the three angels is helping me at the perfect time. She reached the center of town and started to raise the horn up again.

I took this as my cue and wrapped the wings close in on my body. I dropped like a rock and barreled towards Wrath. I was flying really fast and reached her in no time. She looked at me in surprise as my fist collided with her face. It felt even stronger than my first punch on Wrath. Her head snapped to the side and she fell to the ground. I skidded along the ground, and I came to a stop about five yards from Wrath. She got up slowly but looked a little confused. I must have knocked her head really good.

I flapped my wings and went for another punch. She blocked it grabbing onto my arm and tossing me away. This time with the wings though I was able to spin my body and use the speed she gave me to whip around in flight. I flew back and before she could respond, raised up my shotgun and fired a shot into her chest. She was getting incredibly mad as she yelled very mean words and swung wildly at me.

I flew around her as I saw her arms start to glow. She aimed into the sky near me and fired two columns of flame from each arm. I dipped down low and dodged the flames. She lowered her arms towards me. I quickly stopped but part of the fire cut into the tip of my wing. I could feel the burning in my wing and quickly flapped it to put the flame out. The tip of my wing was singed but otherwise okay. I could still feel my ribs screaming in pain but it felt like it fueled me.

Wrath stopped the flames and looked at me. "So, you finally showed yourself in your true form angel," Wrath said. I had no idea what she was talking about.

"Yes and which angel am I?" I asked to see if she could give me some clues.

"You must be the Angel of Humanity. If I kill you it will be much easier to take down the rest of humanity," She explained and threatened.

Angel of Humanity? What was she talking about? Well no time to think about it now I had to take her down, and if this new power helped me then so be it. Even if I somehow was the Angel of Humanity I just hoped it would help me protect the world.

The Horn of Gabriel was between Wrath and me. We stared each other down to see who would make the first move. I focused on her and was able to have the out of body experience. This time I did not see Luci or Orion's soul surrounding me. I looked really lonely down there. What I did see though was a small shining dot in Wrath's throat. That was it, that was her weak point.

I flew for the Horn as quickly as I could as a diversion. She took the bait and jumped quickly towards it. As I reached the horn I spun in the air quickly so I was facing up towards Wrath. I aimed at her throat and took a shot. This was it I had her now. Before the pellets could reach her though she lifted her large stone arm and deflected the shots. With her free hand, she punched down onto my chest. It flattened me on the ground against the horn. The horn bent my back and I felt a sharp pain in my spine. I coughed up some blood as she lifted her fist.

She picked me up by the foot, *I was really getting tired of being picked up,* and tossed me to the side. I landed with a thud and shakily got to my hands and knees. I glanced up and saw Wrath pick up the Horn. She looked over at me and smiled, "Let's end this, angel." With that she rose the horn to her lips

"No!" I shouted. I was not going to let all of this be for nothing. I felt a surge as the wings grew in size and flapped powerfully. The gust of air sent me flying straight for Wrath. I held my arm out and clotheslined her just as she was about to blow. I heard her spurt out a bit of air before falling to the ground with me. Since I hit her in the throat with her weak point she was hurting and gasped for air.

I did it though. I got her before she could blow the horn.

I then heard a noise behind me. It sounded like a lightning crack mixed with something breaking the speed of sound. I covered my ears as the noise grew intensity before fading away. I slowly looked behind me to see a portal. The portal was black. So black it looked like no light came from it at all, and any light that passed into it did not reflect off anything.

I heard a cruel laugh from Wrath next to me. She rubbed her throat and looked at the portal. "You thought you stopped me but it was your clothesline that made me push air into the horn," She sneered. "It is only right that humanity undoes itself."

She had to be bluffing there was no way. It had to be a long drawn out blow for them to be summoned I was sure of it. How could just a small amount of air from her count as a blow.

It was then though that I saw the first hoof stick through.

28

THE BEGINNING OF THE END

The first horse came out of the black portal. It was pure white and extremely skinny. It did not look like it had any fat or muscle on it at all. The skin on its mouth was pulled back revealing its front teeth. The eyes glowed a bright white and stared hungrily at everything. Its body was covered in sores and pus oozed from it all over. The woman on top of the horse looked a little older than me. She wore a black tattered robe and cloak in contrast to her white horse. Her eyes glowed white and her face was covered in pox. She carried a bow and wore a crown on top of her cloak.

I heard another crack of thunder as another horse came out. This one was pure red with eyes of fire. With each snort it blew out a torrent of flame and each step it took onto the earth left a hoofprint of smoldering embers. It was hugely muscular and stood taller than the first horse. On the red horse road another rider. He was a kid shorter than the first but wore a helmet of what looked like obsidian. His eyes glowed red with rage. He carried a long sword with him that seemed too big for him to handle but he carried it with ease. He looked across the town and smiled cruelly.

With a third crack of thunder another horse came out. This one was black and was as skinny as the white horse. Its bones seemed to even crack through the skin. Its eyes were black and seemed to suck any light in around it. Each time the horse stepped frost formed on the ground, and its breath made it seem like it was below freezing. The rider was as skinny as the horse and had white hair at about shoulder length. The hair was dry and looked like it would fall out at any moment. He carried a scale in his hands that was perfectly balanced.

The last of the four horsemen approached out from the dark portal. I felt a deep feeling of dread in my gut as I knew this one was the most powerful. The horse was just a skeleton with dark blue energy wrapping around the bones and into the chest. Its eyes did not glow but rather looked completely dead. Where it stepped all the weeds shriveled up into dust. The rider was beautiful but caused great fear in my chest.

She was an older woman probably about forty years old. Her hair went down to the middle of her back and was a deep dark black. She had pale white skin and soulless black eyes. Her lips were grey and she stared at me with a knowing smile. She a dark robe with the hood down. Underneath she had a corset and a long black skirt. She carried no weapon but instead had a violin that at the end had a small scythe protruding out.

Wrath immediately got up and cautiously approached the Four Horsemen. She lowered herself on one knee and bowed her head.

"Greetings great bringers of the apocalypse. I was the one to release and am ready to accept my place as the fifth horsemen," Wrath said. The horsemen looked at each other and the older lady flicked her hand to the side. Wrath looked up just in time to see the bow wielding girl draw back her bow. Before Wrath could say anything, the arrow was released, and it hit her straight in the throat.

Wrath clawed at the arrow in her throat before her body began to rot. Around her throat the flesh became green and decayed rapidly. It traveled up to her face and down her body. Wrath laid on the ground twitching for a moment before her entire form decayed into a pile of rotting flesh. I stared the whole time with my mouth open.

I stood up and cracked my shotgun open loading two shells. I closed the breach and aimed at the four of them while my hands shook. They all looked at me like I was humorous for even thinking I was a threat. I took a step back as the older woman prepared to play the violin. She drew the bow across the strings but, yet I heard no noise. In fact, everything was silent. The older woman, who I was realizing was Death looked up and a deep frown crossed her face, but she was looking past me.

I felt a hand placed upon my right shoulder. I looked back to see Pitch standing next to me. I also noticed there was shadow covering the sides of my head. I saw Pitch in his skeletal form speaking with the other Death. She seemed angry and was speaking with him as well. Pitch looked mad and deadly serious. I felt his hand tighten on my shoulder as the conversation continued. I could not hear a word of it due to the shadows. I felt tears drip down my face as I realized the end of the world had begun.

The horseman Death then seemed done with the conversation and waved her hand. The other three horsemen charged Pitch and me. I raised my shotgun ready to fight but saw the shadow from Pitch swallow me. The last thing I saw was Death's mouth get them before everything turned pitch black.

"Now what do we do?"

THE END.

S.G. BURSON

Meet Gregory Burson and Stevie Chandler, two writers from Milford, Ohio.

The two authors met in high school, where they immediately started sharing story ideas. They remained together into college.

Stevie had published two novels during that time. Gregory helped her by discussing ideas, along with editing. Last year, both decided to co-author a novel together. Gregory had been wanting to write a book from the moment he met Stevie.

Gregory and Stevie co-wrote *THE THREE ANGELS AND THE SEVEN DEADLY SINS,* their first collaboration.

www.ingramcontent.com/pod-product-compliance
Lightning Source LLC
Chambersburg PA
CBHW071743190726
48292CB00003B/858